MEG DELGADO

1978:
Her ambition: to become an investigative reporter

1994:
Her assignment: to catch a thief

Meg has always wanted an exciting and adventurous life—and she's got it! She and her four brothers have formed a private-investigation firm that specializes in uncovering cruise-ship crime. This time, she disguises herself as glamorous divorcee Meg Newell, dripping with jewels to entice the thief. But her prime suspect is doing a little enticing of his own—with his great looks, his Cary Grant charm and his sexy, roguish smile....

NOAH WEBB

Yes, that's his real name, although Meg knows him as Noah Danforth. *He's* in disguise, too. And while Meg's selected him as *her* suspect, he's chosen "Mrs. Newell" as his. Because Noah's there on assignment, too—a different kind of assignment. And even though the man's name and background are fake, the looks, the charm and the sexy smile are definitely for real!

ABOUT THE AUTHOR

With more than eight million books in print, Elise Title can fairly be described as one of the most popular and prolific novelists around! She's particularly well-known for her fast-paced and witty romantic comedies, like *Too Many Husbands,* the Fortune Boys quartet, the Hart Girls trilogy—and *Meg & the Mystery Man.* In January 1995, watch for *Hot Property,* a Mira Books release.

For a change of pace, Elise writes screenplays. And, together with her husband, she's written a nonfiction relationship self-help book called *Loving Smart.* They're uniquely qualified to tackle this subject—not only does Elise write about relationships in her romance fiction, she worked as a pyschotherapist before she became a writer and her husband is a practicing clinical psychologist.

Besides writing, Elise loves taking long walks with her husband, reading, watching movies (she holds the record for the most movies rented from her local video store!), interior design (she did the design work for a major reno-vation of her current home) and—when she has time—traveling.

Elise Title

Meg & the Mystery Man

Harlequin Books

TORONTO • NEW YORK • LONDON
AMSTERDAM • PARIS • SYDNEY • HAMBURG
STOCKHOLM • ATHENS • TOKYO • MILAN
MADRID • WARSAW • BUDAPEST • AUCKLAND

ISBN 0-373-70618-9

MEG & THE MYSTERY MAN

Copyright © 1994 by Elise Title

Meg & the
Mystery Man

PROLOGUE

"FOR FOUR LONG YEARS, Berkeley School for Girls has nurtured and nourished us. Now the time has come for us to take what we have learned here and use that knowledge to sustain us in the next stage of our lives...."

Meg Delgado, her graduation cap tipped at a precarious angle because of her ponytail, fought back a yawn. She was thinking, as she listened to Chrissie Harris's valedictory address, that it was certainly *long*. At times it felt like forever. Not that she didn't have some terrific memories to look back on. And some wonderful friends, like Sandra, Kim and Laurel. The Four Mouseketeers, as she sometimes thought of them.

They'd become fast friends, working together on the school newspaper, the *Berkeley Crimson*—and had set it right on its ear, Meg thought with a feeling of pride and accomplishment. She bet the paper would never be as controversial or so in the thick of things again once they were gone. On the other hand, she bet plenty of teachers and school officials would breathe sighs of relief now that the staff of the *Crimson* was graduating. "Too provactive," the school superintendent had angrily charged when he'd attempted to get them to back off from certain issues.

Well, there hadn't been much chance of that, Meg thought. They'd told it and photographed it as they saw it. For her, working as an investigative reporter for the school paper had been the best part of high school. She always did have a nose for news, as well as a knack for putting that nose where a lot of folks felt it didn't belong—especially those who stood to lose the most thanks to that refined sniffer of hers.

"...choosing different paths. College for many. Jobs for others. And for some, marriage and even motherhood..."

Meg saw the blush rise in the valedictorian's cheeks. Chrissie was right about the marriage and mother-hood bit, but not necessarily the order.

"...what's important is that we are the women of the future. We have the opportunity to make a real difference. We have the drive, the determination, the intelligence to make the right choices..."

The right choices. Am I making the right choice? She'd chosen to go to the University of California at San Diego, following in the footsteps of her four big brothers, Tony, Alex, Sean and Paul. Family tradi-tion. The Delgados were big on both family and tra-dition.

"...to be responsible, dedicated, unswerving in our conviction to make this place a better world..."

Responsibility. Meg sighed. Oh, sure, responsibil-ity was important, but what she wanted was excite-ment, thrills, life experiences. Okay, she could probably land a job on the college paper, continue digging up dirt on campus for four years, but it al-ready felt *old* to her. She ached for something new.

"...and when this summer comes to a close we will all be going our separate ways. A time of fond but sad farewells..."

Meg felt an uncharacteristic lump in her throat. Saying goodbye wasn't going to be easy. Especially when it came to Sandra, Laurel and Kim. They'd been through so much together, shared so much, laughed together until they cried, cried together until they laughed. Meg didn't dare look at them for fear that if she did she wouldn't be able to hold back the tears. They'd never let her live it down if she started to bawl right out here in the open in front of the whole senior class, her family...

Her family. Saying goodbye to them was going to be awfully hard, too. Her mom would cry. That was a given. Mom always cried whenever one of her brood flew the coop. And since Meg was the youngest, it was going to be at least a three-hanky deal. Then there was her dad. He was as emotional as Mom. Oh, he wouldn't actually blubber, but he'd be hugging her and ruffling her hair, sniffing the whole time he was lecturing her about studying hard, staying out of trouble...

"...our troubles may seem insurmountable at times, but we must steer our course ahead, looking for smooth waters..."

That wasn't at all the course Meg wanted. She wanted choppy waters. The choppier the better. Ever since she'd been a little girl and the family had taken that cruise to Hawaii, sailing right into a hurricane, Meg had loved being at sea. She could still remember how frightened almost everyone on board had been on that trip, even her parents. Not so she or her brothers, who were wired with excitement. For them it was a great adventure.

Great adventure. That's what she wanted. That's what she longed for. Risks, danger, mystery.

"... and we will go forth to make our mark in history. Onward and upward."

Yes, Meg thought with a surge of anticipation. Onward and upward. All she had to do was get through the next four years and then she really did mean to make her mark in history. Just where, when or how exactly... well, she had time to figure that out.

CHAPTER ONE

"WHO IS THAT statuesque beauty who just boarded?" Elaine Harper, a short, stout woman in her early fifties whispered, nudging her husband, Eliot. "She certainly is getting the royal treatment. Not only is the captain himself greeting her, he's fawning all over her. I wonder if she's a movie star. No. She doesn't look familiar. Unless she's foreign. Not really a beauty, but certainly striking. I might go as far as to say regal."

Eliot Harper, a portly fifty-eight-year-old physics professor at Manhattan University, nodded absently. At the moment he was studying the ship's evacuation map, making note of all the lifeboat locations in case of an emergency.

"I'll tell you one thing for sure, Eliot. She's loaded. If that little black suit isn't Chanel I'll eat my hat. Well, I'm not wearing a hat, but if I were... And will you just look at that diamond brooch shaped like a heart on her lapel. And the diamond earrings. Cartiers, I bet. They had to cost an absolute fortune. I do wish she'd take off her gloves so I could see if she's wearing a matching diamond ring. I wonder if she's married to that man she boarded with. If she is, she's certainly married beneath her. Oh, he's attractive enough, but his suit! Definitely off the rack. And do you notice the way he stands behind her a little? What do you think, Eliot?"

Eliot was actually thinking about his seasick patch. He hoped it worked so that he didn't end up sick to his stomach the entire two weeks of this Caribbean cruise. They'd saved for years for this holiday to celebrate their thirtieth wedding anniversary. Not his choice, but then, when was it?

Elaine Harper patted her flyaway brown hair, which was generously streaked with gray, and nudged her husband a little closer to the woman occupying her curiosity.

"Hmm," she murmured after overhearing the captain address the new passenger by name. "Mrs. Newell. Newell. Newell. Why, I'm sure I've seen the name in the society columns. I think they're into oil. Or is it gas?"

Eliot Harper glanced up from the pamphlet he was skimming and gave his wife a look of consternation. "Gas? I do hope you remembered to pack the antacid tablets, Elaine."

Elaine waved off her husband's remark. "Whatever they own, I'm sure they've got more money than they know what to do with. Well, this particular Newell looks like she knows *one* thing to do with it. Buy jewels."

"Did you know that all soft drinks on board are complimentary?" Eliot said. "Well, at least something on this tub's free."

"You can bet she's traveling first-class. Not to mention having a permanent seat at the captain's table."

"Ah. Not only a doctor but a dentist on board!" Eliot Harper turned the page excitedly.

"Oh, look at that man coming up behind them," Elaine said sotto voce. "Now he's more the type I'd have thought would be accompanying a woman in Newell's social position. You can tell he's someone just by the way he carries himself. He positively radiates class, glamour, wealth. Take a look at that suit he's wearing. Certainly not off the rack, I can tell you that, Eliot. Custom tailored, mark my words. Now I'd say almost for a fact he's foreign."

"Says here that every room has its own VCR—"

"Shh, Eliot. Do you hear that?"

Eliot gave his wife a perplexed look. "Hear what?"

"British. He's got a British accent. I told you he was foreign. You know who he looks exactly like? Cary Grant. Cary Grant was British, you know. Oh, remember him in *An Affair to Remember?*" she said dreamily.

"...and you can even order monogrammed robes," Eliot went on, then stopped abruptly, glancing at his wife. "What affair, dear?"

Elaine Harper pursed her lips as she continued her study of the tall, handsome, dark-haired passenger. "Danforth. Hmm."

Eliot Harper scratched his thatch of gray hair. "The Danforth affair? I don't believe—"

"Noah Danforth. The second," Elaine said in a hushed whisper. "I bet he owns one of those marvelous British estates. You know the kind that are listed on the social register and where they're always having fox hunts and that sort of thing." She nudged her husband once again. "And did you see the look those two gave each other?"

"What two?"

"Noah Danforth II and Meg Newell."

Eliot scowled. "Newell. Now why does that name ring a bell?"

Elaine rolled her eyes. "Oh, really, Eliot."

"I HOPE THE SUITE is to your liking, Mrs. Newell," the steward said, opening the door to the first-class cabin and stepping aside to let the elegantly dressed woman and her companion enter.

Mrs. Newell undid the pearl buttons of her black Chanel bolero wool jacket trimmed in white piping as she strolled around the luxurious stateroom, which was done in tastefully subdued shades mixed with vibrant tropical hues. She paused at the glorious five-foot-wide picture window to glance out at the skyline of lower Manhattan. It was early March. A gray time in the city. A perfect time to get away; a perfect time for a Caribbean cruise.

Turning from the view, Meg Newell glanced idly around the exquisitely appointed sitting room with its butter-soft aquamarine leather sofa and matching club chairs squared off around a glass-top coffee table supported by a free-form marble base. Stowed inside a teak louvered entertainment center was a huge color TV, VCR and CD player. Across the room was a fully stocked bar. Next to the bar was an antique writing table replete with gilt-edged white linen stationery.

Off the sitting room was a gracious boudoir with a king-size bed, enormous cherry armoire, a dressing table and a second writing desk. There was even a huge, mirrored walk-in closet. And through the sleeping quarters could be seen a marble bathroom large enough to accommodate twin sinks and Jacuzzi tub.

To describe the suite as opulent would have been a vast understatement. The most jaded world traveler would have been hard put not to view these accommodations aboard the *Galileo,* brand-new flagship of the SeaQuest Line, as the absolute ultimate in ocean-going luxury. And they were. With a staggering price tag to confirm it.

"I suppose it'll do," Mrs. Meg Newell said with a careless flick of her hand when her inspection was completed.

The steward, a thin, middle-aged man with a pleasant face and a high forehead topped by wavy almost white-blond hair, was clearly taken aback by such a bland response. His expression mirrored the surprise he felt as he glanced at the woman's companion, a tall, even-featured man with shaggy red hair who looked to be in his mid-thirties.

"Very nice. Very nice, indeed," the companion said with a bit more enthusiasm.

There was an awkward silence. At least, the steward felt awkward.

"Shall I...show you where your private wall safe is located, Mrs. Newell?" he asked, his eyes darting from her sparkling diamond brooch to the matching earrings. Then she took off her black pigskin gloves, and his mouth almost dropped open when he saw the size of the rock on her finger.

She gave a weary little sigh. "I suppose one can never be too careful."

A shadow of a frown skimmed the steward's angular face, but then he quickly donned an air of confidence. "Not that there's any cause for concern. Merely that it's always wise—"

"Yes, yes, I know. But things do happen, don't they?" Mrs. Newell remarked offhandedly. "Even on the *Galileo*."

"Please let me assure you, Mrs. Newell, that you and your..." He hesitated, his eyes straying to her companion.

"Mr. Madison is my social secretary," she said curtly.

"Yes, naturally. I mean, yes, of course. Your social secretary," the steward was quick to repeat, avoiding looking either one of them in the eye.

"The safe?" she reminded him with a touch of impatience in her voice.

"Yes. It's right here. Next to the entertainment center." The steward hurried over to the wall next to the teak built-in cabinet where an original seascape oil painting hung. The painting proved to be hinged to the wall, a hidden catch allowing it to spring out like a door. Behind it was a small wall safe.

"You've already registered your private code—it happened when you registered for the cruise," the steward said. "Even security doesn't have a copy of it. They're issued directly from SeaQuest's main office. If you should forget it or if somehow word of your code gets out, you must report it immediately, and you'll have to register a new code with headquarters. Of course, you also have the ship's safe at your disposal for those items you might not be needing on a regular basis while you're aboard."

"I haven't brought along anything of particular value other than my jewelry. And my philosophy always has been that there's little point in owning beautiful jewels if you keep them hidden away all the time," Mrs. Newell proclaimed.

"I suppose you've got a point. Will there be anything else?" the steward asked. "If you'd like I'll be happy to show your...social secretary to his quarters."

"That won't be necessary," Mrs. Newell said. "I need him to take some dictation. I'm sure he'll find his way."

The steward nodded and left. No sooner did the door close than Mrs. Newell had to duck to avoid the small pillow her social secretary threw at her.

"Hey, watch it, or I *will* give you some dictation," she said with a laugh.

"Oh, you will, will you?"

"What's got your goat?"

"'I suppose it'll do,'" Paul Madison, alias Paul Delgado, said, in a good imitation of Meg Newell, alias Meg Delgado. "Aren't we putting it on a little heavy with the help, my dear Mrs. Newell? How did you ever come up with that particular name, anyway?"

"Elementary, my dear Mr. Madison. Newell. Rhymes with jewel. A nice touch, *n'est pas?*" Meg said with a wiseacre grin as she pulled out the pins from her chignon and let her thick, wavy, chestnut-brown hair cascade over her shoulders. Then she kicked off her shoes and flopped onto the sofa, running her palm across the soft leather cushion. "These are rather nice digs at that," she said, her amber eyes sparkling.

"Nice digs, huh?" Paul wagged a finger at his sister. "I tell you what, Mrs. Newell. Next time, how about I play the wealthy jet-setter and you be *my* social secretary? Then I get the first-class suite and get to hobnob with the rich and the famous, and you can rough it in a second-class cabin and stroll amongst the common folk."

"Don't be pouty, Paul. Nobody's exactly roughing it on board the flagship of the SeaQuest Line, which, need I remind you, is the beluga caviar of cruise lines. And speaking of beluga—"

"You hate caviar."

"I wasn't thinking about caviar. I was thinking about that fellow who came on board just behind us. Noah Danforth II."

"What about him?"

"Come on, Paul. Does that name sound for real?"

"As for real as Mrs.-Newell-rhymes-with-jewel."

"Exactly. It's a phony. I bet the Brit accent's phony, too. For that matter, there wasn't one thing about him that rang true in my book."

Paul pulled a bottle of mineral water from the complimentary bar. "You got a ten-second look at him."

"I'm not saying he's our man. I'm simply putting him high on my list. Something smells fishy about him, and I always trust this sniffer of mine," she said, tapping her pert nose.

"I know you're feeling your oats after our last little caper was so successful, but really, little sister, don't you think you're putting too much stock in first impressions?"

"Did you see the way those baby blue eyes of his lit up when he looked at my brooch?"

Paul grinned crookedly. "I didn't think it was actually your *brooch* he was ogling."

Now Meg snatched up the pillow and threw it at her brother. He wasn't as quick to duck as she'd been, and it hit him right in the chest. He gasped dramatically.

She laughed. "You're getting out of shape, Paulie. You should take advantage of the state-of-the-art health club on board. Come to think of it, I could use a bit of a workout myself. What do you say we change and head over there, maybe lift a few weights?''

NOAH DANFORTH II was just settling in to his own opulent first-class suite when there was a knock on his door. Slipping back into his Savile Row, double-breasted, chalk-striped wool crepe jacket, he went to see who it was.

The same steward who'd shown Meg ''Newell'' to her quarters greeted the new passenger with a polite, ''Anything I can do for you, sir?''

A young couple walking arm in arm down the corridor was passing Danforth's door. He smiled at them, then nodded to the steward. ''Yes. Would you mind stepping in for a moment, steward? I seem to be having a problem with the catch on one of my suitcases.''

''Certainly, sir.''

No sooner had Noah shut the door than the steward turned to him with a toothy grin. ''What a job. My feet are killing me.''

''Well, by all means, my good fellow, feel free to slip off your shoes for a bit and give your bunions some breathing space,'' Noah said expansively.

The steward chuckled. ''Forget the shoes. What I need's a nice, tall gin and tonic. Care to join me, Webb?''

''Danforth, Chet. The name's Danforth, not Webb. And should you be imbibing on the job, old chap?'' Noah teased, his British accent still quite obvious but less clipped. Anyone with a good ear for accents would have picked up the hint of cockney.

''If you want me to be at my best, most definitely yes,'' Chet Carson declared, heading for the bar.

Noah Webb slipped off his jacket and loosened his blue paisley silk tie. "All right, but talk while you mix them."

"Well, for starters, I gather you caught the baubles our Mrs. Newell was wearing," Chet said as he poured a healthy jigger of Bombay gin into each of two tall crystal glasses.

Noah unpacked his dinner jacket and hung it in the enormous closet. "I'd've had to have been blind not to. What do you know about her?"

"I know that something about her doesn't feel right," Chet said, topping each glass off with tonic water. "A little too blasé. Very easy on the eyes, though. Likewise those diamonds."

Noah ran a hand through his dark brown hair. Tall, broad-shouldered, a face full of interesting character lines set off by cobalt-blue eyes, his skin giving off a healthy golden glow, he looked every bit the wealthy Fleet Street barrister and man-about-town he claimed to be. Hard for anyone to imagine that twenty years back, Noah Danforth II, alias Noah Webb, had been a scrawny, sallow-faced fifteen-year-old kid doing a one-year stint in a work farm for pinching bananas from a London fruit peddler.

Sometimes, though, Chet wondered if that wasn't just another of Noah's colorful stories. He smiled. Noah had a way of always keeping you guessing. Which was one of the reasons he was so good at what he did. There were other reasons, as well. He was shrewd, charming, smart as a whip, and he had a clear focus on his priorities, never mixing business with pleasure. Chet always enjoyed teaming up with Noah.

"Who's the guy she's dragged along?" Noah asked, removing the solid gold cuff links from his custom-made, crisp white shirt.

"She says he's her social secretary," Chet said with a sly little smile, handing his friend a drink.

Noah arched a brow. "He isn't the one who bought her those baubles, I'll wager."

"No, I agree with you there. If anything, she'd be the one doing the buying for him. By the way, she doesn't intend to avail herself of the ship's safe. Likes showing her baubles off."

The two men shared a look. "Is that so?" Noah mused.

"Says the only things of value she brought along on the trip were her jewels. Nothing else."

Noah tapped his glass against Chet's. "Interesting."

"You'll be seated next to each other at the captain's table for dinner tonight," Chet said. "And every night thereafter, unless you decide to move on to other pastures."

"We'll see," Noah said, slipping out of his shirt to reveal a honey-gold expanse of well-muscled flesh. "Right now, I think I'll go down to the gym and work out a few kinks. I want to be at my charming best at dinner," he added with a rakish smile.

Chet took a large swallow of his drink, then wiped his mouth with the back of his hand. "Something tells me you'll have to be. She's not one that's easily impressed."

Noah winked. "It's never fun when they're easy, old man."

"NO GAIN WITHOUT PAIN, Mrs. Newell," the exceedingly well-built athletic director cajoled as Meg lay flat on her back trying to bench-press 120 pounds. Her sunflower yellow spandex leotard was darkened with sweat.

"Breathe now," he chirped, finally taking pity on her and helping her ease the barbell into its rest.

Meg gave him a dirty look. "Breathe, huh? Easy for you to say," she gasped.

The director gave her a grin and went to give a hand to a sweating middle-aged man on the other side of the room. Meg glanced to her left. Working out next to her was a gorgeous, lanky and very shapely redhead by the name of Heather St. John. She returned Meg's glance and gave a light laugh. "I sometimes wonder if it's worth it."

Meg eyed the young woman's body and sighed. "It's certainly been worth it for you."

Heather St. John sat up, draped a fluffy white towel around her long graceful neck and stretched. "Well, I guess I'll call it quits for today. Nice meeting you, Mrs. Newell."

"Call me Meg."

"Okay, Meg. And I'm Heather," the redhead said with a smile, revealing the kind of teeth you see in toothpaste commercials.

Since Meg had gotten the *Galileo* assignment a couple of weeks ago, she'd only had time to do a cursory check on the passengers. She'd dug up very little on Heather, learning merely that her father had a seat on the New York Stock Exchange and that Heather was single, twenty-four and dabbled in art.

Time to find out more.

"Are you traveling for work or fun?" Meg asked conversationally.

Heather sighed. "Neither, really. I'm supposed to be mending a broken heart, you see."

Paul, who'd been working his biceps on one of the machines a short distance away, strolled over and smiled sympathetically at the beautiful redhead. "Nothing like an ocean cruise to mend a broken heart," he said.

She smiled coyly at him. "Oh, it's not really broken. I was only seeing the guy for a few months, and I wasn't hearing bells or music or any of those things you're supposed to hear when you're in love. When he decided to go back to the wife I didn't know he had, I used the breakup as a good excuse to get away."

"Where did you want to get away from?" Meg asked, ever on the job.

"It's a long dull story. I wouldn't want to bore you with it," Heather said offhandedly, adding a little yawn for emphasis.

Before Meg could respond, Paul jumped in.

"I wouldn't be bored. Maybe tonight, after dinner, we could have a drink," he suggested. He followed this up with a quick introduction. "I'm Paul Madison, by the way."

Heather extended a graceful hand, her tapered fingernails beautifully manicured and polished a ruby red. "A pleasure, Paul."

"Oh, no. The pleasure's all mine," he said with a jaunty smile, holding on to her hand for an extra moment. "What do you say to that after-dinner drink?"

"Well . . ." The redhead hesitated, her gaze shifting back to Meg.

"It's fine with me," Meg said. "Paul works for me. What he does after hours is his own business."

Heather still seemed hesitant as she turned back to Paul. "I'm just not sure about tonight. I was planning to turn in early. Maybe you could give me a rain check."

"Sure," Paul said, knowing a brush-off when he heard one.

Heather slid off the table and just as the athletic director returned. She gave him a little wave. "See you tomorrow, Alex."

"I'll be looking forward to it, Miss St. John," he called out as she headed through the double doors.

Both men were still staring in the direction of the swinging doors after Heather St. John exited. Meg, swinging her legs off the bench, eyed the two of them with a mock frown. "Don't look now, but you're drooling, boys."

Alex gave her a narrow look. "Care to lift some more weights, Mrs. Newell?"

"Care to add a bit of black and blue to one of your eyes?" she replied tartly. The athletic director was a brawny man well over six feet with a Mr. Universe build, shaggy reddish-brown hair, a nose that had seen more than its share of punches and a disarming smile, which he was currently displaying.

"The last time you gave me a black eye was when I was fourteen and told Tommy Porter you had a crush on him," Alex said with a laugh.

"Which I didn't."

"Yes, you did," Paul joined in.

"Brothers," Meg sighed. "Can't live with 'em—"

"—and can't live without 'em," Alex and Paul finished off in unison.

Meg wiped the sweat from her face with her towel. "Let's remember, fellows, this isn't the *Love Boat*. Shall we get down to business?"

Alex gave his older brother a playful jab in the arm. "Right. This isn't a pleasure cruise, bro. Any old way, Heather's too young for you, Paulie. She's only twenty-three."

"Twenty-four," Paul corrected.

"You'd still be robbing the cradle," Alex contended.

"Since when is thirty-six old?" Paul countered. "And may I remind you, Alex, you're only a year and seven months younger than me. If she's too young for me, she's too young for you, too."

"Hey, she's not even my type," Alex said, straight-faced.

"Besides," Meg said, "a woman like that isn't going to give the lowly athletic director on a cruise ship the time of day."

"Or the secretary of a rich socialite," Alex added, shooting his sister a dirty look.

"Well," she declared with a wave of her hand, "if she's such a snob, you're both better off without her."

"Yeah, right," Paul deadpanned. Then, catching his brother's lascivious grin, he broke into laughter. Alex joined in.

"Really," Meg said with a sigh of exasperation. "You're such...men."

This made them laugh even harder.

"A little decorum, please. Before someone else walks in," she scolded.

"Okay," Paul said, getting his laughter under wraps. "You're right. Let's get down to business." He looked at Alex, who had also sobered up. "Meggie already thinks she's got a hot one on the line," he told his brother.

"Who is it?"

"His name's Danforth," Meg said. "Noah Danforth II. Or so he claims. He's a real looker with a snooty British accent."

"A real looker, huh?" Alex echoed with a sly smile.

"A regular dreamboat," Paul piped in. "And you should have seen the way his baby blues lit up when he spotted Meggie's . . . diamond brooch. Well, she says it was her diamond brooch." He gave his sister a teasing grin. "And what was it about Mr. Danforth II that caught your eye, Meggie?"

"I want to go on record here and now," Meg stated officiously, "that I am not the tiniest bit taken with Mr. Danforth II's looks, phony accent or anything else about him."

"Right," Paul said. "He's not your type."

"Like . . . what was his name? wasn't your type," Alex mused.

"Drew. Jonathan Drew," Paul said, helping him out.

"That was different," Meg said. "For one thing I was a lot younger. Anyway, may I remind you both that even though I may initially have been a bit starry-eyed over . . . over what's his name . . ."

"Jonathan Drew," Paul reminded her with a broad grin.

"Right. Anyway, the point is, in the end I did pull his cover."

"After you'd been under it with him," Alex teased.

"A mistake I haven't repeated since," Meg said, having learned her lesson the hard way. It was her firm belief that shipboard romances rarely worked out even in the best of circumstances. And ever since she'd formed High Seas Investigators, the circumstances were far from the best. Any romancing required while on the job was strictly business. And strictly above the covers!

"Furthermore," she was quick to point out, "just let me remind you that if it weren't for my very brief shipboard romance with Jonathan Drew, I never would have discovered that he was conning dozens of passengers out of a fortune with his supposed insider information. Which is how all this started, if you both happen to recall."

They recalled quite well. All this was the birth of High Seas Investigators. In the four years since Meg had started the company she ran with her brothers, they'd been responsible for nabbing numerous swindlers, cardsharps, con artists, stowaways and petty thieves aboard a dozen cruise ships. Their successes had allowed them to beat out the competition for this latest and most prestigious assignment on the *Galileo*.

Alex glanced at Paul. "Our little sister's got a point. We do owe Drew a debt of gratitude."

Paul grinned. "While I hate to admit it, we owe Meggie here a lot, too. Even if I am stuck playing social secretary this time out."

Meg smiled at her two brothers. "Kudos all around, fellows. Now, let's get back to Noah Danforth II, shall we?"

"Aren't we jumping the gun? I mean, we don't even know with absolute certainty that our boy's even on board," Alex reminded her.

"In the last six months there have been major jewel thefts reported on four luxury cruise lines," Meg said.

"And there are more jewels per square inch aboard the *Galileo* than on all the others combined."

"Most of them yours," Paul pointed out, then added, "On temporary loan, unfortunately."

Meg shrugged. "Which is fine with me. I don't mind playing the part of a rich socialite, but I wouldn't want to actually have to live it. It's not my thing."

"Well, you're doing a great job of pretend," Paul said with a smile.

"Okay," Alex broke in. "You certainly would draw a jewel thief like a magnet if he's on board. I still say it remains an *if*."

"Are you forgetting that anonymous tip the cruise line received a few weeks ago that he was going to strike again?" Meg reminded him.

"No. But it could be a hoax," Alex said. "Those kind of tips often prove to be just that."

"I don't think so this time. And obviously neither does SeaQuest," Meg said. "They clearly see it as a genuine threat. Otherwise they wouldn't have agreed to our hefty fee, never mind take on loan a cool million in diamonds, rubies and sapphires, which I'll be sporting during this cruise. They feel confident our boy's going to strike. And confident we're going to see to it that he isn't successful."

Paul gave them both a thoughtful look. "You think he sent the tip himself?"

"Why would he do something like that?" Alex asked. "I'd think he'd want to keep a real low profile. If he warned the company he was going to pull another heist he'd have to know they'd respond by tightening security and making his job a lot harder. Not to mention riskier."

"Exactly," Meg said. "My guess is he's feeling it's been too easy for him. He's getting bored. The risk is all part of the excitement, the thrill, the high. I think our thief's so full of himself that he wanted to up the ante. Make it more challenging. Show that he can outsmart anyone the cruise line gets to try to nab him."

Paul grinned at his sister.

"What?" she asked.

"You've got that glint in your eye, Meggie," Paul said. "I don't think our clever jewel thief knows who he's up against."

"Right," Alex seconded. "When it comes to taking on a challenge, you're right up there with the best of them, kid."

Meg frowned. "True, but don't think for one minute that our boy isn't one of the best of them, too."

"The clash of the Titans," Paul said with a broad smile.

"And you really think the Titan we're after is this Noah Danforth II?" Alex asked his sister. "Before we boarded, we'd targeted a dozen passengers as potential suspects." Their focus was on passengers since the cruise line had done thorough checks on their staff, clearing them of suspicion. Especially as none of them had worked on any of those cruise ships that had been hit by jewel thefts during the past six months.

"Granted," Alex went on, "Danforth was one of those high up on our list, but we shouldn't forget about the other eleven."

"I'm not saying Danforth's our only suspect. Just that he caught my eye right off. My *professional* eye," Meg quickly added to avert any further sly innuendos from either or both of her big brothers. Really, you'd think she'd never seen a great-looking guy before.

Great-looking? Okay, so he was somewhat exceptional in the looks department. Not simply handsome in the traditional sense—although he was that, too. It was something more. His face. Strong-boned. Those striking planes and angles. The sensual, bad-boy mouth. A face to be reckoned with. Dangerous. And those baby blue eyes. Paul was right, though she wasn't about to admit it. Danforth's eyes had taken in a lot more than her diamond brooch in that one brief look he'd given her while the captain had formally introduced them.

She became aware that her brothers were watching her. She put her hands on her hips. "Oh, please. Not that again."

Paul looked idly around the gym and whistled. Alex did a few Mr. Universe flexes.

"Look, all I'm telling you is that Noah Danforth II is someone to watch," Meg said. "He has that kind of smug self-confidence that makes him stand right out." She sighed. "Of course, it would've been nice if we'd gotten this assignment a little earlier and had more time to do some serious digging into his background and run a few checks. As it is, I have to trust my instincts on this one."

Her brothers didn't balk at that, since Meg's hunches in the past had more often than not proved to be right on the money.

"If it should turn out I'm wrong about him being our jewel thief," Meg added, "I'll still lay you boys odds that this guy's not on the up-and-up," she finished emphatically, slipping on her pale yellow sweatpants. Still too wet with perspiration to put on her jacket, she slung it over her shoulder.

"You think he'll show up here?" Alex asked her.

"Yes. He looks like a guy who works out," Meg said, poking Paul who was grinning broadly again, then steering him toward the door. "See if you can get chummy with him, Alex. Find out what you can. I'll check in with you tomorrow, same time."

As if on cue, Noah Danforth II stepped through the swinging doors of the health club just as Meg and Paul reached them. His lean, muscular body was clad in a teal blue velour sweat suit. Practically the color of his eyes, Meg couldn't help but notice.

Noah's eyebrows lifted fractionally as his gaze fell on Meg.

"I thought I'd be the first passenger down here," he said conversationally as he unzipped his jacket.

Meg forced her eyes from his rippled, golden chest as he slipped the jacket off. "I wanted to beat the hordes."

Noah glanced around the gym, empty now save for Meg, Paul and Alex. "I think you did."

Alex approached and introduced himself. Noah gave him a friendly smile and shook hands with him. His gaze, however, quickly shifted back to Meg. Now a faint smile played on his lips as he gave her an unabashed full inspection. "Looks like you work out regularly, Mrs. Newell. If it isn't too presumptuous, may I say that you have very nicely defined . . . biceps."

Meg laughed, thinking, despite herself, that Noah Danforth II's biceps were nothing to sneeze at, either. "I don't know about *too* presumptuous, Mr. Danforth," she said with a deliberately flirtatious glint in her amber eyes.

Noah grinned. This one was quick on her feet. Cheeky. He suddenly found himself regretting that this wasn't a pleasure cruise. And that Mrs. Meg Newell wasn't just an ordinary passenger. But then, he thought, under no circumstance would he ever classify the enchanting Mrs. Newell as *ordinary*.

CHAPTER TWO

"HAVE YOU EVER!" Elaine gasped, thumping her husband's back as they sat eating dinner their first night at sea.

Eliot Harper almost choked on the asparagus tip he'd just popped into his mouth. "What? What is it? Is something wrong?" He really should not have seen that disaster movie *The Poseidon Adventure*. He kept expecting the worst at every turn.

"There she is again," Elaine murmured, leaning closer to her husband so that the two other couples at their table wouldn't overhear. Fortunately the foursome was busily engaged in a conversation about their previous cruises. And since this was the Harpers' first cruise, they had nothing to contribute to the discussion.

"There who is again?" Eliot asked his wife.

"That Mrs. Newell. Over by the entrance."

Eliot started to turn his head until Elaine kicked his shin under the linen tablecloth. "Don't stare, Eliot."

"I wasn't—"

"Will you just look at that diamond-and-ruby necklace she's wearing," Elaine whispered in awe.

"How can I look at the necklace if—"

"Why, it makes that diamond brooch and earrings she wore when she boarded this morning look like something from the five-and-dime by comparison."

"Sadly enough," Eliot lamented, "the five-and-dime store is a relic of the past."

"If you want my opinion," Elaine said, scowling, "that woman's asking for trouble."

"What kind of trouble?" Eliot asked nervously.

"Flaunting all those jewels the way she does. I say she's just asking to be robbed."

Eliot pressed his hand to his chest. "Robbed? Here? On a ship like this? You don't really think—"

Elaine's eyes narrowed. "And what if it didn't stop there? What if he broke into her room while she was sleeping and she woke up? Or he could think she was somewhere else on the ship only for her to return unexpectedly to her cabin and catch him right in the act. Just think about that."

Eliot really didn't want to think about such things. He had more than enough to worry about already.

"It's obvious what would happen," Elaine went on.

"It is?" Eliot was beginning to feel decidedly queasy.

"He'd have to take drastic measures."

"Drastic measures?" Eliot simply refused to accept such a scenario. "Really, my dear, I think you've read a few too many mystery novels. What was that one you were reading only last week? *Murder at Sea*, wasn't it?"

Elaine gave a flick of her hand. "It doesn't only happen in novels, Eliot. Julia Peterson, our own travel agent, told me just last month that there's been an outbreak of robberies on cruise ships, but that the companies have managed to hush it up so that prospective passengers won't start to get nervous."

"You never told me."

"Of course I told you, Eliot. You never listen. Anyway, we have nothing to worry about. Why would a jewel thief bother with the likes of us when there are people like Mrs. Newell aboard? But if I were her..."

MEG STOOD at the entrance to the Renaissance Room, wearing an Yves St. Laurent red taffeta off-the-shoulder cocktail dress set off by an eye-popping diamond-and-ruby necklace, an equally dazzling matching ruby-and-diamond bracelet, and a look of studied ennui. The expression on her face didn't come easy. In all her travels, Meg had never seen such opulence as was displayed in every nook and cranny of this five-star luxury cruise ship. Nothing exemplified the No Expense Spared motto of the *Galileo* than the ship's breathtakingly sumptuous main dining hall.

Sweeping seascape murals covered the walls on three sides of the vast room, mirroring the real vista beyond the huge windows running the length of the fourth wall, which looked out over the ocean. Crystal teardrop chandeliers hung from the gilt ceiling, casting a warm glow over generously spaced tables covered in the finest pale peach Irish linen and set with the best crystal and bone china. The Chippendale chairs grouped around the tables were upholstered in peach-and-mint-green-striped damask. In one corner of the room was a small dance floor that led through French doors onto the deck. A few couples were dancing to a combo, who were playing a lilting Sondheim medley.

The delightful aromas of haute cuisine mingled with that distinctly unique scent of well-being and wealth. From all appearances, Meg fit right in with her glitzy, well-heeled traveling companions. And if the attention she and her jewels were garnering from most of

the already seated diners was any indication, she stood
out in the formidable crowd. Which, after all, was the
point of this charade. She was the lure, the bait. *If
you're out there, Mr. Itchy Fingers, I'm the one with
the goods.*

Meg gave a little nod as the maître d' approached.
He was a tall, broad-shouldered fellow with military-
short light brown hair, a ruddy complexion and a cleft
chin—the only Delgado offspring to bear their father's trademark feature. Meg's second-to-eldest
brother, Sean Delgado cut a dashing figure in his blue
serge jacket with shiny brass buttons and gold epaulets, navy tuxedo trousers and spit-shined black shoes.
No one ever would have guessed he wasn't born to the
part.

"Hiya, sis," Sean murmured, the gold-embossed
menu he held carefully raised to conceal his mouth.
"Nice baubles."

Meg maintained her faintly bored, slightly conde-
scending pose, but her lips were slightly parted so she
could speak without being spotted. "Anyone spark-
ing your interest?"

His face still hidden behind the menu, Sean whispered, "Well, there's this dynamite redhead by the
name of Heather St. John..."

"Not you, too," she muttered as he led her across
the dining hall.

"Only kidding. Not my type. Seriously, though, I'd
give this Swede Olson a closer look. A real Don Juan
type."

Meg feigned a little cough so that she could cover
her mouth. "Where is he?"

"At your table. Seated next to that dynamite redhead."

CAPTAIN SIMON, a tall, lean, elegant man in his mid-forties with a head of silver hair, rose as he saw the maître d' escort Meg over to his table. The captain's table occupied a choice spot in one corner of the dining room right in front of an enormous window. It was set for eleven people, the captain and ten of the most well-connected guests—by virtue of celebrity or fortune or both—on board. All of the hand-picked group, save Meg, were already seated at the table. As Meg was helped into her seat she didn't miss the tidy collection of jewels her female dining companions were sporting. While there was little question that her own gems topped the cake, Meg had no doubt her jewel thief would consider these other jewels quite nice icing.

The captain, who was seated on Meg's left, did the introductions, beginning with Danforth, who was seated on Meg's right.

"You've already met our barrister from London."

Meg nodded, favoring her prime suspect with a faint smile. She was playing it cautiously. If Danforth was her man and if, as she suspected, he was itching for a challenge, she didn't want to make this too easy for him. Still, she didn't want to play too hard to get, either, because his suspicions might be raised. "I hope you had a good workout at the health club, Mr. Danforth."

"Most invigorating," he said, his gaze sliding appraisingly over her. "May I say you look absolutely ravishing in that ensemble, Mrs. Newell."

"A bit late to ask for permission," she quipped, thinking that Noah Danforth II looked damn ravishing himself in his full evening regalia: a classic black tux, pleated white shirt, slightly offbeat, gold-and-black paisley bow tie.

The captain continued around the table, introducing Meg to the rest of her dining companions. There was chubby, fortyish Barbara Friers, a noted novelist whose latest political intrigue had been made into a multimillion-dollar film, and her husband, Horace Friers, who was the head of CineCom, which produced the film; Dr. Franz Schmidt, a small, self-effacing seventy-two-year-old Nobel-prize-winning Hungarian botanist and his diminutive, retiring wife, Clara; Alan Delacore, the large, jovial former ambassador to Belgium, and his pretty, much younger Southern-belle fiancée, Louanne Percy; the glamorous and chic Heather St. John; and last, but certainly not least, Lars Olson, a flamboyant Swedish hunk with a wild mane of golden hair. Meg's take on Olson was sketchy at best. Under "Employment" on the cruise-ship registration form he'd written "entrepreneur." Covered a wide berth.

When the captain introduced her to the Swede, Olson gave Meg a polite greeting and a decidedly brief, careless smile, quickly returning his full attention to the woman seated directly to his right, Heather St. John.

It was not only obvious to Meg that Olson's interest lay elsewhere, but she also noted that he didn't give her diamonds and rubies so much as a cursory glance. And it wasn't as if her jewels were in competition with the ones Heather St. John was wearing, since all the gorgeous redhead sported in the way of precious gems was a small sapphire ring and a diamond pendant that would weigh in at a carat at best.

While this didn't rule out the Swede in Meg's mind, or anyone else for that matter, her hunch was that the thief would make some kind of a play for her. Not only would it help him learn her habits firsthand, thus allowing him to plan the best time to carry out the heist, but if her profile of the thief was accurate, romancing his victim would heighten the excitement. And the challenge.

As the evening meal got under way, there was the requisite polite getting-acquainted banter among the guests at the captain's table. When the conversation started to ebb, the captain held court for several minutes, talking about some of their upcoming ports of call. Their first stop, he said, would be Virgin Gorda.

By the time the group was halfway through their gourmet feast, which included savory *mousselines de poisson à la Maréchale* as the first course and moved on to an entrée of succulent *Selle d'agneau rotie Persillade,* the diners had broken off into small conversation groups. Olson almost entirely monopolized Heather St. John, while the former ambassador and his fiancée were deep into a conversation about the vagaries of Hollywood with the studio mogul and his celebrity-novelist wife. The captain engaged the botanist and his wife in a lengthy conversation about the fauna and flora of the Caribbean. That left Meg and Noah to team up, which suited them both quite nicely, each for their own *professional* reasons.

"So tell me, Mr. Danforth, is this your first cruise?" Meg asked him after swallowing a delicious morsel of her lamb.

"I'll tell you if you call me Noah," he said, his eyes drifting to her sparkling diamond-and-ruby necklace.

Has to be worth a hundred grand easy, he thought. *Add another fifty grand for the bracelet.*

"Okay, Noah. Tell me."

He gave her a blank look, his calculations making him forget what it was he was supposed to be telling her. He did like the sound of his name on her lips, though. *Watch it, Webb. You're letting the sparkle in her voice outshine the sparkle around her neck.*

He quickly pulled himself together. "My first cruise? Was that your question?"

Meg smiled to herself. *What's the matter, Noah? My jewels distracting you? Already calculating how much they're worth?*

"Does it take some thought?" she asked lightly, spearing a juicy asparagus tip with her sterling-silver fork.

He took a swallow of champagne and smiled at her. "No. My thoughts just strayed a bit."

"I don't suppose you'd care to tell me where they went."

He gave her a rogue's smile. "Maybe when we've gotten to know each other a bit better," he murmured, finishing off the remainder of champagne in his fluted crystal goblet. "I've actually been on several cruises over the years. Find them quite energizing."

I bet you do, Meg mused.

"And you?" he asked pleasantly.

Meg took a sip of her champagne. "Oh, I feel the same way. I like to take at least one or two cruises every year."

"And what keeps you busy between cruises?" Noah asked after the dining steward rushed over to refill their glasses.

"Oh, well, committees, that sort of thing," Meg said airily. "And you? Do you have a busy law practice in London?"

"Busy enough."

"Any particular specialty?" she prodded.

There was a hint of amusement in his blue eyes as he answered, "Yes, actually. Divorce law." Without missing a beat, he asked, "Have you been divorced long?"

Meg had to smile. "Long enough. How did you know I was divorced?"

"I asked Captain Simon before you joined us for dinner."

Meg lifted her champagne glass, eyeing him over the rim as she took a sip. *Doing a bit of a preliminary check on your target, are you?*

She set the glass down. "What about you? Are you married, Mr.—sorry, Noah."

"No. I'm the confirmed bachelor who gets invited as the extra man to an endless round of dinner parties," he told her in a teasingly conspiratorial whisper. "It can be quite exhausting, but it does give my cook, Alice, most weekends off."

"Are you against marriage or simply too busy enjoying the single life?" Meg asked, telling herself she had absolutely no personal interest in his answer. She was merely gathering data. Getting to know as much about her prime suspect as possible. Not so much facts, which she assumed he'd fabricate if he was her man, but more a psychological profile. Watching the expression on his face when he answered; looking for little clues as to how his mind worked; getting a feel for what she was up against.

Noah gave her a long look that made her distinctly uneasy. Was he growing suspicious of her questions? Was she being heavy-handed?

"Perhaps I've just never found the right woman," he murmured, leaning a little closer to her, his blue eyes fixed on her face. "Would you care to..."

For one insane, dizzying moment Meg actually imagined he was about to propose to her.

"...dance?"

"Excuse me?" she asked, temporarily disoriented.

"Dance? You know. Swaying together to the music? The man taking one of the woman's hands in his—" he took hold of her hand as he spoke, lacing his fingers with hers "—his other hand slipping ever so gracefully around her waist—" which he also did, guiding her to her feet at the same time.

Noah excused them both from the table and led Meg to the dance floor. A few graceful twirls and they were dancing through the open French doors and out onto the deck, which was enveloped by a velvety blackness save for the twinkling of stars overhead. Unlike the chill weather in New York that morning when they'd embarked, the evening was quite balmy, the ship now off the coast of North Carolina.

"This is nice," he murmured against her hair, one hand pressed to her bare back, the other drawing her hand against his chest as they danced. *Okay, so this is work. Still, no reason not to enjoy the work.*

"You're a very good dancer. Very light on your feet," she answered, letting the fingers of her left hand curl ever so lightly around his neck. *In your line of work, being light on your feet must come in handy.*

"It helps to have the right partner," he said, twirling her, then dipping her low.

She felt a little light-headed as he held her poised in that position for an extra-long moment, his gaze slowly cruising over her.

Meg began to think that maybe dancing with her prime suspect wasn't such a smart idea. It put him in the driver's seat, so to speak.

He slowly lifted her back up so that they were face-to-face, their lips only inches apart.

There was no denying the temptation Noah felt at that moment to bridge those few inches.

Don't even think about it, his head cautioned. *It's much too soon. Last thing you want is to scare her off by rushing things. No, this one you've got to take very slow. It's the only way you're going to get what you're after.*

Meg was having her own struggles as his gaze fixed on her. If a woman wasn't careful, she thought, she could lose herself in those sexy bedroom eyes. Meg guessed many women had. If he hadn't been her prime suspect, Meg knew that even she might have found herself tempted. Even though she had sworn off shipboard romances.

"Maybe we should go back inside," she suggested, trying to regain her equilibrium and hopefully gain the lead. "They're probably serving dessert. I hear the pastry chef's—"

"Do you really want to do back in there?" he cut her off in that sexy British accent. They'd stopped actually dancing, but they were still holding each other.

Damn, he's good at this! Meg had to briskly remind herself that so was she.

Okay, Mr. Danforth II, two can play this game, but just remember only one of us can win it. And sorry to tell you this, but it's going to be me.

Meg drew her head back a few inches and lifted one slender eyebrow. "What are you suggesting?" she asked with just a touch of coyness.

Her voice was so breathy and she felt so good in his arms that once again Noah found himself losing his train of thought. This wouldn't do. This was no time to be going soft. He had a job to do. *Job* made it sound routine, and the way he earned his living was far from routine. Any professional endeavor that smacked of routine would have driven him nuts. The boredom, the tedium of it, gave him the shivers. In an altogether different way, so, unfortunately, did Meg Newell.

He started to tell himself that maybe she wasn't the right one. There were several other possible picks on board this tank. Only problem was, this one fit the bill to a T. And then there was this gut instinct he had the minute he'd laid eyes on her. And on her sparkling gems. Yes, he thought with an uncharacteristic bittersweet twinge in his chest, Meg Newell had what he wanted. All he had to do was concentrate on the best way to get it.

He donned a deliberately provocative smile. "Are you a gambler, Meg?"

She gave a little start at hearing him call her Meg for the first time. The way it sounded on his lips . . . Hell, it was only the British accent. The *phony* British accent.

"A gambler?" She smiled faintly. "That depends on what the stakes are."

"The higher the stakes the greater the excitement," he murmured seductively.

"And the greater the risk of losing," she added.

"Does that worry you, Meg? Losing?"

He was baiting her. She was sure of it. This was all part of the game for him.

"No. Losing has never worried me, Noah. Maybe because I've never lost when it really counted."

Okay, so maybe *never* was a bit of an exaggeration, but the point was, she wasn't going to lose this time around. She was ready for him; she was onto his game plan. Better than that, she was one step ahead of him. She had a game plan of her own. One she was certain he wasn't anticipating.

IT WAS CLOSE to 11 p.m. and the ship's casino was humming. Noah and Meg spent some time at baccarat, where they both did quite well, then joined up with Heather St. John and Lars Olson at one of three roulette tables. Out of the corner of her eye, Meg spotted Paul idly dropping coins into a one-armed bandit. Every now and then he glanced in the direction of their table, but Meg wasn't sure if he was keeping an eye on their prime suspect or on the luscious Heather.

"Place your bets, ladies and gentlemen," said Liza Hamilton, a beautiful croupier with dark brown hair, sooty lashes, flawless ivory skin and a svelte body wrapped in gold lamé. Her tapered, beautifully manicured fingers were poised on the roulette wheel.

Meg placed a generous stack of chips on only one number while Noah spread his around on several. They shared a smile as the croupier spun the wheel.

Everyone at the table watched with nervous anticipation as the wheel came to a slow stop. The croupier smiled in Meg's direction as she announced, "Thirty-two red."

"You have a knack for picking the right number, it appears," Olson remarked to Meg as she stacked up her winnings in a tidy pile. He had lost a small pile of chips on twenty-three black.

"I suppose I do," Meg replied cavalierly. A total lie. On the rare occasions she'd gambled, she'd lost every time. Maybe she was having better luck now because she wasn't betting with her own money. SeaQuest Line was footing the bill. And pocketing the winnings. Not that Meg was complaining. High Seas had received a sizable retainer for this job. And there'd be a very big bonus at the end. If they nabbed the jewel thief. Meg preferred to think of it as *when* they nabbed him. There was no way she would allow herself to accept the possibility of failure.

As she started to gather up her chips Noah caught hold of her arm. "You're not quitting, are you, Meg?"

"Don't you think it's wise to quit when you're ahead?"

He grinned. "I've rarely come across a wise gambler. Especially when they're ahead. Have you?"

She smiled coquettishly. "Actually I was just taking a break to go powder my nose."

He gestured to the pile of chips she was about to dump into her beaded purse. "I'll watch those for you. Unless, of course, you don't trust me."

Their eyes met and locked.

"What reason in the world would I have not to trust you?" she asked with feigned innocence.

He gave her a sexy, half-lidded look. "None that I can think of," he crooned.

She smiled beguilingly, then dropped the chips back down on the green felt table beside Noah's stack of chips and headed for the powder room.

SHE MADE A detour on the way, slipping behind an ivy-covered latticework divider at the far end of the casino. After a quick look around to make sure the coast was clear, she knocked firmly on the casino manager's office door.

The nameplate on the paneled oak door read Anthony Ross, but the man who opened it was none other than Tony Delgado, the last and youngest of Meg's four brothers. Tony, who knew his way around more than a few casinos, had been only too happy to nab the part of the *Galileo*'s casino manager for this gig, as he called it.

Meg and Tony were only eighteen months apart and bore a strong resemblance to each other, which was the main reason Tony had grown a beard for this assignment and had even, albeit reluctantly, succumbed to a henna rinse. His brown hair, normally almost the exact shade as Meg's, was now a deep auburn.

Tony stepped aside for Meg to slip into his office, then shut the door behind her and locked it so they wouldn't be disturbed.

"Saw you at the roulette table," he said with a smile. "You're doing well."

"I didn't see you out there."

Tony pointed to the wall to his left. Meg followed her brother's finger. Covering the entire left wall of Tony's temporary spacious office was a bank of monitors each targeting specific areas inside the casino. Tony could sit in his plush maroon upholstered swivel chair and, with a flick of the eye, see everyone and everything going on within his domain.

Meg walked closer to the monitor that showed the roulette table she'd just left. There was Noah, who was now chatting with Heather St. John. Where was the Swede? Her eyes cruised the other monitors until she finally spotted Olson heading for the exit leading to the deck, an unlit cigarette in his hand. Apparently ducking out for a smoke.

Meg turned her attention back to the monitor showing the roulette table. Both Noah and Heather had placed their bets. While the wheel spun, Meg saw Heather lean closer to Noah and whisper something that made him laugh. Meg felt a funny little pang. Jealousy? No, of course not. She simply didn't want someone gumming up the works.

"She's beautiful, isn't she?" Tony remarked dreamily as he came up behind his sister.

Meg sighed heavily. "Not you, too. You're going to have to vie with your three brothers as to who's going to head the Heather St. John fan club."

"Heather St. John? Who's talking about Heather St. John?"

Meg turned to her brother. "You are. Aren't you?"

Tony grinned. "No. I'm talking about Liza Hamilton."

"Who?"

"That drop-dead gorgeous croupier at the roulette table." Tony placed his hand against his chest right over his heart. "Don't tell me you didn't notice her. I'm telling you, Meggie, that woman—"

"Forget that woman," Meg said sharply. Then she threw up her hands. "I don't know what's the matter with all of you. Paul, Alex and Sean mooning over

Heather St. John, you going gaga over some croupier..."

"Well now, little sister, you and Danforth were sure getting real chummy dancing under the stars a little while ago," Tony teased. "Paulie happened to be sitting at a table in the dining room with a great view of the deck. He said that the two of you—"

"I was just doing my job," she snapped. "And I expect the rest of you to concentrate fully on doing yours."

Tony playfully pinched her cheek. "Have we ever let you down, little sister?"

A smile tugged at the corners of Meg's mouth. "No."

Her smile quickly faded. "But we're really up against it this time. The stakes have never been higher, Tony. If we screw up on this one, we can kiss our reputation goodbye. Our name will be mud in the business. We'll be lucky if a banana boat hires us."

Tony gave his sister a reassuring hug. "Stop worrying. We won't screw up."

He held her at arm's length, his gaze shifting to the monitor angled on the roulette table and Noah Danforth II, then back to his sister. All of the playful amusement was gone from his face. "Just be careful, Meggie."

She nodded. Even though she wasn't altogether sure exactly what it was her brother was cautioning her to be careful about.

CHAPTER THREE

CHET CARSON exhaled a long stream of smoke as he fixed an anxious gaze on Noah Webb. Noah had removed his jacket and bow tie and was sprawled on the couch of his suite, staring up at the ceiling. It was nearly two in the morning. He'd left Meg at the door to her suite twenty minutes earlier.

"So, is she the one?" Chet asked, slipping off his shoes. "I mean, we've got a few others we could consider. There's Heather St. John, for starters." Chet grinned broadly. "Not bad for starters, if you ask me."

Noah didn't say anything.

"You think it's the Newell dame, though, don't you?"

Still no response.

Chet was starting to get antsy. He always did before things really got under way. And he hated the guesswork. Always liked it better when there was no question about the target. And something else. Webb wasn't acting like his old self. He seemed kind of moody. Not that he'd ever been what Chet would call garrulous, but now trying to wring words out of him was like pulling teeth.

"Don't you think we should be getting down to the nitty-gritty, Webb?"

Noah shot Carson a disapproving look.

"Okay, okay. Sorry. Danforth." Carson stuck his cigarette in the corner of his mouth and rubbed his palms together. "The question is, when are you going to make your move?" Carson waited. "The sooner the better, if you ask me."

Still no answer.

Chet took another drag of his cigarette. Noah's seeming complacency about this whole business was really putting him on edge. He needed to set a fire under him. "By the way, a pal of mine in the casino spotted Newell slip into the manager's office on her way to the powder room. He says she did a quick check before she knocked on his door. She was in there for a good five minutes. Looked a little flushed when she left."

Noah sat up.

Carson smiled to himself. Mission accomplished. "Curious, huh?" he mused. "Then there's that *secretary* of hers. You may have some competition here, old chap."

Noah wasn't paying attention to what Carson was saying. "There's something about her," he said, mulling over each word as he spoke them.

Carson grinned. "I'll say. Even without those rocks, she's a hot number. No doubt about that. Hey, pal, you're only human. Just like the rest of us. Now, personally, that St. John dame is more my style, but hey, Newell is a knockout in her own way."

Noah scowled. "That's not what I'm talking about." Well, it wasn't *all* he was talking about, anyway. Sure, he was only human. And okay, Meg happened to be the kind of woman he could go for. It wasn't the classy package she presented, either. Or even her looks, although he had no complaints in that department. It was something else about her that drew him. He wasn't sure what. And he wasn't sure he should be spending his time trying to figure it out.

He got up and poured himself a tall glass of plain tonic on the rocks.

Carson joined him at the bar, pouring himself a shot of bourbon. He gave Noah a sideways glance. "You're not having any doubts about pulling this off? That's not like you."

"Did I say anything about doubts?" Noah snapped. "I just want to take it slow. Get a better handle on her."

"You had a pretty good handle on her out there on the deck," Carson said with a grin. "She's a good dancer. Real graceful."

"Don't go getting the wrong idea here, Carson. It was all in a night's work."

"So, how come you didn't drop into her suite for a nightcap?"

"Like I said, I don't want to rush it." Noah cupped his drink in both hands. "We've got two weeks. There's no hurry. And like you said yourself, there are a few other possibilities. We want to keep our options open. Sniff around. And if we do zero in on Newell, I need to play it cool. She's no fool. And she's wary. Oh, she tries to cover it up, but I can feel it. Like she's sizing me up all the while I'm sizing her up. It's going to take a little time to get her to relax and trust that I'm on the up-and-up. Then when her guard's down . . ."

Carson grinned. "Ya stick it to her."

Noah gave him a dirty look.

Carson flushed. "Hey, I didn't mean . . . I'm just saying it's a good game plan. Lay on the charm for a couple more days, and my hunch is she'll be eating out of your hand. Why, I don't know. But women seem to find you irresistible."

Noah scowled. "There are times I feel like a bloody heel. Times I feel like hanging it up. Retiring."

Carson couldn't figure his friend out. "Okay, maybe it looks like more fun from the outside looking in." He paused for a moment, his gaze narrowing. "You worried she might really fall for you?"

Noah shook off the question Carson asked. As well as the one he didn't ask, but Noah knew he was thinking. *You worried you might really fall for her?*

"I'm only worried about one thing," Noah said firmly. "Getting what we came here for."

Carson smiled. "Now that's the way I like to hear you talk, Webb. Because there are a lot of folks counting on you. And it wouldn't help either of our careers to disappoint them. But you know that already."

Noah knew it only too well.

MEG GAVE her brother Paul an uneasy look. "You're sure no one spotted you coming over here. Hard to explain what my *secretary* was doing in my suite at two in the morning."

"Relax, Meggie. No one saw me. I'm a pro, remember? What's eating you, anyway?"

"Nothing," Meg said too quickly and knew it. She fidgeted with the catch of her necklace. "God, this thing weighs a ton."

Paul came over and unfastened it for her. Then Meg removed the bracelet, walked over to the safe, pressed out her secret code, swung the door open and stowed the jewels away for the night.

Paul stared thoughtfully at the safe. "I just don't see how he's going to manage breaking into that baby."

"Maybe that's not his plan," Meg said quietly.

Paul cast her a puzzled look. "What do you mean?"

"Let's say you've had this string of divinely romantic evenings with this suave, handsome, charming man. One night, he's escorting you back to your suite and neither of you wants the night to end...."

"This is getting interesting now," Paul said with a twinkle in his brown eyes.

Meg gave him a humorless smile and went on, "And probably you've had a bit too much bubbly so you aren't thinking clearly...."

"Or you've got other things on your mind?"

"Or so lover boy's counting on," Meg said sardonically.

"So maybe you don't pause to take the time to stow your jewels?"

"Right. You think to yourself you'll do it—after." Meg had trouble maintaining eye contact with her brother. She could feel the color start to rise up her neck.

"Only maybe *after,*" Paul picked up, "you're feeling so relaxed you forget about your jewels altogether. Maybe you drift off to sleep..."

"And lo and behold, next morning you wake up and..."

"They're gone," Paul finished.

Meg sighed. "Gone."

"But wouldn't your shipboard lover be the first person you'd point the finger at?" Paul asked.

"Maybe. Maybe not," Meg mused. "Don't forget if he's as good as I suspect he is—"

"Suspect?" Paul teased. "Seems to me you've already gotten at least a sample of lover boy's charm. Given, may I say again, that he's the right lover boy. But since he's coming on so hot and heavy and not having to beat out any competition thus far..."

"As I was saying," Meg said in her all-business tone, "it's most likely he'd make it a point to leave the suite after...that is, before his lady love drifted off. Probably even make some comment about her jewels lying around."

"I get where you're heading. But what if she wanted him to spend the night?"

"He'd probably say something very gallant like he didn't want to risk gossip spreading among the passengers. Anyway, he'd find some way to make his exit. Later, when she was sound asleep, it would be very easy for him to slip back in and steal the goods."

"I still say he'd be the first person she'd point to come the next morning," Paul insisted.

"First of all, even if she did, he'd be smart enough not to have the jewels in his possession," Meg said. "Without any proof, there'd be no way to charge him with the theft."

"You think he'd hide them somewhere on board?"

Meg thought about that. "Or pass them on to someone else."

Paul's eyes widened. "An accomplice."

"It makes sense."

"You're right," Paul said. "So we should pass the word to the others, and we should all keep a check on who Danforth makes contact with."

"Definitely," Meg said, flashing back on that image of Noah and Heather chumming it up at the roulette table while she was supposedly in the powder room.

"One thing I don't get," Paul said. "If this is the way you think he's going to operate, then I gather you're figuring it's his usual MO. He books himself on a cruise, stakes out some bejeweled woman on board who's traveling alone, romances her and swipes her baubles."

"Look at the reports SeaQuest gave us of the jewel thefts on those other cruise ships," Meg said. "All the victims were women fitting your description."

"But not one of them even acknowledged they were having a shipboard romance, or we'd have something more than practically nothing to go on."

Meg sighed. "And, unfortunately, no one who investigated the thefts thought to question any of the other passengers about whether these victims had been courted while at sea."

"Why would the victims keep mum about it?" Paul asked.

"There could be several reasons," Meg said. "A couple of the victims we got reports on were married, and I doubt they'd want their husbands' learning of their little indiscretions."

"And the ones who were single?" Paul persisted. "No reason for them to keep it a secret."

"Unless he gave them a reason."

"I don't get it. Like what?"

"Like he was going through a divorce. Like he'd lied to his boss and he'd get canned if the boss learned he'd been on the ship, instead of whatever place he was supposed to be. Or like..." She hesitated.

"Like what?" Paul pressed.

"Like he told them he was madly in love with them. That they were special. That he'd never met anyone like them before in his life. If they believed him, how could they ever let themselves imagine it had all been a lie? That they'd been duped? That he hadn't meant a single word? No one wants to think that, do they?" Meg reflected, unable to mask the bittersweet note in her voice. Even though she'd long ago stopped having any romantic feelings for Jonathan Drew, the hurt that came with having been one of those women who had been deceived still hung on. One thing was for sure—she'd never be dumb enough to let that happen to her again.

Paul came over and put his arm around his sister. "None of us are exempt from being made to feel the fool when it comes to matters of the heart."

Meg gave her brother a friendly jab in the arm. "What we're dealing with here is a matter of the mind, Paulie, not the heart. The point is that we don't want Mr. Noah Danforth II to realize that. Let him be the busy little unsuspecting bee buzzing around me. We'll be the busy little spiders weaving the web."

"Right you are, sis."

She fought back a yawn. "Time for us both to get some sleep. I'm wiped."

"A little too much bubbly, Meg?" Paul teased.

She gave him a shove in the direction of the door. "Make sure no one spots you leaving. I'll see you tomorrow at ten. For morning dictation," she added with a wink.

He stuck out his tongue at her.

NOAH COULDN'T SETTLE down. Finally he changed into a pair of gray cords, a black turtleneck, threw an Irish cable-knit sweater over his shoulders and headed over to the glass-domed piano lounge on the Casablanca Deck.

The lounge was almost deserted. Noah spotted a few hangers-on chatting quietly around a table in the far corner, a couple at the bar and a piano player crooning a Sinatra ballad at the baby grand.

As Noah headed toward the bar he heard his name being called. He turned to see Heather St. John and Lars Olson sitting in a partially hidden nook to his right. It was Heather who'd called him. Olson didn't seem particularly thrilled as he ambled over to their table.

"You're ears must be burning, Barrister," Heather said cheerily.

"I beg your pardon," Noah said.

"Lars and I were just talking about you," Heather said. "Well, I was doing the talking, actually."

Noah pulled an extra chair over to the small marble-topped table for two. Heather scooted over to make room for him. Lars was less accommodating and didn't budge. A waitress approached and Noah ordered a martini and a second round of drinks for his shipmates.

"So what was it you were saying about me, Miss St. John?" Noah asked after the waitress left.

"I was saying that you have a definite air of mystery about you, Mr. Danforth II."

Noah donned his roguish smile. "Well, I think I like that."

Heather leaned a little closer to him. She squinted slightly, as if mining his face for clues. "So, is there some mystery about you, Mr. Danforth II?"

"If there is, Miss St. John, and I told you what it was, there wouldn't be any more mystery, would there?"

She trilled a low sexy laugh. "Quite right. Isn't that so, Lars?"

Lars gave Heather a woeful look. "And what about me? Am I not mysterious?"

Heather smiled in much the way one might smile at a pouting child. "Mysterious? No, not really, darling. But you have some other fine qualities."

Lars was only mildly placated. "Like what?" he pressed.

Subtle guy, Noah mused.

Heather glanced at Noah. He got the message that she was stymied as to what those fine qualities were. Apparently Lars Olson's looking like a Norse god wasn't enough for her. Noah felt compelled to come to her rescue.

"Please, you're going to make me blush if you recount them now, in front of me," Noah said to Heather.

"We can't have that," Heather said with an enticing smile.

Lars was clearly not pleased. He glanced at his watch. "It's quite late, I see. May I walk you to your cabin, Heather?"

"Aren't you forgetting? Noah just ordered us another round."

Right on cue, the waitress arrived with the drinks. Lars finished off his cognac in a matter of minutes. Heather, on the other hand, was nursing her Scotch on the rocks, and Noah was taking his time with his martini.

"I love London," Heather was telling Noah. "My mother used to have a flat on Knightsbridge Road. When I was at boarding school in Switzerland, I sometimes stayed with her on holidays. I remember badgering her to take me around to all the sights, but she was always too busy."

"What did she do?" Noah asked.

Heather grinned. "Good question. I was never quite sure."

Noah quirked an eyebrow.

"Oh, I don't mean she was doing anything wicked or illegal. Mother's a very proper woman. Very refined. Not enough so for my father, though. She was a disappointment to him. As was I," she added offhandedly. "They were divorced when I was nine."

"Is she still in London?" Noah asked.

"No. She's seeing a very rich Austrian businessman, and they're currently in Saudi Arabia where Helmut's overseeing his investments."

"I visit England often," Lars interjected. "We must plan to meet there sometime soon, Heather, and I shall take you to see all the sights. Buckingham Palace, the Tower of London, the British Museum, Covent Garden..."

Heather patted Lars's cheek. "That's very dear of you, but I did have a gentleman friend take me around only last fall. A friend of a friend, really."

"Anyone I might know?" Noah asked.

"The friend? Or the friend of a friend?"

"Either. Both. I know a lot of people."

Heather was pensive for a moment or two, then her shoulders lifted in a graceful shrug. "That's funny.

The names are on the tip of my tongue. I just don't seem able to spit them out. I'll probably wake up in the middle of the night and remember."

Lars tapped the face of his watch and smiled at Heather. "It's already well past the middle of the night. Please allow me to walk you back to your cabin, yes?"

Heather smiled back sweetly. "No thanks. I think I'll stay here with Noah for a bit and chat about London. Don't let us keep you, though."

Lars shot Noah a look that could have turned boiling water into an ice cube in seconds. When his eyes shifted to Heather, his gaze warmed considerably. "Well, it's been a most delightful evening. I hope it will be the first of many. Now, if you'll excuse me..."

Heather murmured some pleasantry, but as soon as Lars made his exit, she glanced at Noah with a crooked grin. "Now there's a fellow who thinks he's God's gift to women."

"I imagine," Noah said, "there are many women who would agree."

Heather shrugged. "I suppose you're right. He simply happens not to be my cup of tea." She laughed prettily. "Actually, I hate tea. You probably think that's close to treason, what with you being a proper Englishman." Her smile turned playful. "Or maybe not so proper?"

Noah wagged a finger at her, then gave her a conspiratorial look. "Promise not to spread it about, but I'm not too wild about tea myself. Although I assure you," he teased, "in all other ways, I'm an exceedingly proper Brit."

Heather smiled, then tilted her head and gave him a long study. "Is that what she thinks? That you're a proper Brit?"

"She?" he queried. "Ah, I gather you mean Mrs. Newell."

"You two look very good together."

Noah returned the smile. "I imagine Meg Newell would look good with anyone."

"I find her a bit mysterious, too," Heather mused. After a short pause she sighed. "That's my problem in a nutshell. I lack that elusive, enigmatic quality."

"You have other fine qualities," Noah said with a teasing smile.

She laughed softly. "Unlike my crass Swedish friend, I won't ask you to list them." She pursed her lips slightly. "Besides," she said reflectively, "some things are meant to be, and others aren't."

She stretched gracefully. The woman, Noah noted, did everything gracefully. Maybe he was shopping the wrong side of the street, so to speak. No. Heather St. John simply didn't meet the specifications. She might be a woman with a lot to offer, but he was pretty sure she didn't have what he needed. A part of him wished she had. It would have made his job much less complicated. As beautiful as Heather was, she simply didn't set off any sparks in him.

Unfortunately Meg Newell was another story altogether. Not that he couldn't manage to keep a few sparks from turning into a forest fire.

"Well, I really am tired," Heather said after a long shared silence. "And to think I had planned to turn in early tonight."

Noah grinned. "Well, it *is* early. It's a little after two in the morning." He started to rise as Heather stood up.

"That's okay," she said, giving him a friendly pat on the shoulder. "Stay put and finish your drink. I'll find my way. I've got an excellent sense of direction."

"TONY, HAVE YOU HEARD a word I've said?" Liza Hamilton scolded lightly.

The beautiful dark-haired croupier and the bearded casino manager were sitting at the bar, and while Tony wanted nothing more than to hang on every one of the luscious Liza's words, he was distracted by the tête-à-tête going on between Noah Danforth and Heather St. John in one of the lounge's cozy little nooks a few yards behind him. He was too far away to overhear what they were saying, but he could observe them quite easily through the mirror running across the entire wall back of the bar.

Tony looked into Liza's big brown eyes and took hold of her hand. "Sorry. Tell me again and I promise to give you my undivided attention."

Liza's gaze shot to the mirror, then returned to Tony. She gave him a pouty look. "Now that I don't have to share your attention with that pretty redhead, you mean."

Tony brought her hand to his lips, his eyes cruising her face. "What redhead?"

PAUL STEPPED OUT of Meg's suite, hurried down the empty corridor and was just turning the corner when he bumped smack-dab into Heather St. John.

They both wore awkward expressions as they stared at each other—Heather because she'd turned Paul down for a drink on the excuse that she was going to make an early night of it, and Paul because his presence in that particular first-class quarter had to appear mighty suspicious.

"Well," Heather mumbled, not quite meeting Paul's eyes.

"Well," Paul echoed, his gaze fixed on a spot someplace over Heather's right shoulder.

They stood there with dumb smiles plastered on their faces.

"I...couldn't sleep," she said finally.

"I...uh..." He glanced behind him. "Had some papers to...drop off. For my boss. Mrs. Newell."

"Yes, well..." She looked over at the gleaming brass rail that ran the entire length of the pale-blue-walled corridor.

Paul absently smoothed back his hair, which was almost the same shade of red as Heather's. "I slipped them under her door. Wouldn't do to...wake the boss at..." He paused, glanced at his watch. "Wow, it is late."

"Or early."

"Right."

They shared another awkward smile.

"Well...I guess I'll be turning in," she said. "I'm just around the corner."

"Me, too," Paul said. "I mean, about turning in. I'm one level down."

They started to step around each other, only they both moved in the same direction at the same time, each of them effectively blocking the other from passing. Immediately they stepped to the other side. Again together and at the same time. Another impasse.

Paul smiled with more sincerity now. "I tell you what. You stand still and I'll step around you."

"Sounds like a good plan," she said, looking amused.

"See ya," Paul said with a little wave as he walked past her.

"Right. See ya."

ELIOT HARPER simply couldn't sleep. Every time he closed his eyes visions of disaster swam through his head. Finally he got up, turned on the reading light on his side of the bed, found his slippers and shuffled across the cabin.

He was quietly standing in front of the closed door, carefully studying the card posted there indicating the lifeboat station assigned the "occupants" and the location of the life jackets, when Elaine, her hair in rollers, a grayish green mud pack on her face, was awakened by the light in the room. At first she thought it must be morning, but then she squinted at the clock.

What in heaven's name...? Then she spotted her husband, standing with his back to her, staring at their closed door.

"Have you gone mad? What are you doing standing there like that? It's after two o'clock in the morning, for goodness' sake," she scolded. "Come to bed, Eliot."

"This is important, Elaine. Something we must commit to memory," he said earnestly. "The signal for lifeboat and fire drills is seven short blasts followed by one long blast of the ship's whistle," he read off the card. "And that will be accompanied by indoor alarm bells. As soon as the alarm is sounded, we must—"

"The alarm isn't likely to sound on our first night out, Eliot. Now would you please come to bed."

"Yes, dear," Eliot said with a sigh of resignation.

He started across the room.

"Eliot, you did remember about my amethyst ring?"

"What about it, dear?" he asked as he sat down on his side of the bed.

"You did lock it in the safe? With my gold watch and my sapphire choker?"

"Yes, dear. I did that hours ago," he said, stepping out of his slippers.

"Granted they're not all that valuable when compared to those gems of Mrs. Newell's or some of the others on board, but they're still worth a pretty penny."

"Yes, dear," Eliot said, slipping under the covers.

"Of course, they are insured. You did remember to pay the premium before we left? You can be so forgetful. There was that time you forgot to mail the Christmas card to the paperboy, and if it hadn't been for the woman at the cleaner's who discovered the card in one of your jacket pockets the boy might not have gotten that card and the five dollars inside it until Easter."

While his wife droned on, Eliot pulled up the blankets, thinking, Was it seven long blasts followed by one short blast or one short blast followed by seven long blasts?

"Eliot?" Elaine said sharply.

Eliot gave a little start. "Yes, dear?"

"The insurance premiums."

"Life insurance?"

"No. For heaven's sake, Eliot. The premiums on my jewels."

"Oh. Those premiums. Yes, dear. Don't you remember, we—"

"Still, they have a sentimental value that insurance money can't ever replace. Especially the amethyst ring. It was my mother's."

"I'm sure everything will be quite safe, my dear."

"Yes, I suppose you're right. But you can never be too careful."

Eliot stared up at the ceiling, worry lines creasing his brow. Or was it seven short blasts followed by one long blast, or one short—

"Eliot, the light. Turn out the light."

"Yes, dear."

He tried to settle down, but then the thought struck him—what if it wasn't a drill? What if real calamity struck?

ALAN DELACORE gently pulled the covers up over his fiancée as she lay in bed, then bent low and kissed her lightly on the lips. "Good night, gumdrop."

Louanne Percy sleepily slipped her arms around the former ambassador's thick neck. In his college days he'd been a linebacker. Now much of the muscle had turned to fat. Louanne didn't seem to mind.

"Are you sure you won't just stay the night, sugar?" she drawled.

He planted another kiss on her lips. "You know I'd love to, sweetie pie, but what with my divorce not being final yet ..."

"I don't know what you ever saw in that woman, sugar."

"Now, now, gumdrop. She is the mother of my two children. And you know how I feel about those little darlings. We don't want to put them through any ugly custody battles. As long as I maintain certain proprieties, Annette promises not to cause any difficulties with the visitation agreement."

"Oh, well, it just seems dumb to me." Louanne sighed petulantly. "I mean she's got to know we're sleeping together even if we don't share a dumb old suite while we're on this cruise. It's nothing but a farce."

Alan stroked Louanne's cheek. "Annette has always been very big on maintaining the appearance of propriety. So we each have our own suite. Now, we've been all through this, sugar. You get some beauty sleep and I'll see you bright and early in the morning."

"You most certainly will not. I intend to sleep till midafternoon. I'll meet you at the pool at four."

"That's a date, you sweet thing."

They shared another kiss, this one far more passionate. Then Alan Delacore started to leave. Halfway across the room, he snapped his fingers. "My watch. I almost forgot."

He turned back to the bedside table to retrieve it. The watch was tangled up with the jewelry Louanne had removed before getting into bed—her three-carat diamond engagement ring, a pair of sparkling sapphire earrings, and a twenty-four-carat gold charm bracelet. "Hey, gumdrop. You really shouldn't leave your jewelry lying around."

"Mmm," Louanne murmured, already starting to doze off. "I'll put them away first thing in the morning."

"I can do it for you now if you like. What's your code?"

"What?" she asked sleepily.

"Your code, sweetie pie."

"Oh, I can't remember..." She yawned. "Don't worry, sugar. They'll be ... fine."

"Well, stow it all away first thing when you get up, you hear, sweetie pie?"

"Mmm. Night, sugar. Love ya."

"Love you, too, gumdrop."

CHAPTER FOUR

"IT'S FORTUNATE I'm an inveterate insomniac, Captain," Barbara Friers said at four-fifteen that same morning. "And that Horace and I happen to have the suite right next door to Louanne Percy's."

"Yes, it certainly is," Captain Simon agreed. As soon as the anxious call from the Friers woman had been put through to him, he'd hurriedly dressed in his crisp blue-and-gold uniform and sped over to their suite.

Horace Friers, dressed in white silk pajamas and a plaid silk robe, padded across his suite carrying a glass of water and a tablet in his hand. "Here you go, dear. This will settle your nerves," he said, handing his wife the glass and the pill.

"It's one thing to write about intrigue and quite another to come face-to-face with it in real life, I must say," the buxom novelist said, then paused to take the tablet, explaining to the captain that, like all creative people, she was high-strung.

"Could you tell me once again exactly what happened?" the captain asked after she'd swallowed half the glass of water.

The novelist pulled her floral silk robe with its bright swirls of tropical colors more tightly around her as she sat on the coral sofa. Horace took a seat beside her, and the captain sat in one of the matching coral leather armchairs across from her.

"First of all, when I say face-to-face I'm taking a certain literary license," Barbara Friers qualified.

"Then you didn't actually see his face?" the captain asked.

"Like I said before, when I spotted him his back was to me. And he was wearing one of those sweatshirts with a hood, so I couldn't even see what color his hair was."

"And the sweatshirt itself? Anything special or distinctive about it?"

"It was just like the one we all received as a boarding gift. Pale gray and it had the name of the ship—*Galileo*—in aquamarine lettering across the back."

Horace rose. "I can show you one of ours, Captain."

"No, that's all right. I'm well acquainted with them," Captain Simon said. He turned his attention back to the novelist. "What else was he wearing?"

"Gray running pants. The kind that match the sweatshirt. Again like we all got. Actually, it's quite an astonishing coincidence."

"What is that, Mrs. Friers?" the captain asked.

"In my last book, the male protagonist—his code name was Starling—dressed quite similarly for a break-in in my novel, *Beyond Hope*. He was a double agent. The Soviets—of course this novel was set before the downfall of the Soviet Union—believed he was one of theirs, as did the readers. But then in a very dramatic scene late in the book he confides to the woman he's fallen in love with—Julianna, who's with the CIA—that in truth he, too, is working for the CIA. Only to discover, to his horror, that Julianna is herself a double agent working for the KGB. One night he has to sneak into her apartment and steal back certain plans, and he dresses in a hooded gray running suit and white tennis sneakers..."

"Then the man you saw at Miss Percy's door was also wearing white tennis sneakers?" the captain interjected, trying his best to keep the impatience out of his voice.

"Yes. Didn't I already say that?" The novelist shrugged, then her eyes lit up. "Wouldn't it be something if the intruder had actually read my novel?"

Horace beamed. "Make a great story for the media."

The media? Captain Simon felt his stomach knot. That was all he needed.

"I do think it behooves us to keep this quiet for the present," the captain said solemnly. "After all, we don't have the full story yet. There may be another explanation."

"I seriously doubt it," Mrs. Friers said haughtily. "In *Beyond Hope,* I threw in several red herrings, but usually it's the explanation that best fits the situation that wins out in the end."

"Could we go over it once more?" the captain asked, dabbing the bead of perspiration on his brow with his linen handkerchief. "Not your novel. I mean what you saw," he quickly qualified.

Barbara Friers pursed her lips. "It didn't start with what I saw, Captain. If you want me to be precise, it began with what I heard."

"And what exactly did you hear?"

"I heard this funny scratching sound." She put her hand up to her chest. "I hope you won't be insulted, Captain, but the very first thing I thought was, Good grief, I certainly hope there aren't any mice or rats aboard. You do hear some horrific tales. Have you ever heard of Catherine Jamison?''

"No, I'm afraid I haven't," the captain said wearily.

"Well, she wrote *In Defense of Honor*. Not a particularly good book, if you want my opinion, but it did do well. Anyway, that's beside the point.''

The captain of the *Galileo* was beginning to lose track of the point himself.

"The point is," she said, "Catherine took a cruise around the Greek Isles on a very reputable first-class cruise ship and one night she found herself vying for pillow space with... a rat!"

Horace shuddered. "Dreadful. Simply revolting story. Are you sure she didn't make it up?''

"Quite sure, Horace," Barbara said firmly. "And if it was a rat I heard earlier, a lot of good you'd've done me.''

She looked back at the captain. "When I heard the noise and thought it might be a rat, I poked Horace, but he was sound asleep and I couldn't get him to budge. I have never met a man who could sleep so soundly. Do you know that once, when we were in Kyoto where Horace was filming some silly action-adventure movie—"

"It wasn't silly, Barb," Horace objected. "Nothing that brings in twelve million in its opening weekend is silly.''

Barbara gave her husband a placating smile. "He's so sensitive. Anyway, where was I?''

"About the..." That was as far as the captain got before he was again interrupted.

"Oh, yes, Kyoto, where Horace was filming a *very successful* action-adventure yarn." She gave her husband a broad smile. "There, dear. Is that better?"

"Much," Horace said airily.

"Anyway, Captain," Barbara said, turning her attention back to Simon, "the point I was trying to make was that one night Horace actually slept right through an earthquake. It shook the entire hotel. I was literally thrown off the bed. Horace, being rather overweight at the time, didn't budge."

"I don't know why you always have to tell that story, Barb. Isn't it old, already?" Horace said testily.

Barbara sighed wearily. "You're so sensitive, Horace. I'm just trying to explain to the captain why it was that I was the one who went and peeked out into the corridor, not you."

"And you're quite sure the person you saw wasn't simply passing Miss Percy's room?" the captain quickly inserted before the couple got into another disagreement. "Or... leaving it?"

The novelist smiled knowingly. "He was trying to pick the lock on her door, captain. I don't imagine he'd find that necessary if he was an invited guest of Miss Percy's."

"You saw him actually—"

"Well, if we're going to be strictly technical I didn't actually see him picking the lock. I made certain deductions from the sounds I heard. And from the way he bolted like a shot as soon as I popped my head out the door and said, 'What...?' That's it. That's all that I got out of my mouth before he took off like a shot as I just said."

"You keep saying *he,*" the captain said. "Are you quite sure...?"

"Well, I can't be absolutely certain," the novelist conceded. "What with the hood pulled up and, well, you know how bulky those sweat suits can be. Personally, I prefer spandex, which I think is ever so much more flattering to the figure."

"Then it could have been a woman?"

"A tall woman."

"Tall? How tall?"

Barbara Friers scowled. "I can't say for sure. First he—or she—was sort of squatting at Miss Percy's door. Then when he—or she—bolted, well, when you run you don't actually stand up straight. But I got the distinct impression of tallness."

The captain nodded. "An impression. Of tallness. Is there anything else you can tell me, Mrs. Friers?"

She pondered his question for a long minute. "Well, there is one thing you might be curious to know."

"Yes?" the captain asked eagerly.

"In the end, he goes back to his wife."

"Excuse me?"

"In *Beyond Hope.* Starling had separated from his wife in the beginning of the novel, then had this affair with Julianna, which turned out badly once he found that she'd duped him, but then in the end he realizes he never truly stopped loving Jessica, his wife. So it worked out well for everyone, by the finale. Except for Julianna. She dies in this incredibly dramatic denouement—"

Horace cut her off. "You always do that, Barb."

"Barb" was not pleased by her husband's interruption. "Do what, Horace?"

"Give away the plots to your books. Why should anyone read them after you've told them every twist?"

"I don't think I need to worry about readership, Horace. Considering *Beyond Hope* sold over 300,000 in hard cover and we're already over a million in paperback."

"That's not the point, Barb."

"Then what is the point, Horace?"

"The point is . . ."

Captain Simon did not stick around to find out the point. He doubted either of the feuding Frierses even heard him as he politely excused himself and left.

AT SIX THAT MORNING, Meg and Captain Simon were having breakfast in the captain's private quarters. In addition to a sleeping alcove and a sitting room, the captain's spacious suite had a lovely skylit dining area with a spectacular panoramic view from the windows on three of the four walls of the eating nook. The sunrise over the ocean was breathtaking, but neither Meg nor the captain gave it much notice. They had more pressing matters at hand.

Meg took a sip of the delicious freshly brewed black coffee in her white china cup. Despite having had less than four hours of sleep, the report of a near break-in of one of the passenger cabins had sent a rush of adrenaline through Meg's bloodstream, and she was feeling remarkably alert.

She spread some mango jam on her croissant. "And that's all Friers could tell you?"

The captain smiled sardonically. "Unless you want the plot of her last novel, *Beyond Hope*. Or a dreadful tale about a rat."

Meg set down the sterling-silver jam knife and stared at Simon. "You aren't serious."

"Believe me, I am." He sighed. "I'm afraid she was of very little help in this most distressing matter."

"And how about Louanne Percy? Did she hear anything?"

"Mrs. Friers woke her after the alleged intruder took off. Apparently, Miss Percy was sound asleep and hadn't heard a thing. I had a brief word with her after I left the Frierses' cabin."

"Was she alone when you went in to see her?" Meg asked.

"You mean, was her fiancé, Mr. Delacore, with her?"

Meg smiled faintly. "Him or... anyone else."

"Oh, I see." The captain gave a knowing smile. "No. No, she was quite alone. Unless someone was hiding in the closet or the bathroom."

"What was her reaction when you told her that Mrs. Friers saw someone trying to break into her cabin?"

The captain sighed. "She really thought it was all a big fuss over nothing. It was her opinion that Mrs. Friers imagined the whole thing."

"Do you think it's possible?"

He gave Meg a level look. "Do you?"

She pressed her lips together. "No. Louanne was wearing some very enticing jewels last night."

"Yes, you're quite right. When I was in her suite, I saw those same jewels carelessly lying about on her bedside table. If our thief had broken in, he'd have had very little difficulty snatching them. I did encourage her to lock her valuables in her safe whenever she wasn't wearing them. She mumbled something to me about her fiancé having told her the same thing."

"Interesting," Meg mused.

"Miss Percy may have been nonchalant about this ugly business, but I'm quite worried that the rest of the passengers might not treat the news so casually," the captain said, his deep baritone evincing real concern. "And thanks to the loquacious Mrs. Friers I'm sure that everyone on board will have heard about the would-be break-in before the morning's out."

Meg took a bite of her croissant and washed it down with another sip of coffee. "Well, it might not be so bad if the word gets out. It'll make things harder for our thief, because the passengers will be more cautious with their valuables."

"Unfortunately it also makes it harder for all of us affiliated with the SeaQuest Line in general and the *Galileo* in particular to maintain our fine reputation," the captain said glumly.

Meg nodded sympathetically, then her brows knit together in consternation. "I'd really hoped I'd be the one he would make his first move on, but maybe he's decided to do a few practice runs first. The thing is, how did he know Percy had her jewels lying about?"

"Her fiancé knew," Captain Simon reminded her.

"You mean you think he might have planned to pilfer them? That the former ambassador to Belgium is our jewel thief?"

"Well, one doesn't know what financial difficulties a man might have, whatever his position. Or former position. He isn't really doing anything currently. And Miss Percy comes from a very affluent and influential Atlanta family."

"He must have bought her that diamond engagement ring, though," Meg pointed out. "It had to have cost a tidy sum."

The captain nodded. "But what if subsequent to that purchase he fell on some hard times? Needed money?"

"I should check with Tony and see if our former ambassador did any heavy gambling in the casino," Meg said.

"And there wasn't only the diamond ring. Miss Percy's other jewels are worth a good deal of money, as well. Furthermore, he may have felt that his fiancée wouldn't suffer greatly since I'm sure the jewels are insured. And it's unlikely she would ever suspect the thief was the man she was planning to marry."

"It does fit one of my theories about how our thief operates," Meg admitted. "Under the circumstances Delacore certainly has to be added to my list of prime suspects."

She stared off into space. "But I still have this gut feeling the man we're looking for is this Danforth character. Something about him simply doesn't ring true."

"You're quite right about that."

Meg looked sharply across at the captain. "What do you mean?"

"There's reason to believe that Mr. Noah Danforth II is not actually a barrister as he claims. Granted, that doesn't mean he's a jewel thief, but—"

"Are you telling me you have proof that Danforth isn't a legal eagle?"

The captain rose and retrieved a single sheet of paper from his desk in the adjoining room. He returned and handed Meg the paper, which turned out to be a fax he'd received only a few minutes before she'd arrived.

Meg silently read the fax.

Records indicate that there is no listing in the London Bar for a Noah Danforth II. Further investigation into the office quarters listed on Mr. Danforth's ship registry card as his place of employment indicate that while said office has been leased to a gentleman claiming to be a barrister by the name of Noah Danforth II, none of the tenants in the building recall ever seeing anyone using that office.

Meg stared at the paper. How odd. Here was a piece of news that confirmed, at least in part, her suspicions that Noah was not who he claimed to be, yet instead of feeling elated, patting herself on the back for her brilliant intuition about him, she was—what? She wasn't quite sure how she felt. Had she wanted to be proved wrong about him? That wasn't like her at all. But then, she wasn't feeling completely like herself at the moment.

"Are you all right, Meg?" the captain asked solicitously.

She looked up from the fax, but it took her a few seconds to get the captain back in sharp focus. "Oh, yes. Fine. This is...very helpful. It's obviously not enough...yet, but it's a good start." She tried to sound enthusiastic about the discovery, but she couldn't quite pull it off.

"I suppose we should count our blessings," the captain said.

"Our blessings?" Meg asked, her throat oddly dry.

"He—whether it's Danforth, Delacore or whoever—was foiled in his attempt to steal Miss Percy's jewels."

"It was unlucky for him that he picked the suite next door to an insomniac," Meg said with a humorless smile.

The captain frowned. "I only hope he doesn't get lucky next time round. If there is a next time. As you say, once the word gets out, the passengers will all no doubt be far more careful to stow their valuables in their safes."

"One passenger won't," Meg said pointedly.

The captain gave her a puzzled look, but then his mouth curved in a smile. "Oh, I get it."

AT SIX FORTY-FIVE that same morning, Meg and her brothers held a secret rendezvous in Tony's cabin on the lower deck, where the ship's staff were housed. After Meg filled them all in on the near break-in of Louanne Percy's suite, she asked Tony if he'd spotted Alan Delacore in the casino the previous evening.

"As a matter of fact, he spent a good deal of time playing blackjack," Tony said.

"Did he win or lose?" Meg asked.

"I'm not sure. But I can check on it."

"Do that," Meg said. "You didn't happen to spot any other high rollers? I know Danforth didn't gamble much, but that may have been because we were together. And from what I saw of Lars Olson, he wasn't bidding too extravagantly at roulette."

"No, but I did notice him going at it a bit heavier at the craps table shortly after dinner. I saw him sweep up a rather high stack of chips and look quite pleased about it."

"Anyone else?"

Tony scratched his beard. "Actually, I did see Horace Friers lose a sizable sum at blackjack. Not that he can't afford it. I'm sure the head of a movie studio would look on that loss as peanuts."

"Unless his studio was in trouble," Sean pointed out. A while back, Sean had spent a few months in Hollywood trying to break into the acting game. He had the looks and the talent, but he soon found out that the same was true of thousands of other would-be actors.

Alex snapped his fingers. "I just thought of something. What if it was Friers?"

"What do you mean?" Paul asked.

"He and the wife could be in it together," Alex said excitedly. "She makes up this cock-and-bull story about a mysterious intruder trying to break into Percy's suite so that when her husband really does strike, who'd ever think it was him?"

"Hey," Tony said, "I like that."

"I don't know," Meg said, tapping her index finger against her lips.

"You did say that the thief could be working with an accomplice," Paul reminded her.

"Yes, that's true," Meg conceded, "but even if Horace Friers's studio was going under, which we have no idea about, his wife makes a fortune selling her books."

"Still," Alex persisted, "if he's an inveterate gambler—"

"Wait a sec," Tony broke in. "If we're thinking about a pair working together, I've got another possibility for you to mull over." He proceeded to tell them of his sighting of Noah and Heather in the piano lounge in the wee hours of the morning.

"What time did Danforth leave the lounge?" Meg asked tightly. She'd assumed he'd gone directly to his suite after leaving her at the door to hers at 2 a.m. The fact that he went, instead, to have this late night rendezvous with Heather St. John left her feeling decidedly on edge. Especially after remembering the way they behaved in the casino while she was gone. Remembering that she'd thought then that they might be a team. And not liking the thought at all. Were they merely business partners, or did they have an intimate relationship as well? All Meg had to do was conjure up the image of the sultry redhead to know the logical answer to her own question.

"She left at around two-thirty and he finished up his drink and left maybe five minutes later," Tony said.

"Like maybe they didn't want to be seen leaving together," Sean suggested. "But he could easily have met her back in her suite. Or she in his."

"They could have been planning the Percy heist," Alex said excitedly.

Sean grinned. "Or they could have been involved in other extracurricular pursuits."

Meg felt a constriction in her chest.

"Hey, they could have killed two birds with one stone, if you catch my drift," Alex said with a chuckle.

"Let's just say that Danforth and the St. John woman were real cozy in the lounge," Tony told them, then zeroed in on Meg. "If your hunch about Danforth is right and we're scouting an accomplice for our cat burglar, my vote definitely goes to the luscious redhead."

"She looks good to me," Alex said. "I mean that in the literal sense, but also as a top choice for Danforth's partner in crime."

Paul, who'd been unusually quiet during this discussion, finally said in a low, firm voice, "I don't believe it. Heather just doesn't seem the type."

"They never seem the type," Sean returned wryly. "That's the whole idea."

Alex gave his brother a closer scrutiny. "You don't really have a crush on her, do you, Paulie? We were both only joking around yesterday in the health club, weren't we? I mean, because I was. Sure she's a knockout, but to tell you the truth, I've always been a little wary of redheads."

Sean put a brotherly arm around Paul. "Do you dig her?"

"Be serious," Paul said, shrugging off his brother's embrace. "Anyway, even if I did, which I don't, she's way out of my league." The "which I don't" part sounded less than convincing.

Meg felt a pang of sympathy for Paul. Maybe it wasn't just for him.

"There are a few hot-looking numbers on the dining staff I could introduce you to, Paul," Sean said. "In fact there's this perky little blonde..."

Meg glared at her brothers. "I don't believe this. I feel like I just stepped onto the set of 'The Dating Game.' Could we please keep our minds on our work here?"

All four of her brothers donned contrite smiles and nodded.

"That's better," Meg said as she sat down on Tony's bunk only to feel something sharp jab her thigh.

"What the heck . . . ?" She reached under the cover to see what the culprit was and came out with one of those brass name-tag pins worn by the *Galileo* staff. The name on this one was Liza Hamilton.

Tony tugged on his beard and smiled sheepishly. "Oops."

MEG, DRESSED IN a flattering pale yellow sundress set off by a pair of earrings and a matching choker of exquisite natural pearls, was having her *second* breakfast of the day, al fresco on the topside veranda. Several other diners, including the Friers, had invited her to join them, but she had declined.

When Noah strolled over she was sitting alone at a table for two. "Good morning," he said.

Meg glanced up from her bowl of granola. Noah, dressed in tan slacks, a pale blue shirt and a navy cashmere vest, looked amazingly cool and rested. He also looked exceedingly handsome.

"Hi," she said cheerily. "Would you care to join me?"

"I'd be delighted," Noah said after a moment's hesitation. He hadn't expected an utterly unsolicited invitation from Meg, especially after the cool handshake at her door the night before. Still, it was what he'd hoped for even if he hadn't anticipated it. He could imagine Chet's big smile. *See, mate. You do it to them every time.*

No sooner did he sit down than a steward came scooting over with a breakfast menu. Noah didn't glance at it. "Just coffee."

The steward nodded. He already had a silver coffee carafe in hand. He quickly turned Noah's white bone china cup right side up in the saucer and poured him a steaming cup of aromatic Colombian coffee.

"That isn't much of a breakfast," Meg commented.

"I've already eaten," he said, taking a sip of coffee. "Had a heaping plate of kippers and eggs a couple of hours ago. I've been up since seven."

"Really?" she said, marveling at how good he looked on so little sleep considering he'd turned in well after two in the morning. Or, if she was on the right track, quite possibly well after four. After his failed attempt at breaking into Louanne Percy's suite.

Noah was studying her unabashedly. "You look a bit tired. Have you been up a while, as well?"

Meg hesitated. There was always a chance he'd spotted her some time earlier that morning coming or going from one of her secret meetings, although she'd certainly tried her best not to be observed.

"Yes," she said finally. "I tend to be an early riser."

"Then I apologize for keeping you up so late last night."

Her smile held a faintly seductive tinge. "Oh, don't apologize, Noah. I had a very nice time."

"Did you?"

Meg frowned inwardly. Was she slipping? Had she finally met her match? Her confidence took a decided dip. Would she really outsmart him in the end?

"What makes you doubt it?" she asked, lifting her juice glass to her lips, the morning sun glinting off her five-carat diamond ring.

She didn't miss the way Noah's eyes lingered on her hand. Or more to the point, on her ring.

"You have some beautiful jewelry, Meg. Family heirlooms? Or a generous husband?"

Ah, now we're getting somewhere. "Ex-husband, remember?" she corrected coyly.

"Was he generous when he wasn't your ex?" Noah followed up.

Meg held out the hand sporting the diamond. "He was quite generous."

"And since then?"

"I don't think I follow," Meg said.

Noah wore a contrite smile, but it didn't quite fit. "I'm sorry. I am being presumptuous."

"Oh," she said, one eyebrow arching, "you mean, have I had some generous men friends since Phillip?"

He held up his hand. "It's none of my business. Forgive me for asking." It wasn't as if he didn't already have a damn good guess about the answer.

Meg slid her bowl of granola away from her and folded her hands, one over the other, on the edge of the table. Then she looked square into Noah's face, which was dominated by those penetrating and what she now viewed as conniving blue eyes. "There hasn't been anyone since Phillip, Noah."

Noah stared back at her. *She's good,* he thought, not believing her for an instant. And, damn it all, wishing that he could.

Meg saw the faint line form on Noah's forehead as his brows drew slightly together. What was worrying him? How he was going to obtain her lovely gifts from her ex-husband? Well, she was doing her best to make it easy for him. Like taking candy from a baby. Maybe not that easy. Again she had to remind herself that he was looking for a challenge.

"Have you signed up for one of the guided tours of Virgin Gorda?" he asked. They would be docking there the next morning and would have the whole day to spend on the island. There was a varied assortment of planned excursions, everything from scuba diving and hiking to a nature jaunt and a visit to the eerie grottoes and crystalline pools the island was famous for.

"Why, no," Meg said. "To be honest, I prefer exploring on my own."

"Fancy that. My preference exactly."

They both fell silent for a few moments.

"I don't suppose," Noah said, "that we could each explore the island on our own . . . together?"

Meg pretended to ponder his offer. "I suppose we could give it a try. See how it works out. If we find we have different interests we could always split up." *If you knew how different our interests were you'd run for the hills, Barrister. Barrister, indeed!* Afraid her face might in some way betray her sardonic thoughts, she smiled at him.

Noah took in the ersatz smile and returned one that was equally fraudulent. "I suppose all I can do is hope that our interests coincide, then," he said, all the while thinking how very unlikely that was. If there was a prize for the two people whose interests were most at odds, they would surely win it hands down.

The steward arrived to refill their coffee cups. When he left, Meg looked across at Noah. "Have you heard about the mystery intruder?" Her tone was deliberately casual and offhand.

"What I heard," Noah said, matching Meg's tone, "was that he didn't actually manage to intrude. Barbara Friers waylaid me on the Promenade Deck first thing this morning to fill me in on all the excitement. I also had to hear about several of her novels and only managed to escape when she and her husband got into an argument over something to do with earth-quakes."

Meg laughed. "She is a character. But a very successful one."

"Oh, indeed," Noah said, grinning. "Did you know that her last book sold over a million copies in paperback?"

"So what do you make of Mrs. Friers's latest tale?" she pressed lightly.

"About the would-be intruder?" Noah gave a careless shrug. "Don't writers, especially successful ones, have very fertile imaginations?"

"Then you think she made it up?"

"Or dreamed it possibly." He regarded her thoughtfully. "What do you think?"

She matched his careless shrug. "Oh, I think you're probably right."

CHAPTER FIVE

CHET CARSON carried the newly pressed dinner jacket into Noah's suite. "Hope this will be satisfactory, sir," he said solicitously for the benefit of the elderly couple walking down the corridor.

Once Noah closed the door to the suite, Chet draped the jacket over a nearby chair and lit a cigarette. "So, what's the plan?"

"I'm spending the day with her touring the highways and byways of Virgin Gorda," Noah said, looking very tropical and elegant in a tailored mint green shirt and summer wool slacks in a pale shade of heather.

Chet grinned. "So your charm worked like a charm once again. Have her eating out of your hand yet?"

"Sniffing around it is more likely, mate," Noah said sardonically, running a comb through his hair.

"You think she's still wary of you?"

"Like a hound is wary of a fox," Noah said. "Although she's doing her best to conceal it."

"Well, after a glorious day and evening on the beautiful and romantic isle of Virgin Gorda, she should be in a more receptive mood or your name's not Noah Webb," Chet said. His mouth tugged into a wry smile. "But I forget. That isn't your name at the moment."

Noah shot him a grimace as he patted his face with some woodsy after-shave.

"Lot of buzz about that near break-in of the Percy suite in the wee hours," Chet remarked. "Although the general consensus is the Friers woman imagined it. From what I hear, Mrs. Friers isn't too happy she's not being taken seriously." He paused. "She probably wishes the jewels had been swiped just to show 'em."

"I'd say," Noah said slyly, "that Mrs. Friers isn't the only one who's disappointed."

PAUL DUG HIS HANDS into the pockets of his khaki chinos. "All I'm saying is I don't think it's Heather."

Meg tied a floral silk scarf around the waist of her white linen dress. "That's not all you're saying, Paul." She spun away from the mirror in her bedroom suite and faced her brother. "What do you think? Does the scarf work?"

Paul nodded absently. "Meggie, my plan makes sense no matter which of us is right."

"First of all, you have little chance of putting this so-called plan of yours into operation. Second of all—"

"Hold it. Let's tackle the 'first of all' part. I know Heather gave me the brush-off the other day in the health club, but I'm telling you, Meg, I picked up different vibes when we bumped into each other in the corridor in the middle of the night. I think she might have had a change of heart about spending time with me."

"She's probably going to spend the day sightseeing with Lars Olson."

"I don't think so. I saw Olson getting chummy last night with a pretty blonde who's traveling with her rich maiden aunt. And from what Tony says, when Olson left Heather and Danforth alone together in the lounge the other night, he didn't look like a happy camper. My guess is our handsome Swedish hunk's a guy who isn't used to getting brush-offs, like some of the rest of us mere mortals are,'' Paul added with a disarming smile.

"Okay, Paul,'' Meg said, switching the scarf for a wide, woven leather berry-red belt. ''Let's say for argument's sake that you can make some headway with Heather St. John. I'm just not sure you can . . .'' She hesitated.

"Be objective?'' Paul queried. ''Look Meggie, if she is Danforth's partner in crime, I want her brought to justice as much as the rest of you. And even if she's innocent, which is certainly possible, don't go thinking I have any unrealistic expectations here. Sure, Heather's very attractive and appealing, but I'm fully aware we're from different planets. And the planets never cross.'' He gave his sister a pensive look. ''At least I don't think they do.''

"Oh, this belt looks awful,'' Meg said, scowling at her reflection in her full-length mirror. ''Or maybe it's the dress. Slacks. I think slacks make more sense.''

"You certainly seem to be going out of your way to make a good impression on a jewel thief, Meggie.''

She turned to her brother. ''Meaning?''

"Meaning, I hope you aren't doing with Danforth exactly what you're so afraid I'll do with Heather.''

Meg folded her arms across her chest. ''What are you talking about, Paul?''

"Just that from where I'm standing there seems to be a little touch of stardust in those amber eyes of yours, Meggie.''

"You're crazy. You can't seriously think I have even an ounce of romantic interest in that…that no-good, shifty, rogue of a jewel thief."

Meg was at her closet now, pulling out a Donna Karan pantsuit in a mauve linen tweed.

"Okay," Paul said, "so how about we make a pact? You don't fall for Don Juan and I don't fall for the redheaded siren."

He crossed to his sister, extending his hand. As she reached out to shake on it, Paul abruptly lifted his hand. "What if you're wrong about him?"

Meg scowled. "I'm not wrong."

"You're absolutely positive he's the jewel thief?"

"No," she conceded. "He could simply be your average con artist. The point is, he isn't who he says he is. And that's enough to keep me on the straight and narrow."

Paul once again extended his hand. This time they did shake.

NOAH WAS WAITING for Meg on the Promenade Deck. In one long sweep, he took in her exquisitely tailored linen slacks, the sexy off-white silk halter top under the open linen jacket, and her hair pulled gently back from her face by tortoiseshell combs to reveal the diamonds sparkling at her ears. She was quite a sight. At once elegant and dazzling. And what he marveled at the most was that she was so seemingly without guile.

Meg was well aware of Noah's thorough survey. He looked as if he knew some secret about her. It made her decidedly uneasy. As did her own general appearance. All this haute couture simply wasn't her. She was pretending to be someone she wasn't. In her own way, she felt as much a fraud as she knew Noah to be. She hastened to remind herself that the difference was that her masquerade was based on honorable intentions, and she absolutely could not shake the feeling that Noah's intentions were anything but honorable. She still wasn't certain what his game was, but she was sure he had one. And she was determined to find out exactly what it was.

Their eyes met as she came up to him. Noah looked as if he'd just stepped out of the pages of a *Gentleman's Quarterly* "Dressing for the Islands" edition.

"You look dazzling," he said.

Dazzling. Yes, she thought, that was the word that would come to a jewel thief's mind. She accepted his compliment with a deliberately nonchalant smile.

He gestured toward the large canvas tote she'd slung over her shoulder. "I hope you've got your bikini stowed in that."

"What makes you think it's a bikini?"

He grinned. "Isn't it?"

She had debated back in her suite between her one-piece red tank suit and the peach bikini. After going back and forth several times she'd finally settled on the bikini. Now she wished she'd chosen the tank suit.

Letting Noah's question hang—he'd find out soon enough that he was right—Meg headed for the *Galileo*'s first port of call.

"ELIOT, WILL YOU LOOK at that!" Elaine exclaimed.

"Absolutely exquisite," Eliot murmured in awe. "I always heard The Baths were spectacular, but I never dreamed... Why, those boulders are as big as houses. They look like some supernatural force reached down and toppled them over. I really do think we ought to do some exploring of those grottoes and caves, Elaine.''

''Really, Eliot. I'm not talking about those rocks and caves. Don't you see them down there?'' Elaine pointed in the opposite direction, to a secluded alcove farther down on the beach.

''I don't see anything of any particular interest,'' Eliot said, squinting where his wife was pointing.

She passed the binoculars to her husband as they stood on one of the cliffs overlooking the beach.

Eliot gazed through the binoculars.

''No, no, Eliot. To your right. More. There. Now they should be in view.''

''Do you mean the couple lying on that blanket?''

''They're not just any couple, Eliot. Don't you recognize them?''

''They do look familiar. Have we met them on board?''

''Oh, for heaven's sakes, Eliot. Of course we haven't met them. Formally, that is. It's that debonair English barrister, Noah Danforth II, and Mrs. Newell, the one that's just dripping with jewels. Didn't I tell you they were a perfect match? Didn't I say the minute I laid eyes on them when we boarded in New York that they were simply an ideal pairing?''

Eliot's brow wrinkled into a series of little lines. ''Did you, my dear?''

Elaine threw up her hands. ''Really, Eliot. You never listen to me. I don't know where your mind is half the time.''

At the moment, the truth was that Eliot's mind, as well as his binoculars, were fixed on Mrs. Meg Newell, who looked like a sea nymph in that peach bikini. Indeed, for a moment when he first sighted her, what with the color of the bikini so closely matching her skin, he'd actually thought she wasn't wearing any bathing suit at all. But if that had been the case he was certain his wife would not have pointed her out to him.

"Here now, you can stop ogling," Elaine said sharply, snatching the binoculars from her husband. No sooner did she regain possession than she stuck them in front of her own eyes for a closer view of the man she thought so resembled her old heartthrob, Cary Grant. Although she'd seen every one of the movie star's films, she could not recall ever seeing him in a skimpy pair of black bathing briefs like the ones the barrister was wearing. Really, she thought, they were rather risqué. Not that that thought in any way stopped her from "ogling."

THIS WAS MEG'S FIRST TRIP to Virgin Gorda, and as she stretched out on the blanket Noah had thought to bring along, she couldn't help feeling like she was in the midst of a natural wonderland.

"Ready to go for a dip?" Noah asked, stretching out beside her.

"In a few minutes," Meg murmured, her eyes closed.

Noah moved perceptibly closer. He planted a friendly, good-natured kiss on her lips.

Meg's eyes popped open. "Why did you do that?" she demanded.

"A better question might be, why didn't I do it sooner?" he quipped.

Meg sat up, putting her hand over her eyes to block out the sun as she stared at him. "I'm serious."

There was faint irony in his smile. "Are you?"

"I don't even know you, Noah. I know absolutely nothing about you."

"It's no different for me, I assure you. Why don't we spend the day getting to know each other better?"

"I'm not sure I'm comfortable with your method."

He laughed softly. "Was it so awful?"

"No. You're quite good."

"Then you were pleased."

Meg scowled. "I didn't say that."

He dismissed her denial. "Imagine how pleased you'd be if I truly applied myself."

"I'm not amused, Noah." She was, however, aroused. A dip in the cool aquamarine sea was definitely in order. She rose from the blanket. "I'm going for a swim."

He caught up with her where the hot bleached sand met the first ripples of water and snatched hold of her wrist. "Are you going to go in with those?"

She didn't understand at first what he meant, but then she realized he was referring to her diamond earrings. "Oh. They'll do fine. Safer on me than if I left them lying about, don't you agree?"

He shrugged. "I suppose so. Someone might be watching you from the cliffs and sneak down and steal off with them while we're having our dip."

She looked him straight in the eye. "Then you do think there might be a jewel thief about."

"I really don't know," Noah said. "But if there is one, I promise to look out for both you and your jewels."

Meg smiled. *I bet you will. I just bet you will.*

They ran together into the cool, inviting water, Noah diving under first, Meg following suit. They were both strong swimmers and they swam quite vig-

orously and independently for several minutes. Then
Noah began cutting through the water toward Meg.
Before she knew it, he was right in front of her.

The water was shallow enough for them to stand.
Meg gave a little start when she felt Noah's hands on
her hips.

"I truly would like to get to know you better," he
murmured.

She started to slip away from his embrace, but one
of his hands surfaced from the water and cupped her
chin.

"Please, Noah."

"Please yes? Or please no?"

"Please . . . no."

She was lying through her teeth and she knew it.
What was worse, so did he. It was as if the warm,
tropical ocean had enveloped them both in a blanket
of desire.

Their eyes locked. He gave her ample opportunity
to escape before his mouth descended. Nothing
friendly or good-natured about this kiss. Ardent was
the only way to describe it. His tongue slipped unob-
structed past her lips. Touching her tongue. For a few
moments Meg simply gave in to the kiss with equal
passion, her wet arms circling his wet neck, her own
tongue doing some exploring of its own. But then, just
when she was almost lost to the intoxicating feeling of
their kiss, a disturbing flutter of alarm skipped across
her stomach. And a litany sprang forth in her head.
*This is all playacting. It doesn't mean anything. A kiss
or two. Okay, I can handle it. I can keep things from
getting out of hand.*

To Meg's surprise—and damn it all, to her dismay,
as well—Noah ended the kiss abruptly. "We should

dry off. We've got those dinner reservations." His voice was husky, even a bit brusque. And he didn't even wait to lead her back to shore.

No one was as surprised as Noah that he'd pulled away from Meg at the precise moment he should have made his next seductive move. And certainly would have done with any other woman in a similar situation. Indeed, had done with a number of women in such situations in the past. With the desired success.

That was the problem. It wasn't success he was thinking about when he was kissing Meg Newell. Making the grand coup was not on his mind. It was desire, pure and simple, that he'd felt. And right on the heels of that fierce longing had come this inexplicable, uncharacteristic feeling of guilt.

Guilt. Of all the feelings alien to him, guilt had to be right up there with the best of them. But there it was.

Guilt and desire. A most troublesome blend of emotions. Well, if he was going to move ahead with his plans, which he certainly was, he'd simply have to do away with them.

"Is anything the matter?" Meg asked him when she reached the blanket. She picked up a towel and draped it around her shoulders.

"No. Nothing," Noah said, already toweling off. He tried to smile at her but couldn't quite manage it. "That's a lie."

Meg regarded him quizzically. For a moment she wondered if he actually meant to confess to her. Her palms got sweaty. Her pulse started to race. "Something is the matter, then?"

"Yes. Very much so," he said softly, moving closer to her.

Meg could feel her heart start to shift into over-drive. "What is it?" *Say it, Noah. Confession is good for the soul. Maybe if you come clean, you'll be able to start fresh.*

"It's you, Meg."

"What . . . what about me?"

Now his smile was disarming. And alarming. "Everything about you, I'm afraid."

"That bad?"

"That good. Extraordinarily good."

The next thing Meg knew she found herself wrapped, not in her towel, but in Noah's strong arms. And then something inside her simply went haywire. She felt this incredible, primitive sexual thrill. It was unlike anything she'd ever experienced.

This time, Meg was the one who sought his lips, invaded his mouth. She didn't let herself think about it or try to put the proper spin on it. Little chance of her succeeding if she had.

There she was, on a wild, glorious tropical island with a man who made her head spin, her heart race, her whole body tremble with desire. She wasn't playing by the rules. She knew that. But she'd made the rules in the first place, so she could break them. No, just bend them. Bend the rules a little. What harm . . .

They fell together half on the blanket, half on the sand, their mouths still locked in a fierce greedy kiss. He covered her body with his, and Meg found herself clinging to him with an urgency she was wholly unprepared for.

She didn't even realize he'd unclasped the bra of her bikini until his head lowered and she felt his lips on her nipple. Rockets went off in her head. Wantonly, recklessly, she arched against him.

He planted a circle of hot kisses around each breast and all she could do was grab his hair with her fists. She felt a sensual rush that stunned her. Just how far would she let herself bend those rules?

What were those rules? She couldn't think. His palms were cupping her breasts now, his mouth leaving a trail of kisses up along her throat. Her whole body throbbed. All her senses throbbed.

The rules. What the hell were the rules? Oh, the delicious feel of his hard powerful body pressing down on her. Every touch, every caress, sent another wave of longing through her.

His lips moved to her cheek, the tip of her nose, her eyelids, her brow. Then finally back to her lips, which were already parted, eagerly waiting to be claimed. Her eyes were closed. A moan stirred in her throat as his tongue penetrated her mouth. Her arms circled his hard shoulders.

Meg knew she was in trouble, but somehow she couldn't fight this furtive wanting that had been held in check from the first moment she'd set eyes on him. She felt as if the blueprint for what was happening now had been drawn up and sealed at that moment, and there was nothing she could do about it.

Noah felt in no less trouble than Meg. He'd meant to prove to himself that he could coldly, calculatedly, make love to this woman. But it wasn't working. What was wrong with him? Was he losing his touch? Going soft? Hell, he was anything but soft. He was hard and throbbing, and he knew without a doubt he could easily press his advantage. . . .

He rolled off her, his arm curving over his eyes as he lay flat on his back on the hot sand. His breath was raw and ragged. It had taken every ounce of strength to pull himself away from her and now he felt utterly depleted.

Meg reacted quite differently. The instant Noah's body broke contact with hers, she came abruptly to her senses. Hurriedly, she fumbled with her bikini bra, struggling to reclasp it. Her breathing was shallow and her whole body was trembling, but her head was working properly again, thank heaven.

Without a word, Meg gathered up her clothes and slipped behind a boulder to dress. When she returned to the blanket a few minutes later, Noah was also dressed and looking remarkably composed. Still not speaking, they folded the blanket together, their eyes never meeting.

They headed up the cliff, Noah leading the way, to the spot where he had parked the red convertible he'd rented for their island jaunt. Almost near the top, Meg slipped. Noah turned and reached out his hand for her, but she shook her head, managing to regain her footing without his help. It wasn't that she was feeling so self-reliant. It was that she didn't want to risk what it might do to her insides to feel the touch of his hand again.

PAUL FOUND HEATHER browsing in the outdoor market. She approached a street vendor selling woven bags and pointed to one. He took it down for her to examine more closely.

"I like that one, too," Paul said, coming up behind her.

Heather gave a little start as she turned her head in his direction. Then she smiled. "Hi."

"How much?" Paul asked the vendor.

"Thirty-five dollars," the vendor said in a clipped accent.

Paul reached into his trouser pocket for his wallet. Heather started to protest, but he was already handing over the bills.

"Really, you shouldn't," Heather said as Paul led her off.

"Was there one you liked better?" he asked.

"No. I love this bag. It's beautiful. In the States it would be triple the price."

"So, it was a steal." Paul almost choked on the word *steal*. He patted his chest. "Parched. How about a nice cool tropical drink?"

"You could have bargained him down to half the price. They expect it, you know," Heather said, letting him steer her across the street to a white hotel with pale pink shutters and a large columned veranda where tables with colorful umbrellas were set up for dining and cocktails.

"Well, then, I made his day," Paul said brightly.

Heather gave him a sideways glance and a winning smile. "And mine. Thank you, Paul."

He slipped an arm around her waist as they climbed the steps leading to the veranda. "Thank you, Heather."

She gave him a curious look. "Whatever for?"

"For your smile. For having this drink with me. And then for having dinner with me."

"Are we having dinner together?" she asked demurely.

"Unless you have other plans." Paul hesitated. "Or another date."

Heather gazed coquettishly at him. "If I tell you something will you promise not to let it go to your head?"

The fact that Paul had gotten this far with Heather St. John had already gone to his head, but he nodded.

"If I did have another date, I would have broken it."

He smiled suspiciously. "That isn't a line, is it?"

"I always thought it was the man who handed the woman the line," she teased.

Paul grinned. "Well, it *is* the nineties."

They waited by a podium for the maître d' to come over and show them to a table.

Heather tilted her head to the side as she looked over at him. "Would a line have been necessary?"

His expression sobered. "No. No, it wouldn't have."

"I like you, Paul."

"Any particular reason?" he prodded.

She gave his question some thought. "You seem like one of the few men aboard this cruise who isn't after something."

Paul groaned inwardly. Great start.

The maître d' arrived and led them to a table beneath a bright red-and-yellow-striped umbrella. As they settled into their chairs, Paul spotted another group of shipmates a few tables away—Alan Delacore, his fiancée, Louanne, and Lars Olson. Delacore was settling the bill while Olson helped Louanne out of her seat. They headed out in the opposite direction from Paul and Heather.

Heather, who had followed Paul's gaze, groaned under her breath. "Really, that man is such a bore."

Paul turned back to Heather. "Olson or Delacore?"

She grinned. "Both, really."

"What about Danforth?" Paul asked, idly glancing at the cocktail menu on the table. "Do you find him a bore, as well?"

"No," she said simply.

Paul had to admire her frankness even as he felt a stab of jealousy. "Well, that was certainly an unequivocal answer."

"It's my impression your boss doesn't find Noah Danforth boring, either."

"My— Oh, my boss. You mean Mrs. Newell."

"Do you have any other bosses?"

"No. One is quite enough. Especially when that one is Mrs. Newell."

"Tough, is she?"

"Oh, yes. Very demanding. Work, work, work."

Heather gave him a measured look. "What kind of work exactly do you do for your boss?"

"I guess you could say I'm sort of her guy Friday," he said offhandedly. "Take dictation, type reports, that sort of thing. She does a great deal of charity work. Right now she's working on a memoir of sorts."

"Has she led a fascinating life?"

Paul pressed his palms together in a tentlike fashion and rested his chin on the tips of his fingers. "When it comes to leading a fascinating life, my guess is few women could hold a candle to you, Heather."

She smiled, but Paul couldn't help but notice the smile didn't reach her beautiful sapphire blue eyes.

"You'd be surprised," she said hollowly, "how dull it really is."

TONY RAPPED LIGHTLY on Liza's door. It took her a few minutes to open it. She was a bit flushed. "Hi, babe. You caught me right in the middle of my exercises."

He grinned. "I thought I'd have given you enough of a workout last night."

The svelte brunette wagged a finger at him. "You are a naughty boy, Tony."

"You ain't seen nothin' yet, sweetheart," he said in a husky Bogart voice.

Liza laughed. "Hey, I'm starting to cool down. Gotta go." She started to close the door.

"Whoa. Wait a sec."

"Don't you dare say you could warm me up. I expect better from a guy like you."

Tony sighed. Of course that had been precisely what he'd been going to say. He quickly changed course. "I'm just curious. Why don't you work out in the health club? We've got staff privileges."

Liza grinned sexily. "When I sweat, I like to do it in private," she said with a wink.

Tony grinned. "Will I see you tonight? After we get off?"

"Sure," she said brightly, starting to jog in place. "Now get out of here." She jogged right up to him and planted a moist, noisy kiss on his lips, then pivoted around and jogged back into her room, closing the door behind her.

Tony lingered there for a couple of minutes, then started to head back to his cabin, only to spot his brother Sean leaning against the wall a few yards away.

Tony sauntered over to his brother who stood with his arms crossed and slowly shaking his head.

"What?" Tony asked.

"You know what," Sean countered with a sly smile.

"You mean Liza? Don't worry. It's nothing serious."

"You're sure about that?"

"Sure I'm sure. Come on. Let's go rent a couple of motorbikes and take a spin around Virgin Gorda. We can stop by the health club and see if Alex wants to tag along."

Sean shook his head. "I don't think it would be such a good idea for the three of us to be seen hanging out together. Anyway, Alex's on duty."

"At the health club? But just about all the passengers are onshore."

Sean swung an arm around his brother. "No, dummy. Not that kind of duty."

Tony slowly nodded. "Oh. I get it."

ALEX CAUTIOUSLY TURNED the corner after peering around it to make sure there was no one in the corridor. He hurried past Meg's suite and several others until he arrived at his destination. The suite belonging to Noah Danforth II.

Once again he glanced up and down the empty corridor to make sure it was clear, then reached into the pocket of his sweatpants for the key ring that he'd "borrowed" from one of the maids who was working out in the health club. Getting his hands on the keys had been a cinch. All he'd had to do was slip undetected into the women's locker room and there was the maid's uniform hanging on a peg in one of the metal lockers, her key ring right in her apron pocket. She hadn't even bothered with the combination lock, although that wouldn't have presented a problem to

Alex. He'd given her the lock himself. Having first committed the combination to memory.

Alex estimated that the maid would be working out for at least forty-five minutes. To play it safe he'd get the keys back in thirty. That gave him a good fifteen minutes to have a look around the phony barrister's suite. And hopefully dig up something more concrete on Danforth so they wouldn't have to rely only on Meg's intuition.

CHAPTER SIX

MEG MOVED some of her baked grouper around on her plate. Although the dish was excellent, she'd only managed a few bites. She stared out at the bay dotted with yachts and sailboats as she and Noah dined in the open air under a banana-leaf-thatched roof.

Noah looked at her. "Don't you think we ought to talk about it, Meg?"

She pulled her gaze away from the view and focused on her dining companion. "All right," she said. "Why don't you start?"

"Where would you like me to begin?" he asked, pushing aside his barely touched dish of conch fritters.

Meg gave him an appraising look. "You could begin by telling me what you're after." Granted, it was a direct approach, but she seriously doubted any other approach would work with a man like Noah. Not that she had much hope for this approach, either. Although a confession would certainly be nice.

Or would it?

Noah leaned forward, fixing those bedroom eyes on her. "What are you offering?"

Meg hesitated. "Understanding."

Noah cocked his head, his expression puzzled. "Understanding?"

"Yes," she said pointedly. "I can be a very under-standing woman, Noah. You could try trusting me." Was it a lie or could he trust her? Meg found herself thinking that if he did confess his crimes and was willing to make restitution and promised to go straight...

Who was she kidding? She was just letting what had happened between them on the beach cloud her rea-son. If the man was a criminal, it was her responsibil-ity to turn him in. She was just trying her best to lure him in and desperately trying to justify her deceit to herself at the same time. She doubted she'd have any luck with the first, and she certainly wasn't having any with the second.

Noah sighed inwardly. *If only you knew how much I wish I could trust you, love. I wish it far more than I should.*

"Do you know that ever since we were first intro-duced I had this feeling we'd met somewhere be-fore?" Noah mused.

Meg rolled her eyes. Okay, so he wanted to change the subject, but she'd expected better than that tired old line.

He smiled, having read her thoughts accurately. "No, seriously. Have you been in London at all dur-ing these past few months?"

Actually she had spent a couple of weeks there just before Christmas. Still, it was unlikely they'd have bumped into each other.

He was watching her closely. "You have been there."

"Yes, but—"

"When?"

"Mid-December." Curious, she thought. Why was he so interested in whether she'd been in London? Did he suspect she suspected something about him? That she'd been checking up on him even then?

He snapped his fingers. "The New Castle Ball."

"Excuse me?"

"Wait, wait. It's coming back to me. Weren't you with Monty Lyons and his party?"

"I don't—"

"Lyons. You remember. Britain's minister of finance."

He was staring at Meg so intently she found herself feeling inexplicably uneasy. What was he getting at? Where did this minister fit in? Was this Lyons fellow onto Noah's sideline, as well?

Play it very cautious here, Meg, she told herself. "Tell me a bit more about this minister."

She wished he'd stop staring at her like that. Like she was somehow the guilty party here. Clever maneuver on his part to try to turn the tables.

"You want to know more about Lyons?" He folded his hands together. "Well, what can I tell you that you might not know?"

Clearly he assumed she knew this minister. That they'd had some dealings with each other. The question was, should she play along with him? It was the only way to find out where he was leading.

An idea hit her as to what this might be about. She leaned forward slightly. "Is this minister, Mr. Lyons, married?"

An enigmatic smile played on Noah's lips. "Yes, he's very much married."

That's it, Meg thought. *That's the answer.* Noah must have stolen some of the minister's wife's jewels.

And now he suspected that the minister may have hired someone—her—to track him down.

This won't do, she fretted. If he believed she was onto him he'd back off, cancel any planned heists while he was on this little seagoing jaunt.

Or would he? Maybe this was just the kind of challenge he was looking for. A true battle of wits.

"Do you play chess, Noah?"

"Strange question. But yes, as a matter of fact I do. And you?"

"Yes. I'm quite fond of the game," she said airily.

"And no doubt quite good at it," he murmured.

She smiled. "As I'm sure you are."

The confident smile he gave back was all the answer she needed.

Meg could almost feel their kings arming for battle. It was only a matter of who would be calling checkmate.

IT WAS A LITTLE AFTER TEN that evening when Meg and Noah returned to the cruise ship. The instant they got on board, Meg sensed that something was up. She could practically feel the disquieting currents in the air. Yes. Something definitely had happened. She didn't have to wait long to find out what.

No sooner did they step into the *Galileo*'s main lounge than they saw Barbara Friers in tears, her husband, Captain Simon and several other passengers, including Paul and Heather, all grouped around the novelist, trying in vain to comfort her.

Meg and Noah hurried over.

"What happened?" Meg asked, already guessing what it might be.

Barbara Friers stopped midcry and looked up at Meg. "I'll tell you what happened. I've been robbed, that's what. No one would believe me. No one. Oh, I know you all thought that thief was just a figment of my imagination. Well, I don't suppose you'll think so anymore. Not now that he's broken into my suite and absconded with every piece of jewelry I brought on board this . . . this boat."

Captain Simon made brief eye contact with Meg.

"When did it happen?" Noah asked quietly.

"How should I know when?" Barbara Friers snapped. "We left this morning around eleven and we got back about twenty minutes ago. I had a frightful headache—I'm sure it was something I ate."

The novelist glared at her husband. "You and your idea of eating where the locals eat. Wanting local color. Asking a shopkeeper who, for all you know, has ulcers, about his favorite restaurant." She shuddered. "The place was ghastly, but you insisted—"

Horace eyed his wife defiantly. "Did I or did I not tell you to stick with the fish? But no. You decided on the beef because it was flown over from the States."

"It wasn't the beef. I'm sure it was that awful tamari rind they spread all over the top."

"Tamarind rind, Barb. Tamari is a kind of soy sauce."

"Well, since you know everything, Horace," Barbara growled, "maybe you can tell us all how this jewel thief managed to open our safe and make off with my jewels."

Barbara Friers wasn't the only one who wanted to know the answer to that million-dollar—or close to it—question.

Horace gave his wife an imperious look. "It shouldn't be all that difficult to figure out."

"How's that?" Captain Simon asked.

Horace cleared his throat. "The safe had a four-letter code, correct?" He addressed this question to the group in general.

They all nodded.

Horace Friers eyed them all in turn. "Four letters." He clapped his hands together four times. "What might we have chosen as our code, do you suppose?"

No one answered.

"Please," Horace encouraged. "Give it a try. It doesn't matter now, after all, since the jewels are gone, for one thing and for another we'll be changing the code."

"B-A-R-B for Barb?" Heather suggested. "You do call your wife Barb."

Paul looked over at Heather, then surreptitiously caught his sister's eye.

"No, but that's a good guess," Horace Friers said with a smile. "Try again. Any of you?"

Meg glanced at Noah. She was baffled. Noah couldn't have lifted the jewels, because they'd been together all day, all evening. Oh, they'd been apart for a few minutes once or twice, but certainly not enough time for him to make his way back to the ship, steal the jewels and get back to her. If he hadn't done the heist, then who? Simple, Meg thought. Noah's accomplice.

She looked over at Heather, then at Paul, who had his arm rather protectively ensconced around the red-head's shoulder. When had they returned to the boat? And had Paul been with Heather from eleven that morning until twenty minutes ago?

"Might I wager a guess?"

All eyes, especially Meg's, turned to Noah.

Horace smiled at him. "Do you mean wager literally, my friend?"

Noah's blue eyes sparkled. "I'll wager you one hundred dollars that my guess is right."

Horace stuck out his hand. "You've got yourself a wager."

They shook on it.

Noah grinned as all eyes focused on him, none so intensely as Meg's. "I say the code letters your wife chose were H-O-P-E. As in her highly successful current novel *Beyond Hope*. My guess is the thief probably hit upon it after no more than a few other tries. Maybe even hit the jackpot the first time round."

Barbara Friers gave a little gasp. "How remarkable!"

Alan Delacore stood a few feet away and applauded. "Should have figured that one out myself."

Paul caught Meg's eye. She knew what he was thinking. That quite possibly the former ambassador had done just that. But her gaze shifted back to Noah. She had to hand it to the guy. Instead of playing dumb, he'd played it real smart. An exceedingly shrewd move on the chessboard.

Horace gave Noah a friendly slap on the back. "Clever fellow. You didn't happen to pinch the gems yourself, did you?"

Noah laughed. "Sorry to disappoint you, old man, but I've got a solid alibi." He smiled at Meg. She didn't smile back. Her throat felt as if it was closing up. So that's what this day of wining and dining had been all about. She'd allowed herself to be set up. As for the rest of what had happened between them, Meg realized that Noah had a two-pronged attack. One, set her up as his alibi; two, do his best to make her fall for him so that either she'd stop being suspicious of him or she'd be too much in love with him to turn him in. What was so awful was that he'd come disturbingly close to achieving both those goals.

Meg became filled with new resolve. She was going to stop at nothing to nail Noah Danforth II, master jewel thief. He might have gotten her into check a couple of times that day, but the game was far from over.

MEG HADN'T BEEN in her cabin for more than five minutes when a steward arrived at her door.

"I'm sorry to disturb you at such a late hour, Mrs. Newell," Chet Carson said obsequiously, "but I have a message for you."

He handed her a sealed envelope. Meg nodded, absently thanked him and shut the door. As soon as she did, she tore open the flap and slipped out the single sheet of paper: "News flash. Meet Paul at lifeboat station six ASAP. Alex."

Meg considered the typewritten note for a moment. While it certainly could have been sent by Alex, it could also be a fake—a ploy to get her out of her suite. If Noah suspected her of being on his tail, it wouldn't take much for him to figure out that Alex was working with her.

Meg glanced back at her dressing table, where the diamond earrings she'd just taken off sat glittering in a shell-shaped china dish. She stared at them for a long moment, then turned and left her suite.

NOAH PACED his sitting area. "Alex, huh?"

"I'll wager a guess who Alex is," Chet said.

"Who?" Noah asked impatiently.

"The guy who's in charge of the health club."

Noah stopped pacing. "What makes you think it's him?"

"Could be because I saw him sneaking into your suite this afternoon."

Noah could feel all the muscles tighten down his spine. "What the hell . . . ?" His features darkened. "Then she's onto me. Or she's made a damn good educated guess and sent her lackey over to see what he could dig up."

"There isn't anything to dig up, is there, old chum?" Chet asked cautiously.

"No," Noah said sharply. "What could—" He stopped abruptly. "Damn," he muttered, spinning around and storming into his bedroom. He headed straight for the closet, flung the doors open wide and pulled out the jacket he'd worn when he'd boarded. Immediately he began fishing around in the pockets, cursing under his breath.

"What is it? What'd he get?" Chet asked anxiously.

Noah stared at Chet without really seeing him. And to think for a few minutes back there at the beach that afternoon he'd actually thought that maybe he wouldn't end up getting to this moment.

"Webb? What is it?"

Noah cleared his mind of everything but the task at hand. "It doesn't matter. We've got to make our move now," he said grimly.

"You want me to go with you?"

Noah shook his head. "No. You head down to that lifeboat station and keep your eye on her."

As Meg and Paul hovered together in a dark corner, he pulled a sheet of paper out of his pocket. "Alex passed this to me a few minutes ago. You better look at it."

Meg took the paper and Paul shone his penlight on it. The note was brief.

Attention: Noah Webb

Woman most likely traveling under alias. Brown hair, brown eyes, approx. 5′ 8″, slender, striking, glamorous, exceedingly cunning. Proceed with caution. Success crucial.

Meg could feel her chest constrict. "I knew it."

Paul shone the light on her face, but she swatted it away. "What do you mean, you knew it?"

"I knew he was onto me. He thinks some minister hired me to track him down."

"A minister? You mean a man of the cloth?"

"No," Meg muttered. "In the British government. A minister of finance. Lyons. And Minister Lyons has a wife. My guess is Mr. Danforth II, alias Mr. Webb, stole some of Mrs. Lyons's jewels—" She stopped. "But since Lyons obviously didn't hire me, how the hell did Noah get a description of me? Who gave it to him?"

Paul shrugged. "None of this is making any sense, Meggie. And as for Heather—"

Heather. Meg had almost forgotten. "Did the two of you spend the whole day and evening together?"

Paul swallowed hard. "No, but listen, Meg—"

"When did you hook up?"

"I don't know. Early. Maybe around two. Or three. But, Meg—"

"And after that?"

"We were together the whole time. She's not the one, Meg. You've got to trust me on this. We spent something like seven straight hours together. We talked a lot, Meg. I really feel like I got to know her."

"And do you feel like she got to know you, Paul?" Meg challenged.

"What's that supposed to mean?" he asked defensively.

"Everything you told her about yourself was a lie. Your last name, what you do for a living... Don't you see what I'm getting at here? If you can play a role effectively why imagine she can't?"

Meg reached out and took her brother's arm. "I'm sure she's good at her part, Paul," she said softly. "They're both good."

"I still say it isn't Heather. If your boy's got an accomplice it's someone else on board this ship. It could be anyone, Meg. You've got no real reason to link those two."

"Oh, Paul," Meg said softly.

"It's not what you're thinking."

"Isn't it?"

"Okay, but it isn't only that. You have no proof it was her."

"You could..." Meg hesitated.

"What?"

"Forget it."

"Say it, Meg."

She relented. "Okay. I was just thinking that if you two spent enough time together and... some of that time was spent in her suite, well, at some point she might open her safe and you might be able to spot the code letters she pressed.''

"No," he said quietly. "I can't do that, Meg. If you want to get a look into her safe then you're going to have to blast it open or something.''

"I understand, Paul.''

"Do you?''

"More than you realize,'' she said softly.

CHET WAS MAKING a beeline for Meg's suite to warn Noah that she was heading back and that he needed to clear out of there on the double, when he was waylaid by Louanne Percy. She'd popped her head out of her suite just as he was passing her door. She pulled her terry robe closed as she smiled at him.

"Oh, Steward, I seem to be having some trouble with my bathtub. The hot-water tap is jammed. I was just about to go knock on my fiancé's door to see if he could help, but since you're right here..."

"Well, actually I...was on my way to deliver a message..."

"Oh, I'm sure it will only take you a second or two. Please." She gave his sleeve a little tug.

Chet Carson realized it would save more time to simply run into her suite and take care of the problem than to argue with her.

As it turned out he was wrong.

CHAPTER SEVEN

MEG SAW HIM the minute she opened the door to her suite. Caught him red-handed right there at her safe.

Noah turned to face her. "Hello again," he said wryly. Not much else to say really.

Meg thought about her .22 tucked in her top dresser drawer. If only she'd thought to carry it on her that evening.

Noah smiled pleasantly. "I think it best for you to come in and close the door."

She could take a couple of quick steps back and make a run for it. Get help. No way for Noah to escape unless he wanted to jump overboard.

"Please, Meg," Noah said.

It wasn't his persuasive voice that impelled her to obey him. It was the .22 he'd removed from his jacket pocket and was now pointing at her.

The gun looked familiar. He'd obviously been through her drawers, as well as her safe.

She stood very still just inside the door of the suite.

"Come in and have a seat," he said. "We need to talk."

"What is there to talk about?" she asked flatly.

"Let's not pretend anymore," he said coolly. "I know your game."

"And obviously I know yours." She couldn't quite keep the disappointment out of her voice. Or the fear. Her king was in serious danger of checkmate.

She did sit down in one of the leather armchairs, not because he'd told her to but because her knees were feeling a little wobbly.

"How did you manage the safe?" she asked, staring at the safe door, which was gaping open, her large velvet jewel case now sitting on a nearby table, all of its glittering contents lying beside it in a jumble.

"Ah, we in the trade have our ways." Noah spoke in measured tones. Now that everything was out in the open, instead of feeling relief at ending the charade, he felt as if a big rock had settled in the pit of his stomach.

Meg looked away. She felt on the brink of tears and she was determined not to let them fall. The man was worse than a mere jewel thief. He was without conscience or decency. Had she let him, he would have coldly, heartlessly made love to her that afternoon on the beach for no other reason than to gain an advantage. And now that she was forced to face the truth about him, she also confronted the grim truth about herself. She'd wanted him. She'd let herself feel something for him, despite her best efforts at fighting it. Something so intense and powerful that even now, even knowing the truth, she couldn't make those feelings disappear.

"Where are they, Meg?"

She gave him a dazed look. "Where are they?" she echoed. "They're right where you left them. You might have treated them with a little more respect."

He still had the gun on her. "I'm serious, Meg. You must know that."

"How could I not know that?" she countered icily.

"Then let's not waste any more time. Give me what I came for and maybe we can cut a deal."

"What are you talking about?"

"The letters, Meg. Or whatever your real name is. The photos. And, naturally, all the negatives."

"Are you crazy?"

"This isn't any more pleasant for me than it is for you." He gave her a long, appraising and deliberately provocative look. "I can see why Lyons fell for you the way he did. You're very... appealing. Yes, very appealing, indeed."

"I've never met Lyons," Meg said impatiently. "You've got that part wrong. He didn't hire me."

"Who said anything about hiring you? I said he fell for you. A foolish infatuation. I don't condone married men being unfaithful, but he actually feels quite awful about his brief indiscretion."

"You know what I think, Mr. *Webb*..."

He smiled humorlessly. "So your pal from the health club did find that note. A bad slip on my part. Your pal—"

"He isn't my pal," Meg said dully. "He's my brother."

"Sounds a bit like a song."

"Very droll, Mr. Webb."

"Well, since you now know my real name, perhaps you'll share yours with me. It isn't Newell, is it?"

"No."

"Or Alison Baker?"

"Who?" Meg was beginning to think the guy wasn't only a cad and a thief, but off his rocker. Who the hell was Alison Baker? And why was he fixated on that minister of finance?

"So?" Noah pressed. "What is your name, mystery lady?"

"The name's Delgado. Meg Delgado."

"And is there a Mr. Delgado?"

Meg shrugged carelessly. "Several of them."

"My, my."

"There's Alex, as I've already mentioned. Then there's Paul, Sean and Tony."

"You certainly do run through husbands, Mrs. Delgado. I assume Paul's the current one. Since we've already established, haven't we, that Alex is your *brother?*"

"Paul's not my husband, Mr. Webb. He's my brother, too."

"Oh, I see. Paul and Alex are both *brothers.*"

"And Sean."

"Ah, Sean's a brother, too. I look forward to the pleasure of meeting him."

"You already have. He's the maître d' in the Renaissance Room."

"So, it's a regular family affair."

"Don't forget Tony."

Noah arched an eyebrow. "Tony?"

"The fellow with the beard who runs the casino."

"A brother, as well?"

"Yes," Meg replied insouciantly. "Oh, and there's one other man in the family."

"Ah, yet another. I'm all ears, love."

"Georgio."

Noah raised a hand. Not the one still holding the gun on her. "Don't tell me. Another brother."

Meg smirked. "No."

"The husband at last."

"He is a husband," Meg said dryly. "My mother's husband. I happen to be, and have always been, happily unattached, Mr. Webb. And yourself?"

"Oh, the same. Ecstatically unattached."

"I doubt Heather St. John would be very happy to hear you say that."

"I really wouldn't know how Miss St. John would feel about it."

"So, as far as you're concerned, it's...strictly business."

"Precisely," Noah said. Now, if only he meant it. Somewhere along the way the line between business and pleasure had begun to blur. He tried to refocus. "Now that we've gone through your family tree, so to speak, perhaps we can return to business."

Meg's eyes strayed to the pile of jewels on the table. "Quite a good catch, Mr. Webb. Your best to date? Of course, you won't get very far this time round."

"Nice try, Miss Delgado. But it won't work. Tell me, do you and all your *brothers* work together?"

"Yes, Mr. Webb. We're very much a team."

"How nice for you. And I suppose you're quite successful. I imagine what with thefts, blackmail..." He paused. "Am I leaving anything out?"

Meg gave him a hard look. "We cover the gamut. Cons, scams, thefts, blackmail. We're very broad-based."

"I am impressed, Miss Delgado."

Meg crossed her arms in front of her chest. "Well, frankly, Mr. Webb, I'm a bit disappointed. I thought you'd be more of a challenge."

"Did you? Not to cast aspersions, Miss Delgado, but I felt much the same way about you. Perhaps you thought I'd be as easy as Lyons."

"You really are fixated on this minister, Mr. Webb."

"If you hadn't set your sights on him, all this could have been avoided. As it is, I simply must have what I came here for, Miss Delgado."

Meg gestured to the pile of jewels. "You want them, they're yours."

"That isn't what I want," he said sharply.

"You mean you have another problem."

"Precisely."

They stared at each other. A thin bead of sweat broke out on Noah's brow. Meg's throat went dry.

"The problem is," she said very slowly, "what are you to do about me? Isn't that right?"

"That's a problem, too" Noah said tightly.

For all her bravado, Meg's panic was beginning to escalate. They couldn't keep up this congenial banter for much longer. She'd caught him in the act and the only way he was going to get away with his crime was to keep her from talking. And the only way to keep her from talking...

Meg could feel her pulse start to pound in her head.

"It simply can't go on, Meg. It's over. If you're smart, you'll cooperate fully. And advise your *brothers* to do the same."

"And what will you do in turn, Mr. Webb?"

"Please. Let's go back to Noah and Meg. Rather silly to go by last names after we've, er, become fairly well acquainted. Is Meg really your first name?"

"Yes."

"All right, then, Meg, here's the deal. You turn over the negatives, the photos and the letters—oh, and Mrs.

Friers's jewels—and I'll use whatever influence I have—"

"What the hell are you talking about?"

"I do have a certain degree of influence, Meg."

"Really?"

"Yes. As a member of British intelligence . . ."

Meg burst out laughing.

"I don't see why that's amusing. Surely, a clever girl like you would have put two and two together by now. Who else would a top minister turn to for assistance in such a delicate matter?"

"First a barrister and now a secret agent. How versatile you are. Next you'll be telling me you've got a double-O number. Like James Bond. OO7," she said between laughs. She'd seen several Bond films. "License to kill, isn't that what it means?"

Meg abruptly stopped laughing, her eyes falling again to the gun in Noah's hand. *License to kill.* Nothing very funny about that.

Noah came a little closer to her. "Meg, listen to me. I imagine you have a long sad tale of why you felt compelled to resort to such criminal pursuits as blackmail and grand larceny—"

"Why I've resorted to criminal pursuits? Aren't you putting the shoe on the wrong foot, Noah? *You're* the bad guy. *I'm* the good guy."

"Oh, no. I assure you the shoe's on the right foot, Meg. And a very lovely foot, I might add."

"Wait a second. Are you seriously telling me you think I'm a bad guy?"

"Do you consider blackmail and grand larceny and all the other tawdry activities you listed as being ones that a respectable young woman engages in?"

She stared at him in astonishment. "I don't do those things."

"Now, now, Meg. You've already confessed. It's a bit late to deny it."

"No. You don't get it."

"Oh, but I do," Noah said earnestly, coming right up to where she was sitting. He knelt on the plush mauve carpet so that they were eye to eye. "And I want you to know, Meg, that I, too, can be very understanding. Believe me, once we're squared up I'd love to hear your whole sad tale."

"I am not the bad guy here," Meg said between clenched teeth. "I'm not the one just caught redhanded trying to make off with close to a million bucks in jewels."

"Are Mrs. Friers's jewels worth that much?"

"I'm not talking about Mrs. Friers's jewels," she said, exasperated. "I'm talking about *my* jewels. Well, not literally *my* jewels, but—"

"No, I didn't think they were, Meg," Noah murmured dryly.

"I have them on loan."

"Well, that is one way of putting it. I gather you mean until you and your 'brothers four' fence them."

Meg threw up her hands in frustration. "I don't believe this."

"I'll confess something to you, love. I'd truly hoped I was wrong. Even though you fit the physical description so perfectly. And then there were the jewels. Not that I imagine the blackmail money you've already extracted from Lyons was enough to buy more than a brooch or two. But as you say, you and your *brothers* are multitalented."

"Will you stop saying brothers like that!" she snapped.

"Like what?" he asked, so close to her now she could smell his woodsy after-shave.

"Like you don't believe they *are* my brothers."

He smiled sardonically. "Why, if I didn't believe that, love, I'd have to conclude you've been lying to me about everything else."

Meg glared at him. "Okay, I lied to you. But you lied to me, too."

"Unavoidable."

She pressed her hands to her head. "I'm very confused."

"It's all very simple, Meg. You deliberately placed a minister of the British government in a compromising situation and then proceeded, according to plan, to blackmail him with certain letters and titillating photographs that, no doubt, one of your *brothers,* snapped."

"There you go again. Sean, Tony, Alex and Paul are my brothers. And none of them are into photography. And I did not put your minister in a compromising situation. I never met your bloody minister."

Noah smiled. "You're quite radiant when you're angry."

"I have one question to ask you, Noah Webb. Did you or did you not intend to steal my jewels?"

"I thought you said they were on loan."

"I'm serious, Noah."

"You mean you're seriously worried that I might be in competition with you and your gang of thieves?"

Meg rolled her eyes. "We aren't thieves. We're private eyes. Hired by the cruise-ship company to smoke out a notorious jewel thief."

"That's good, Meg. That's very good. You keep right on plugging even at your darkest hour."

"This isn't my darkest hour, you jerk."

It was, in a manner of speaking, Noah's. While the pair were going at it, Alex Delgado had managed to sneak into his sister's suite. By the time Noah sensed there was a new arrival on the scene and turned to look up, Alex's fist met squarely with his jaw. The next thing Noah knew everything went black.

A SEA OF FACES rotated in front of Noah's eyes. He opened his mouth to say something, but all that came out was a low moan. He closed his eyes again.

"You shouldn't have hit him so hard," Meg scolded.

"I suppose I should have just let him shoot you," Alex countered.

"He wasn't going to shoot me."

"He had a gun on you. What was I supposed to think?"

"I tried to tell this brother of yours that he had it all wrong," Chet Carson groused, rubbing his own sore jaw. After finally getting Louanne Percy's hot-water tap unstuck—a task that took him a good ten minutes—he hurried to Meg's suite and was in the process of jimmying open her lock when Alex spotted him and threw him a punch that sent him sprawling.

"What hit me?" Noah whispered, his eyes fluttering open again. The sea of faces was still staring down at him, but at least they were all staying in one place.

"My brother Alex," Meg said. "How does your jaw feel?"

"Like someone slugged me with a brick," Noah muttered. Then he squinted over at Chet. "What are you doing here?"

"I was on my way to help you when I got hit by a similar brick," Chet said dryly.

There was a knock on the door. Alex, who was now in possession of the gun, held it on Chet and Noah as he went to see who was there.

It was Captain Simon. Meg had phoned him right after Alex had KO'd Noah. The captain arrived with the rest of the Delgado clan—Sean, Tony and Paul.

"We've got your jewel thieves," Alex announced proudly to the captain.

"Is this guy dense or what?" Chet Carson belly-ached.

Noah sat up on the floor, gingerly rubbing his jaw. "If it's jewel thieves you want, Captain, meet the lovely ringleader—" he paused to gesture in Meg's direction "—and her merry band of *brothers.*"

"There you go again. What's it going to take to convince you they *are* my brothers?" Meg demanded.

Noah looked from Meg to Sean, then to Alex, Tony and Paul, then back to Meg again. "Well, well. Do you know, there is a family resemblance."

"Could somebody please tell me what's going on?" Captain Simon asked wearily.

"Mr. Webb here," Meg began. "Oh, you know him as Mr. Danforth II. Anyway, our Mr. Webb here has conveniently switched professions. It appears he's not a barrister, after all, but 007 of Her Majesty's Secret Service. Well, maybe I have the exact number wrong, but you get the idea, Captain."

Alex grinned. "And this character here," he said dramatically, pointing to Chet Carson, "isn't a steward in real life. No, by golly. He's a secret agent with the CIA," he added facetiously.

Noah heaved a sigh as he addressed the captain. "And this lovely lass and her partners in crime claim to be private eyes," he said dryly.

"They are private eyes," Captain Simon said flatly.

Noah squinted at the captain as if he couldn't possibly have heard right. "Did you say—?"

Before he could finish, Meg broke in. "The captain said we are private eyes."

Noah stared up at her. "You aren't serious."

"Deadly serious," Meg replied tartly. Then she turned to the captain. "I caught Noah Danforth II alias Noah Webb at my safe. He'd managed to open it. Said it was a trick of the trade. He already had the jewels out, but apparently that wasn't enough for him. He kept going on about this minister of finance he thinks I seduced and was blackmailing with certain indiscreet letters and photographs. Either he's very fast on his feet and was trying to throw me off by fabricating ludicrous charges against me or, what I think more likely, our jewel thief may be a bit touched in the head."

Noah pressed his palms against his temples. "Maybe I am at that," he muttered, shaking his head back and forth.

"You sure screwed this one up, Webb," Chet Carson grumbled.

Noah gave his partner a narrow look. He didn't need a second opinion. Especially when it echoed his own.

The captain cleared his throat and looked from Noah to the steward. "I'm afraid I'll have to place you two men under house arrest until we reach Saint Martin, our next port of call, tomorrow afternoon."

Chet started to reach into the inside jacket pocket of his uniform.

"I wouldn't try any funny stuff," Alex warned, waving the gun at him.

Chet smiled crookedly. "I'm just getting my wallet out." He retrieved it from his pocket and tossed it to the captain. "There's a secret compartment behind the billfold section. My ID's there."

The captain looked at Meg for an instant, then examined the billfold. A few moments later, he extracted a photo ID. Simon studied it intently, then muttered, "Oh, dear."

He lifted his gaze and took in the whole group. "It would appear from this card that Mr. Carson is telling the truth about his affiliation with the Central Intelligence Agency."

"The card could be a phony. Just like it's owner. And his partner," Meg said.

"It's easily verified," Chet said. "Call Langley."

"And you can follow that up, Captain Simon, with a call to the British intelligence," Noah added, rubbing his sore jaw. "You'll learn that Mr. Carson and I are working together to trap a woman on board this vessel who's blackmailing a certain British minister involved in very delicate Euromarket negotiations. If a scandal broke out, it could disrupt those negotiations and the economic repercussions would be felt throughout the world."

Noah looked over at Meg. "Mrs. Newell, alias Miss Delgado, fit the minister's description of the woman to a T. Oh, and the minister also happened to mention that his blackmailer was particularly fond of jewels.''

Everyone's eyes strayed to the tangle of gems still piled on the table. Then the captain cleared his throat and reached for the phone.

Meg found herself holding her breath as he began to dial.

CHAPTER EIGHT

IT WAS JUST before midnight when Noah rapped on the locked door to Meg's suite. After the captain had verified both his and Chet Carson's identities, Meg had ushered everyone out of her suite without a word. Noah had returned a short while later, but she'd refused to let him in. He'd gone off and had a drink with Chet in the lounge, then gone back to his own suite and tried to settle in for the night. He couldn't. Pulling on a pair of jeans and a navy T-shirt, he'd walked back down the corridor to Meg's suite, determined to see her.

After a firm rap, he pressed his face against her door, cupping his mouth so he wouldn't be overheard. Not that there was anyone in sight. And the rooms were exceedingly soundproof. Still, he didn't want to take any chances.

"Meg, I know you're still awake."

He paused, pressing his ear to her door now. There was no sound, no response.

"I know you're still awake," he persisted, "because you can't sleep any more than I can."

"Go away," she shouted from inside.

"I'm not going to go away, Meg."

"I'm not going to unlock my door," she retorted, than added icily, "Not that that's stopped you from entering in the past."

"I could break in, but I'd rather have your cooperation."

"My cooperation? Ha!"

"We've got to talk, love."

"We have nothing more to say to each other."

"Professionally speaking, Meg."

There was silence. Noah was about to rap on her
door again when she opened it. Without a word, she
stepped aside to let him enter. When he saw her, he
almost did a double take.

She was wearing a simple beige linen blouse, dark
cotton trousers, and there was not a jewel or even a
smattering of makeup on her. Her hair was swept
carelessly back from her face and gathered into a ponytail. Gone was the cool, elegant sophisticated Mrs.
Newell. In her place was this down-to-earth California girl.

Noah found himself gazing into Meg's bright and
lovely face and thinking to himself that he'd never seen
her look more beautiful. And this, despite her som-
ber guarded expression. A surge of warmth that was
more than just arousal suffused him.

He smiled, but for once he appeared unsure of
himself. "Quite a mix-up," he murmured.

Although she'd steeled herself for this confronta-
tion, Meg found herself disarmed by this new smile of
his. She felt herself weakening. "Want a drink?" Her
voice sounded raspy. Even before he answered, she
spun away from him and headed for the bar.

"Whiskey," he said.

She nodded, her back to him. She poured them both
a whiskey, even though she rarely drank hard liquor.
When she turned to take his drink to him, she was
startled to find him right beside her.

"Thanks," he said, and took the glass from her hand.

Her eyes shot to his face. Did he know how nervous she was? Had he felt the tremor in her hand when he took the glass from her?

She swallowed a large gulp of whiskey only to break into a coughing fit. Noah hurriedly poured her a glass of water.

"Here," he ordered, "drink this."

She waved it away, still coughing, her whiskey spilling over her glass onto the carpet. Noah persisted, putting the water to her lips. "Drink."

This time she did as he insisted.

The cough slowly subsided. Noah took her whiskey away. "Come sit down."

She resisted his efforts to guide her to a chair, the same one he'd guided her to earlier that evening. With a wave of a gun.

"I think better on my feet," she said archly.

Noah exhaled a weary sigh. "Look, I was wrong about you and you were wrong about me."

"Oh, I was wrong all right. Completely wrong," she muttered.

"Well, I don't know about you, love, but I happen to be glad I was wrong. It wasn't particularly pleasant thinking of you as a blackmailer."

"Really? You seemed to be enjoying yourself well enough," she said sarcastically.

"I assume you're referring to our little..." He hesitated.

Meg's eyes glared. "Yes, what would you call it, Mr. Webb?"

Noah's eyes turned a darker shade of blue. "Whatever either of us call it, you seemed to be enjoying yourself as much as I was. Maybe even more."

"More?" She was incensed. "More?"

They were practically nose to nose. "You heard me. More."

"That's a complete lie."

"Is it?" he challenged, his eyes taking on a hard, defensive glitter. "Maybe you're right. Maybe you're a better actress than I gave you credit for."

"Meaning?" she demanded icily.

"Oh, I think you understand my meaning," he retorted.

"So you think I was just doing my job?" she challenged. "Just like you were just doing your job?"

"Weren't you?"

Meg opened her mouth to speak, but then she realized she was doomed regardless of which position she took. If she told him the truth and admitted she wasn't just doing her job, that implied she'd completely lost sight of her job because she was so attracted to him. If she lied and said it was just a job, she was saying she was as callous and coldhearted as he was.

"Cat got your tongue, love?" he pressed.

Meg felt suddenly like collapsing. The problem was she was standing so close to Noah that, if she did let herself go, she'd fall right into his arms. Which would be awful. Or would it?

Noah regretted having made the charge. What he didn't regret was the intimacy they had shared that afternoon; the feel of her warm, inviting body; the way she'd responded to his kisses, his caresses; the way he'd responded to her. It had been a long time since any woman had had quite that effect on him. And now the feelings were even more intense. He knew those feelings were dangerous. They threatened his focus, his need to concentrate fully on what was an extremely vital assignment. He knew the smart thing to do was to turn on his heel and get out of there. But he felt rooted to the spot. And he couldn't stop staring at her. It was all he could do not to touch her.

He whispered her name softly. "Meg."

She couldn't meet Noah's gaze, knowing if she did all her resolve would instantly melt away and she would fall helplessly into his arms. So much had happened in such a short time. Normally she prided herself on being able to go with the flow, but she felt as if she was going down a stretch of white-water rapids and she'd lost her oars and her boat was starting to fill with water. Any second now she would capsize unless she exerted every ounce of energy she had making it to calm waters. And as long as Noah was within arm's reach, there was nothing but turbulence.

"Oh, go away," she pleaded. "I'm too mixed-up to talk about anything right now."

"It wasn't just a job. Not for me, anyway," he confessed tenderly.

Her eyes met his. "What are you saying?" she asked hoarsely.

"I desperately longed to make love with you on the beach," he found himself confessing. "The only reason I pulled back was that I thought... Well, we've been all through that."

"You mean you were attracted to me?"

He smiled playfully. "I do believe desperate longing would signify definite attraction."

"Don't make fun of me."

"Oh, Meg, believe me, that's the last thing I want to do right now," he murmured.

There was no missing the first thing he wanted to do.

Noah reached out one hand and placed it lightly on the side of her face. The touch was innocent enough, but there was nothing innocent about the fantasy it sparked inside Meg's head. She could already picture the two of them naked on her big king-size bed, limbs entwined, finishing what they'd begun that afternoon beside the Virgin Gorda lagoon.

She was well into the sensual fantasy when she felt Noah's mouth against her ear. A sudden attack of nerves made her jump back. Okay, so he wasn't a criminal. That was only one issue here. There was also the matter of her firm resolve against ever again getting involved in a shipboard romance.

And then another problem popped into her mind. Maybe if she could just focus on the problems she'd be safe.

"Damn," she muttered.

Noah gave her a puzzled look. "What is it?"

"Don't you see what it is?" she countered.

Noah was completely baffled. "Aren't you relieved I'm not the nefarious jewel thief, after all? I must tell you I'm enormously pleased you aren't a cunning blackmailer."

He tried to pull her back into his arms, but she resisted. She went and sat down on the sofa, staring pensively down at her hands.

Noah came and sat down beside her. "What is it, Meg?"

She gave him a sideways glance. "We're back to ground zero again."

He smiled roguishly. "We can work our way back up," he said, cupping her chin and planting a feather-light kiss on her lips.

"Oh, Noah."

"Oh, Meg," he responded, slipping his arm around her waist only to find her hands firmly planted on his chest as he tried to draw her closer.

"This is terrible," she muttered.

"What's terrible?" he asked, baffled.

"You said it yourself. Now you know I'm not the cunning blackmailer you're after and I know you're not the nefarious jewel thief I'm after."

"That's not all we know," he murmured seductively.

"Right," she agreed emphatically, on a different track altogether. "We know that we've wasted all this time on the wrong suspects."

Noah let his hand fall from Meg's waist. "I don't know that I'd call it *wasted* time."

Meg smiled faintly. "Maybe I'm overstating it a bit." Her smile vanished. "But you know what I mean."

Noah heaved a sigh. "Yes, I suppose I do."

They both leaned back against the couch, side by side. Neither of them said anything for a long time.

"Who do you suppose your femme fatale is?" she finally asked.

"I don't bloody know."

"Heather St. John?"

He shook his head. "I don't think so. She doesn't fit Lyons' description. She's smaller. Her hair's the wrong color."

"It could be dyed. She could have worn spike heels when she was seducing your minister."

"I suppose it's possible."

"I thought the two of you were...working together."

"Fellow spies? Oh, no. Fellow jewel thieves."

Meg hesitated. "I thought you might also be...lovers."

"Not very likely."

"Why's that?"

"She isn't my type. You, on the other hand—"

"Don't. Don't say it, Noah. We have enough to cope with here without, well, adding further complications."

Noah gave her a level look. "Meg, it isn't just me. You feel something, too. You felt it at the beach. Both of us let our guards down. That's true, isn't it?" His voice fell into a soft whisper as he spoke.

Meg sighed. "All right. I admit I had a few weak moments." She wasn't feeling altogether strong-willed at the moment, either, despite her best efforts.

"But that was then and this is now," she said, trying to sound firm.

"Now I want you more than ever," he said without guile.

"No..."

Those blue eyes were burning with desire. "Yes, Meg. And you feel the same."

"No. No, I don't, Noah."

"Let's be done with lies, Meg. There's no reason for them anymore. We're both good guys, remember?" he murmured, a seductive smile playing on his lips. "Let me show you how good I can be, love." His voice deepened, grew husky.

She compressed her lips, trying to ignore the longing exploding in her body like a firecracker. "It's late.

My head...is spinning.'' That was certainly true enough.

His eyes were burning into her. He cupped her face with both hands and pressed his lips ever so lightly to her forehead.

When he drew back, Meg stared at him. He looked so incredibly appealing and alarmingly dangerous at the same time. She wanted to pull her gaze away but couldn't. Any more than she could pull her body away when he drew her to him and wrapped her in his arms.

His mouth descended on hers. Their tongues met and greeted each other like long-lost friends. No. Friendliness had nothing to do with this kiss. Or with the way they clung so tightly to each other. Desperate longing. That was the feeling, all right. For both of them.

Noah's hands tugged Meg's shirt out of the waistband of her trousers. He wanted to feel her warm satiny flesh. He wanted to touch and caress her, take possession of her.

A little groan escaped Meg as she felt his fingers skate up her spine. His touch made her hungry for more. She suddenly felt starved. Every inch of her body tingled and throbbed. All her resistance was gone. She was burning, glowing, wanting.

Seemingly with a will of their own, her clothes and Noah's began floating to the carpet. Until there they were, she in nothing but her lacy white bra and silk panties, and Noah in a pair of navy bikini briefs.

Their eyes locked. His warm breath fanned her face, but she felt the cool air of the room on her body. Along with another flurry of alarm. This wasn't smart. She was getting in over her head. Only trouble lay ahead.

But it wasn't too late. She could still stop it from happening; stop herself from passing through that point of no return. She tried to tell herself that nothing was going to come of this. Nothing but heartache.

Noah had no trouble reading Meg's thoughts. They were written all over her face. Nor could he ignore them, since they sparked some concerns of his own. Emotional entanglements were a serious hazard when he was on assignment. Hell, he found them a hazard even when he wasn't. Sure, he used his line of work as a handy excuse for not getting involved, but he knew it went deeper than that. Commitment scared the dickens out of him. And yet, for the first time, that fear just wasn't taking hold in the same old way. It couldn't compete with the desire he was feeling so intensely.

Meg folded her arms across her chest, feeling awkward and vulnerable. "This doesn't make any sense," she muttered.

"Isn't that what we do in our professions?" Noah murmured softly.

"What?"

"Try to make sense out of things that appear not to make any sense?"

"I don't think we can in this instance."

"The way I see it, love, we have two choices here."

"Yes?"

"Either we put some more clothes on and discuss the various complexities of our brief but intense relationship..."

Meg managed a wobbly smile. "Or?"

"Or," he said with a raffish glint in his blue eyes, "we take the rest of our clothes off and proceed without further delay or discussion to your big inviting bed and figure it all out later.''

''It might be too late—later,'' Meg whispered as her heart hammered in her chest.

''It might be,'' he conceded.

Meg was trembling badly. She felt as if she was racing toward the edge of a cliff.

''Then again,'' he murmured, ''maybe we have no choice. Maybe we just have to risk it because...in our hearts we always were and always will be risk takers.''

Their eyes met and locked. Meg smiled tremulously. Yes, she thought, risk was what it was all about for both of them. Risk was what had drawn them together right from the start. And it would very likely be what drew them apart in the end. But now there was no beginning or end. There was just living for the moment....

Noah leaned forward, pressing his mouth to Meg's bare shoulder. His fingers tugged off her ponytail holder and her hair cascaded over her shoulders. He put his hands through the silky strands and drew her face toward him.

He meant the kiss to be gentle, but as soon as her lips parted and she gave a soft moan, he couldn't hold back. He kissed her with all the heat and urgency erupting inside him. He pressed her body to him so that she could feel how hard he was, how excited he was to claim her. Meg's fingers dug into Noah's shoulders. She was infused with a wild recklessness. She wanted this man. There was no denying it, no escaping it. No stopping it.

When he rose, extending his hand to her, she clasped it like a lifeline, her fingers entwining with his. He drew her to her feet and led her into the bedroom.

They fell together on the bed and within seconds those few remaining undergarments lay in a small heap on the floor.

Noah gave her a long rapturous study. "You are a work of art, love."

"If I am, I'm a work in progress," she murmured huskily, drawing him to her.

They kissed with wild abandon, each of them casting aside their cardinal rules even as they knew somewhere in the back of their minds that they'd be castigating themselves tomorrow. It didn't matter. An unstoppable force was rushing them toward an unavoidable fate. They didn't have a choice. Or at least that's what they both eagerly told themselves.

"Oh, Meg, you feel so good. You taste so good." His hands and mouth were everywhere, as if exploring a newly discovered terrain and wanting to claim every inch of it as his own.

His tongue slid around a taut nipple.

Meg arched up to him. "Mmm, that drives me crazy,"

He'd moved on to her other nipple. "That's the idea, love."

"I have a few ideas of my own," she whispered with a naughty-girl smile.

Amusement and desire radiated from his eyes. "Do you, now?"

With a boldness she had amply displayed in all other arenas of her life but this one—until now—she rolled Noah onto his back and climbed astride him. Slowly, she ran her fingertips lightly over the muscles in his arms, shoulders, down his chest.

"A very nice idea," he said huskily.

She dipped her head to his chest so that her hair fell like a fan over his skin and the tip of her tongue darted out and drew a circle around his nipple. Then she sucked it into her mouth as he had done for her.

Noah groaned audibly, filling Meg with intense pleasure. Her hand reached behind her and she took hold of him. He was already hard, but he grew harder still under her sensual ministrations.

"Meg, you're driving me crazy," he gasped.

"That's the idea, love," she whispered, her amber eyes glowing.

His hands came up and cupped her breasts. Then he lifted his head and buried his face in them. Meg clung to him.

Only one shared idea remained and it obliterated everything else from existence. Their mouths met and this time their lips crushed together. Noah's hands circled her rib cage and he lifted her just high enough to find his passage home.

"Oh," she cried as he pushed up inside her at last. They kissed fiercely as he filled her, their hands roaming hungrily, their bodies moving with a fierce greedy desire.

Noah was a strong and intense lover, a perfect match for Meg who had thrilled for so long at living life on the edge. She held on fiercely to him so as not to slip off completely and fall into the abyss.

Neither of them wanted it to end, nor could they hold themselves back. Meg arched her back encouraging Noah to thrust deeper and deeper. In what felt like the space of a heartbeat they took a trip to eternity and beyond.

Spent at last, she rolled off him and fell limply onto her back on the still made-up bed. Noah couldn't move at all.

Neither of them said a word.

It had been the best, the most intense sexual encounter of their lives. Still, the afterglow lasted all of a few minutes. Once the heat of passion began to cool, doubts and self-recriminations began to surface.

"Noah..."

"Meg..."

They'd spoken at the same time.

"You first," he said, a strained politeness in his voice that hadn't been there before.

"No. You," she insisted.

Slowly, he rolled onto his side, but as soon as his eyes swept over her naked body, which he now knew so intimately, he was instantly aroused again. He hastily returned to lying on his back and stared up at the ceiling.

Meg shivered. "Would you mind if we got under the covers?"

"No. No, I wouldn't mind at all."

The next thing he knew, instead of slipping under the blankets, she sprung out of bed.

"What's wrong?"

"Nothing," she said hurriedly, awkwardly. "I realized I really should...shower."

"Oh. Right."

"Besides, it's awfully late."

"Yes, I guess it is," he said quietly.

She grabbed her robe off the chaise and slipped into it. "I was just thinking that...it probably wouldn't...that we shouldn't...that is, you shouldn't..."

"You want me to leave?" he offered.

Meg clutched her robe lapels in her fist. "What I want—" She stopped. What the hell did she want?

He stared across at her. "Are you sorry, Meg?"

"No." And then a more emphatic, "No!" She squirmed. "It's just that, well, we both have very important jobs to do. And if we get too...distracted, well, it wouldn't be a very good idea, would it? For either of us."

He smiled rakishly. "I don't know. It seemed like a very good idea a few minutes ago."

"Please be serious, Noah. Too much has happened too fast. I need some time to sort it all out. I've still got a jewel thief to catch. And you've got to...to save your minister from exposure. And talking about... exposure, could you please get dressed? I can't... concentrate with you...like that."

Noah grinned. "I'll have to keep that in mind."

"The thing is, separate from everything else, meaning the assignments we both have to handle, I've sworn off shipboard...dalliances."

Noah furrowed his brow. "Dalliances?"

"You know what I'm trying to say."

"Have you had many dalliances?"

She knew he was teasing her and she wasn't at all happy about it. "No. Not...many."

"I see."

"Have you?" she shot back.

A mischievous smile tilted the corners of his mouth. "Are we talking dalliances in general terms or dalliances that occurred specifically aboard a seagoing vessel?"

"Don't be cute." Cute and naked was truly more than she could handle.

Noah rose from the bed. Meg saw it as a hopeful sign he would get dressed and leave her to her tumultuous thoughts and emotions. Instead, he came toward her.

"Please don't, Noah," she said.

"I will be perfectly frank with you, love. I have had my share of dalliances. On land and sea."

"Your frankness is so refreshing," Meg said acerbically.

He smiled at her, getting closer and closer. "I would not, however, classify this as a dalliance."

Meg swallowed hard. "You . . . you wouldn't?"

He was now only inches away from her. "I wouldn't."

"What would you . . . classify it as?" she stammered, trying to keep her eyes on his face only to find them drifting of their own will down his gorgeous naked body.

Before he could answer her, there was a knock on her door.

They both jumped.

"Meggie? Meggie, are you up? It's me. Paul."

"Oh, God," Meg moaned. She gave Noah a panicked look. "Don't just stand there." Then she shouted toward the closed door. "Hold on a minute, Paul. Just a minute. Be right there."

She grabbed Noah's arm. "Quick. In the bathroom." She started nudging him in that direction, but then tugged him back. "Your clothes. Get your clothes," she whispered.

"What's the problem? He's on our side," Noah whispered back.

"Meggie? Everything okay in there?" Paul called from the other side of the door.

"Fine. Fine. Coming." She raced wildly over to the pile of clothes in the sitting room, gathered them up, dumped them in Noah's arms and shoved him in the direction of the bathroom.

She waited until Noah disappeared from sight. Then taking a long steadying breath, she made sure her robe was fully closed and went and opened the door.

Paul gave her an assessing look when she finally appeared. "What's the matter?"

"What's the matter?" she echoed. "I was practically fast asleep. You . . . woke me up."

"Why are you out of breath?"

"I was . . . having a bad dream."

"A bad dream left you panting?"

"I was running. In my dream." She put her hands on her hips. "Did you want something, Paul? It's the middle of the night."

"Can I come inside? We can't talk in the hall."

Meg hesitated. "It's awfully late, Paul. Couldn't we talk in the morning?"

"You're up, anyway. And it could be important."

Reluctantly Meg stepped aside. "Just for a few minutes." She manufactured a dramatic yawn. "I'm beat."

Paul frowned. "You're acting weird."

"I'm not *acting* weird," Meg countered defensively. "I'm acting tired. I mean I'm not acting tired. I am tired. Now what is it?"

"Okay, okay. But I know what it's about."

"What what's about?"

"Your weirdness."

"Paul—"

"It's about Danforth. Or should I say Webb?"

Meg felt her face heat up. "That's absolutely untrue."

"I know you like a book, Meggie. We all do."

"All?"

"Sean, Tony, Alex, me. Your big brothers, remember?"

"Paul, what are you talking about?"

"We all know how you hate being wrong. You had Webb pegged as our jewel thief. You were so sure about it. And now you have to accept that you were wrong about him. That your instincts didn't come through for you this time around."

Meg sighed. Well, it was true about some of her instincts, anyway. "Okay, I was wrong," she said, impatient to send her brother on his way. "Maybe it is bugging me a little, but I'm sure I'll feel fine about it in the morning." Not very likely.

Paul wagged a finger at her. "I bet you weren't really sleeping."

Meg blanched, surreptitiously glancing over at the bathroom door. "What do you mean?"

"I bet you were just lying in your bed tossing and turning, racking your brain about who to finger now that Webb's off your list."

"Well . . ."

"I'll give you someone to mull over."

"Who?"

"Larson."

Meg gave him a blank look, trying to get her breathing under control. "Who?"

A thud came from the direction of the bathroom. Paul looked over there, then at his sister. "What was that?"

Meg's heart started to race. "Nothing. I didn't hear anything."

"You didn't hear something drop? Like a shoe?"

"Oh, that. From the corridor. Probably a steward picking up passengers' shoes from in front of their doors. You know, for polishing."

Paul looked dubious.

"Oh, Olson. The Swedish hunk, Olson. Yes, right," Meg said loudly to cover up the possible sound of another shoe dropping. Noah did have two...

Wrong, Meg realized with a sickening sensation in the pit of her stomach as she spied Noah's second shoe a few feet off to Paul's left. She'd missed it when she'd frantically gathered up all the clothes.

"Why are you shouting?" Paul asked.

Meg pressed her fingers to her lips. "Was I?" She took several steps to her left, forcing her brother to turn further away from the spot where Noah's shiny cordovan loafer rested on the carpet.

"Something is the matter," Paul said adamantly. "Is it Webb?" He drew a little closer to her. "You haven't gone and fallen for him, have you, Meggie?"

"Don't be ridiculous."

"Not that it would be a crime. Falling for a jewel thief would have been one thing. But, heck, he's on the up-and-up, so what's the problem?"

"I really don't want to discuss this now. What about Olson?"

"Well, I was just thinking about the way he hit on Heather. Then I saw him having drinks today with Delacore and Louanne Percy, acting real chummy. And Sean saw him chatting it up with the Frierses at breakfast yesterday morning. I'm sure she told him all about her novel *Beyond Hope*. I think he's been scouting all his marks...."

"Not me," Meg pointed out.

"He could be saving his biggest score for last. Working his way up. Probably picked Friers because she made it so easy for him. I mean, if Webb figured out that HOPE was the code, why not Larson?"

Meg pondered Paul's remarks, even forgetting about Noah for the moment. "Larson didn't particularly impress me as being very bright. But maybe that was deliberate. You know something, Paul, you just might have something there."

"One other thing," Paul said.

"Yes?"

He hesitated. "About Heather. I know I can't account for every minute of her time today, but I did spend enough time with her to know that she simply isn't the sort of woman to be mixed up in this ugly business."

NOAH HAD JUST CRACKED open the door to see if Meg was making any headway in getting rid of her brother when he picked up Paul's mention of Heather.

Noah's brow furrowed. So Paul and Meg had pegged Heather St. John as a potential jewel thief. He carefully closed the bathroom door and sat down on the edge of the large Jacuzzi tub. Hmm. Had he vetoed Heather as Lyons's femme fatale too hastily? If Heather was involved in the jewel theft, it might be but one of her many talents. Another being blackmail.

There was still the matter of Lyons's description of "Alison Baker," but as Meg had pointed out, dyeing one's hair was an easy enough matter. And the woman could have worn high heels most of the time she was with the minister. Except when they were in bed naturally. But then, in those moments, it wasn't likely Lyons was thinking about how tall his seductress was.

"ALL I'M SAYING IS we could be after one and the same person," Noah argued as he and Meg stood facing off in the sitting room shortly after Paul's departure.

"That's not all you're saying," Meg retorted, handing him his errant loafer. He was now fully dressed again except for the shoe.

"All right, what else am I saying?" he challenged, slipping it on.

"You're saying that I should cooperate with you in your investigation."

"So?"

"What about *my* investigation? What about you cooperating with me?"

Noah smiled condescendingly. "Meg, I happen to be a professionally trained agent of Her Majesty's Secret Service. I've been in this business for close to fourteen years. I think it would be safe to say I have rather a bit more experience and savvy in these matters than a young woman who's played at being a private eye for a few years."

"Played at?" Meg's nostrils flared. She was incensed. "Played at? Do you think SeaQuest Lines would hand over a retainer of ten grand to someone who *played* at being a detective?"

"All right. You're very clever and astute. And you and your brothers have clearly had a bit of luck in your endeavors. But we're dealing with master criminals here, love. All I'm saying is you'll do well to follow my lead in this particular investigation."

"Why you smug...prig," Meg hissed.

Noah clasped his hand to his heart in mock distress. "Prig? You cut me to the quick, love."

"Smug prig," she corrected. "In equal parts."

Noah clasped his hands together. "Be reasonable. We don't want to be working at cross-purposes, stepping on each other's toes now. All I'm saying—"

"You've said all there is to say." Meg strode over to her door. "Good night, Mr. Danforth."

"You're being very childish, Mrs. Newell."

"I think we've done enough name-calling for the night." She hesitated, averting her gaze. "I think we've done enough of everything."

Noah came up beside her. "Look, we needn't confuse apples and oranges, love," he said softly.

Meg's chin jutted out defiantly. "This isn't a question of fruit."

Noah sighed. "If you do run into trouble, give a whistle."

"The same goes for you," she said airily.

Noah combed his fingers through his tousled hair. For just a moment, Meg couldn't help thinking how those fingers, those hands, had such a short while ago incited riotous passion in her body.

Their faces were inches apart. She made out for the first time a faint scar just below the corner of his right eye. A battle scar?

"Meg," Noah crooned softly.

He started to lean toward her.

It would have been so easy, so simple, so much what a part of her desperately wanted, to put up no impediment to the progress of his lips toward hers.

Only it wasn't easy. Or simple. It was giving in. Not just physically. Or even emotionally. But mentally. It meant admitting he was rightfully in charge. The boss.

No way. She hadn't worked this hard, this long, for someone else to come waltzing into her territory and take over.

Like a boxer who saw the hit coming, Meg ducked to her right. The hit Noah had intended for her irresistible lips got lost somewhere in her hair.

With a sigh of disappointment, he reached for the doorknob.

"Be careful." The words spilled from her lips of their own volition.

He smiled. "You, too, love."

CHAPTER NINE

THE PAIR MET in the shadows near the bridge. It was almost one in the morning. The seas were rough and a tropical night wind blew. The woman pulled her shawl more tightly around her shoulders. The man lifted up the collar of his jacket.

"Well, you're very pleased with yourself," she said.

"Shouldn't I be?" he replied. "Are you complaining about the haul?"

She smiled. "No. And there is some poetic justice in your choice."

"Yes. That'll teach Mrs. Friers to go poking her head where it doesn't belong."

"Still..."

He scowled. "I know what you're thinking."

"You always loved a challenge in the past," she murmured, nuzzling his neck.

He pushed her away. "I like challenges, but I'm not stupid."

"I think you're afraid," she taunted softly, running her tapered finger down the lapel of his jacket.

"Don't play that game with me, darling. It won't work," he said acidly.

"But think about all those glorious jewels, baby. You could manage it, even if you are right and Newell is out to set you up. I know you can do it."

He grinned crookedly. "You're a boost to the ego, I'll say that for you."

Ignoring his earlier rebuff, she pressed her lips to his cheek. "And just think of the satisfaction you'll have outsmarting the little bitch."

"I'll sleep on it."

She draped her arms around his neck. "Let's sleep on it together."

"No, we can't get sloppy now. Besides, I thought you were going to be otherwise occupied tonight."

"I thought so, too." She slid the tip of her tongue across his lower lip. "Doesn't it make you even the tiniest bit jealous to imagine me with another man?"

He gave a low callous laugh. "Not the tiniest bit."

"He's really taken with me, you know."

"I'd be disappointed if he wasn't."

She pouted. "You can be so hard."

He pressed her roughly against him. "See how hard?"

She laughed throatily. "We could do it right here," she said eagerly.

He swatted her playfully on the buttocks, then eased her away from him. "We could, but we won't. I've been successful because while I've taken many risks they've never been foolish ones. Now, go to bed like a good girl."

"But I'm not tired. And I'm not a good girl, darling," she added coyly.

"No. You're not. And that's why I adore you."

ELIOT HARPER rolled over in bed. Once again he was having trouble sleeping. He squinted at the illuminated dial of the clock on the bedside table. Almost one in the morning. He sighed audibly, then nervously glanced over at his wife, afraid he might have awakened her. To his relief, she was snoring peacefully.

He closed his eyes, trying to will himself to sleep, but after five minutes he gave it up. He felt restless and nervous. The ship seemed to be swaying. Fortunately his antiseasick patch was working, but he still worried about the rough seas. What if there was a storm? What if the ship sprung a leak? Did cruise ships spring leaks?

As if natural disasters while aboard ship weren't enough to worry about, there was this ugly business of the jewel theft. Elaine had been so agitated she'd insisted that all her jewels remain locked in the ship's main vault until they docked back in New York. She wasn't taking any chances.

Now that she'd removed the jewels, Elaine felt greatly relieved. Eliot, however, remained agitated by the very idea that there was a thief on board. He'd known right from the start that this cruise was a bad idea. But had he been able to convince Elaine?

Never again would he let his wife talk him into something like this. Never.

AFTER PAUL LEFT Meg's suite he was surprised to run into Heather on the Promenade Deck.

"Hi," she said with a bright smile as the wind whipped her hair around her face. "I see you couldn't sleep, either."

"Care to get a drink or something?" he asked, falling into step with her.

"I just passed the lounge. The Frierses are holding court there."

"On second thought..."

They both laughed, but then Paul grew serious.

"Terrible business," he muttered.

"Yes, terrible," Heather readily agreed. "Still, she is insured."

"True," Paul said.

"And she'll probably use it as the basis for her next novel and make a fortune."

Paul shot Heather a look. She sounded awfully nonchalant about the matter. A flurry of disquiet rippled through him. "I suppose you're right. Mrs. Friers will make the best of it."

She glanced at Paul and smiled. "Don't get me wrong. I certainly don't condone thievery."

Paul was relieved to hear that. The question was, could he believe her. He wanted to believe her? Oh, how he wanted to believe her!

"I don't suppose you have any idea who it might have been," he asked in a tone he hoped sounded offhand.

Heather shrugged. "Oh, I don't know. Someone hard up for cash possibly."

"That would narrow it down some, since most of the passengers aboard this ship are pretty well-heeled."

"Well, we all give that appearance, anyway."

Paul felt his stomach constrict. Was she trying to tell him something? She certainly gave the *impression* of being well-off. Is that what it was? Just an impression?

"Say, if you're in need of a helping hand..." He kept his tone light and let the rest of the sentence hang in the brisk sea air.

She laughed softly, then surprised him by slipping her hand in his. "You're very sweet, Paul."

He squeezed her hand. "I try my best," he said earnestly.

She gave him a sideways glance. "We could go back to my suite. For a drink."

Paul's mouth quirked into a smile. "For a drink. Sure."

"LOUANNE, BABY. My sweet little gumdrop. Don't sulk," Alan Delacore cajoled. "You know I love you. I told you I was going to be tied up this evening. If I don't look after my investments while we're cruising these tropical waters I could find myself in a sea of troubles when we get back to New York. What with interest rates rising and all these trade wars brewing... Come on, sugar. Why don't I walk you back to your suite and tuck you in."

"I don't see why you can't tuck me in right here," Louanne Percy pouted.

"Now, gumdrop, we've been all through that."

"And that's another thing. I just don't know why we have to wait six whole months to get married. Your divorce is final."

"It's all a matter of appearances, sweet pea."

"Oh, who cares about appearances?"

"I do," he said firmly.

Louanne sighed. "Sometimes I wonder, sugar..."

Alan Delacore drew his fiancée into his arms. "What do you wonder, baby?"

"You do love me, Alan?"

"Love you? How could you even ask such a thing? I'm wild about you, gumdrop."

"It's just that I feel you've been so distant since we started on this cruise. So preoccupied."

"Like I told you. The stock market's going kind of crazy lately, and I've got to make sure I keep on top of things."

"There isn't anything to worry about? I mean, you're not going to lose all your money or anything? Not that it would make one iota of difference to me, sugar. I'd love you rich or poor."

He chuckled. "But given a choice, I bet I know which you'd prefer."

She swatted him playfully on the chest. "Now, that isn't fair. I really, truly mean what I said."

He gave her a big moist kiss on the lips. "I know you do, gumdrop."

She snuggled against him. "So, am I going to be marrying a rich man or a poor man in six months?" she cooed.

He grinned. "Gumdrop, I've been poor and I've been rich. And I like rich a lot better. You can bet I'm going to look after all my assets."

"Does that include me, sugar?"

"You bet it does," he murmured, his hands moving to the tiny pearl buttons of her blouse. One by one, he undid them.

Louanne gave a sexy little laugh. "I thought you wanted me to go back to my suite."

He pulled her blouse out of the waistband of her slacks. "I changed my mind."

Louanne smiled a victory smile.

AT CLOSE TO ONE-THIRTY in the morning Tony rapped lightly on Liza's door. After a few seconds the door swung open.

He smiled. "Hi."

Liza smiled back. "Hi."

"Mind if I come in?"

"It's late. I gave you up for lost."

He stepped inside. "You can't lose me that easily."

"That's nice to know," she murmured as he took her in his arms.

"Want to see what I bought this afternoon on-shore?" she asked. Liza had dragged Tony with her to half a dozen shops in the town of Virgin Gorda, but then took pity on him and sent him off to have a nice cool drink at one of the colorful bars while she finished up.

"I didn't think you'd bought anything. When you met me at the bar I didn't see any shopping bags."

She grinned seductively. "I hid what I bought in my tote. I wanted to surprise you. Close your eyes."

He did as she bid. A few moments later she told him he could open them.

When he did, he saw her standing before him in a very lacy, very sheer hot pink teddy. Tony decided there and then that Liza Hamilton had the best body he had ever seen or was ever likely to see again.

She smiled seductively at him with lips painted the same shade of pink as her teddy. "Well? Do you like?"

"Come here," he said huskily, "and I'll show you just how much I like."

IT WAS VERY LATE and the only ones left in the lounge to listen to Barbara Friers's never-ending tale of woe, besides her husband, was the botanist, Dr. Franz Schmidt, and his wife, Clara. The novelist, quite tipsy after several martinis to "quiet her nerves," was dramatically describing how she would use this recent "most unsettling event" of the theft of her jewels in her next novel.

"Of course there'd be several red herrings," she was saying.

Clara Schmidt looked blankly at the novelist. "Herrings?"

"As a boy I remember visiting the Netherlands with my parents," the botanist reflected, "and we enjoyed the most marvelous herring."

Horace Friers chuckled. "No, Franz. Barb's not talking about the kind of herrings you eat."

"Oh, I'm sorry," Dr. Schmidt said. "I misunderstood."

"Not the herrings you eat?" Clara Schmidt repeated with a muddled look.

"Surely you read mysteries, intrigues," Barbara Friers said with a deprecating tone. "My books, for example, do exceedingly well in Germany."

"We are from Hungary, Mrs. Friers," Dr. Schmidt corrected politely.

The novelist gave her husband a bleary-eyed look. "I sell big in Hungary, too, don't I?"

Horace Friers scowled. "Actually, I don't believe sales have been really brisk in Hungary, Barb."

She shrugged. "Where was I, anyway? I seem to have lost my train of thought."

"I believe you were talking about herrings, Mrs. Friers," the botanist reminded her.

"Yes," Clara Schmidt added shyly. "Red herrings."

"Yes, yes," Barbara Friers said. "Red herrings. Exactly." Suddenly she paused and shrewdly eyed the scientist and his wife. "The point is, I'd toss in all these red herrings, deliberately leading the reader astray at every turn. And all along, it's a party or parties they never would suspect."

Clara Schmidt gave her husband a nervous glance.

"Aha!" the novelist exclaimed so loudly that the botanist's wife emitted a little gasp of alarm.

"You see," she said, narrowing her gaze on the couple, "the guilty parties are always the ones who appear quiet and self-effacing on the surface, but peel away that innocent veneer and you discover the true evil that lurks within their black hearts." Quite drunk at this point, Mrs. Friers's words erupted in one long slur.

Dr. Schmidt and his wife were aghast at her outburst. The botanist shot to his feet. "Surely, Mrs. Friers, you're not suggesting that my wife and I had any involvement whatsoever in the theft of your jewels."

The novelist gave him a baffled look. "What?"

"Now, now, Dr. Schmidt," Horace Friers soothed, "no reason to get hot under the collar. You misunderstood my wife." He grinned. "Don't worry. She gets a lot of people confused. Even me. You know how it is with creative people. She wasn't accusing you of anything." He turned to his wife, who was motioning to the waiter for another martini. "Were you, Barb?"

"Was I what?"

Clara tugged on her husband's sleeve. "Please, Franz. Do not make a scene. Sit down."

"Yes, have another drink, Franz," Barbara Friers said magnanimously. "I was just getting to the best part." She blinked several times. "Oh, dear, I seem to have forgotten what it was now. But I'm sure it will come to me."

She looked around for the waiter with her drink. Instead, she spied another shipmate. "Lars. Oh, Lars. Over here. Come join us. I was just telling the Schmidts all about the plot to my next novel."

The Swede, who'd just walked up to the bar, rolled his eyes at the bartender.

The bartender grinned. "Tough luck, my friend."

"Tough luck is right," Lars muttered.

"WHERE'VE YOU BEEN?" Chet Carson asked as Noah opened the door to his suite. "Or should I bother asking?"

"Don't you have your own room, Carson?" Noah snapped.

"Yeah, but yours is a lot nicer," he said with a wiseacre grin as he stretched his legs out in front of him on the sofa, crossing them at the ankles.

"Look, I'm beat, Carson. Let's butt heads in the morning," Noah said.

"Yeah, you must be beat. You got your T-shirt on inside out," Carson returned drolly.

Noah looked down and saw the seams showing on his shirt. He heaved a sigh. "I must be nuts."

The steward-cum-CIA agent's grin broadened. "I'll second that."

Noah crossed the room and sank wearily into one of the leather chairs facing the sofa. "I told her we ought to work together. I have a feeling there's a tie-in here. That we might be after the same folk."

"Sounds reasonable. She didn't agree?"

"About the tie-in, yes. About working together..." He raised his eyes to the ceiling. "She's got this bloody thing about me running the show. Doesn't feature having me in charge of this operation. Total disregard for my expertise, my training, my years in the field. She's as stubborn as . . .''

"As you?"

"I'm serious, Chet. This is a very tricky situation."

"You're telling me? Hey, old chap, neither of our chiefs are too happy with our handling of this operation so far. This isn't exactly what you'd call deep cover anymore. We blew it."

"Don't be kind. It doesn't become you. We didn't blow it. I blew it."

"Don't beat yourself over the head with it. Who'd've figured we'd have competition? The question is, what now?"

Noah ran his fingers through his hair. "I've been thinking more about the St. John woman. Meg seems to think she may be involved in the jewel theft. Could be she's the greedy type. Why not theft and blackmail?"

"You've got a point."

"To give her her due, the point was Meg's first. As much as I hate to admit it, I really didn't think Heather was the sort of woman who could make a man take the kind of chances Alison Baker made Lyons take."

"I don't know," Carson said. "She's real easy on the eyes."

Noah shrugged. "Oh, she's pretty enough, but she doesn't set off any sparks."

"Hey, no saying your taste in women and your minister of finance's taste are the same," Carson pointed out.

Noah nodded. "St. John certainly does seem to be setting off some sparks in Meg's brother."

"Which one? She's got a whole gaggle of 'em," Carson said with a laugh.

"Her social secretary. Paul."

"Maybe he's just feeling her out," Carson suggested.

"No. That's the problem. He's stuck on her. And you know what that means."

Carson laughed dryly. "No, but I bet you do."

CHAPTER TEN

SHORTLY BEFORE NOON the next day, the *Galileo* docked in Philipsburgh on the Dutch side of Saint Martin, or Sint Maarten as the Dutch called it. Meg was one of the last passengers to disembark in this southern section of the island. Dressed in a comfortable pink-print cotton sundress, she donned a pair of sunglasses as she headed down the ramp, scanning the dock area for any sign of Noah. She finally spotted him with Heather St. John heading over to a rental-car company across the road. A knot twisted in her stomach. He certainly didn't waste much time.

"I don't get it," Paul muttered as he came up behind her.

Meg glanced back at her brother and saw that he, too, had sighted the pair. "I get it," she said dryly.

"No, honestly, Meg. I thought Heather and I were really hitting it off. I had a drink back at her suite last night and we ended up talking until close to four in the morning. She's not anything like she appears on the surface."

Meg smiled sardonically.

"I don't mean that and you know it," Paul said sharply.

Meg nudged her brother when she saw Lars Olson standing alone on the dock checking a map. "We'll talk about it later."

Leaving Paul, she ambled over to the Swede. "Trying to find a particular spot?"

Lars gave her a distracted nod. "Yes. I'm trying to see how far is Marigot. It's on the French side of the island and I was told it's quite charming."

"I heard the same thing," Meg said pleasantly. "In fact I was thinking of renting a car and driving there. I don't suppose you'd want to..."

He nodded. "I'd be delighted. And you'll be doing me a great service."

Meg gave him a puzzled look. "I will?"

"Oh, yes. I'm afraid that endlessly talkative woman, Mrs. Friers, has taken a fancy to me. She suggested I join her and her husband for a sight-seeing jaunt. Now I can explain that I have made another plan." He smiled charmingly. "A most delightful plan at that."

Taking her arm, Olson pointed at the very same car-rental company Noah and Heather had entered moments before. Meg hesitated, not particularly keen on bumping into the twosome.

She frowned. Then again, why should she avoid them? She and Noah both had jobs to do and they were doing them. Noah was feeling out Heather just as she planned to feel out Lars Olson. There was nothing personal here.

Not on her part, anyway.

The Swedish hunk intruded into her thoughts. "Are you changing your mind, Meg?"

"What? Oh, no. I was just thinking that with so many people renting cars we may be too late."

"Then we should hurry, yes?"

Her smile held an edge of determination. From here on out, it was business first and foremost. "Yes," she said emphatically.

ELAINE HARPER tsked when she saw Lars Olson take Meg Newell's hand to dash across the street. "Now that's a disappointment," she muttered.

Eliot Harper, who was reading the guidebook, gave his wife a distracted look. "What's that, dear?"

"I didn't take her for the flighty sort."

"Who, dear?"

"That Mrs. Newell," Elaine said impatiently. "And personally I can't see what she sees in that Swedish Casanova."

Eliot gave his wife a bemused look. "Can't you?"

"Why, he flirts with everyone. I even saw him make a pass at one of those skimpily clad croupiers in the casino the other evening."

Eliot smiled. Some of those skimpily clad croupiers were quite alluring. If he'd been thirty years younger and single—

"And what's so amusing?" Elaine asked sharply.

Eliot's smile vanished in a flash. "Nothing, dear."

"ARE YOU SURE you want to do this?" Noah asked Heather as he was filling out the car-rental form.

Heather was looking out the window of the shop as if searching for someone. Noah wondered if it was her accomplice she was trying to spot.

She turned back to him. "Oh, yes. Sure. Why not?" Both her voice and her smile were strained.

Heather's lack of enthusiasm for the jaunt was painfully obvious. Noah wondered why she'd consented. To establish an alibi? She could have done that with Meg's brother, Paul. Noah was sure Paul had invited Heather to spend the day in Saint Martin with him. Why had she refused? Because Paul wasn't a suitable mark for her blackmail schemes? Or had he been sloppy and raised her suspicions that he was onto her? Maybe he'd asked too many questions, somehow given himself away. The guy was clearly gaga over the woman.

Noah sighed inwardly. If only he could have made Meg see that she and her brothers were out of their league here.

Noah finished filling out the form. Just as he handed it to the pretty brunette behind the counter, he heard the bell over the front door jingle.

His features darkened as he saw Meg and Lars Olson step into the office.

All four smiled in greeting, but there wasn't an authentic smile among them.

"I hope you haven't gotten the last rental car," Lars said.

"I doubt that," Noah replied.

Noah was wrong.

"I'm very sorry, sir," the rental agent told Lars and Meg. "But this gentleman has signed for our last available car. It's the white Peugeot parked directly across the street."

"Sorry, old chum," Noah said to Lars, lifting the car key off the counter.

"It doesn't matter," Meg muttered. "I'm sure there's another—"

"Oh, I don't think you will find another car to rent today," the agent, who spoke with a French-patois accent, apologized. "Several other cruise ships have docked this morning and I'm sorry to say there's been a run on rental cars here in Philipsburgh. Perhaps in Marigot.''

"How can we get to Marigot without a car?" Meg asked.

"There is a bus, but it doesn't leave for two hours."

Noah and Heather were heading for the door when Lars called out to them. "Your car would seat four comfortably. Perhaps you can give us a lift to Marigot."

Meg, who could imagine nothing she'd rather do less than double-date with the pair, quickly shook her head. "No, Lars, that's silly. We can explore Philipsburgh and then take the bus."

"It's crazy to take the bus," Heather said amicably enough. "Lars is right. There's plenty of room."

Lars smiled brightly, swinging an arm around Meg's shoulders. "Then it's settled."

Noah said nothing. He felt very much the way Meg felt, but he could think of no way short of blatant rudeness to get out of it. Besides, the professional in him couldn't help thinking of the irony of the two pursuers ending up together, after all—quite possibly with the dastardly duo they were both pursuing.

With the pretty rental agent wishing them a lovely day together, the foursome headed out of the agency, crossed the bustling thoroughfare and climbed into the Peugeot, Noah and Heather in front with Noah at the wheel, Lars and Meg settling into the back.

As he pulled away from the curb, Noah said with a note of resignation, "Well, we're off."

They hadn't been driving for very long when Lars suggested they stop for a bite of lunch. Neither Meg nor Noah had much of an appetite, but Heather seconded the motion. A few minutes later Noah swung into a charming octagonal peak-roofed bay-side restaurant surrounded by large sandbox trees and garlanded with lushly aromatic frangipani and oleander shrubbery. The cool inviting interior was decorated with tropical furnishings—rattan tables and chairs, huge potted palms and primitive artwork.

Lars suggested they dine on the outdoor terrace. Meg told the group she'd meet them there and excused herself to go to the powder room. Heather tagged after her.

"Don't you find him a bore?" Heather asked her as they repaired their makeup at the long mirrored counter.

"Noah or Lars?"

"Lars," Heather said with a smile. "Noah isn't boring. He is a bit..." She hesitated, glancing at Meg's reflection in the mirror. "I was surprised when he asked me to spend the day with him. I thought the two of you...well, I had the impression there was something brewing between you."

Meg looked at Heather's reflection. "My secretary, Paul, gave me the impression that there was something brewing between you and him. I suppose we both got it wrong."

Heather flushed. "Oh, you didn't get it wrong. Not exactly."

Meg squinted at her. "I don't understand."

"Paul's incredibly sweet," Heather said earnestly.

"Sweet?"

"It's just that I don't want him to get the wrong idea."

"What is the wrong idea?"

Heather made a big fuss about searching in her purse for her lipstick. Meg waited patiently.

"Oh, damn," Heather muttered, then set her purse aside and looked Meg square in the eye. "I lied to you that first day."

Meg felt her pulse speed up. "You did?"

"Yes. That story about my breakup and my telling you both that I didn't really care for him. I don't know why I said that. Pride, I suppose."

Pride was something Meg could certainly relate to.

"You're saying you did care for him?"

Heather sighed. "I made an absolute fool of myself over him." She shivered. "I'll tell you something, Meg. Love is a messy business. It turns you into a babbling idiot, makes you do utterly insane things, things you'd never do if you were in your right mind."

Things like blackmailing prime ministers or being an accomplice in jewel heists? Meg wondered.

"I came on this cruise to regain my sanity and then your sweet charming secretary has to pop into my life and..." Heather pressed her lips together. "I just can't let myself go crazy again, if you know what I mean."

"What about Noah?" Meg asked.

"Oh, he's entertaining and a very pleasant distraction. But you know up front with a man like him there's no future in it." Heather gave Meg a close scrutiny. "Or do you know it?"

Meg stiffened. "Of course I do. It's plain as the nose on his face." A damn appealing nose, unfortunately.

"So it's easy to spend time with Noah. Certainly better than spending it with Lars." Heather pressed her hand to her mouth. "Sorry. That was terribly rude of me. Obviously you like him or you wouldn't have agreed to spend the day with him."

Meg shrugged. "He's a pleasant distraction."

Heather combed her hair off her face and fastened it with a silver-inlaid barrette. "It's funny. At first I thought Paul might be just another fortune hunter. A lot of men seem to think because my father is loaded that I must be, too."

"And you're not?"

Heather gave Meg a funny look.

Meg flushed. "Sorry. It's none of my business."

Heather resumed her search for her lipstick, Meg cursing herself for running off at the mouth. Then to her surprise, Heather gave Meg her answer.

"The thing is," Heather said quietly, "my dad and I have never gotten along. He's a very forceful figure, very dynamic and very demanding. His love was always conditional. I had to earn it."

Heather sighed. "I finally got fed up trying to win his approval and told him what he could do with his money."

"And did he?" Meg asked wryly.

Heather laughed. "Not in the literal sense. But he did cut off my allowance and took my name out of his will."

Meg hesitated. "So, how do you manage?"

Heather blotted her lips with a tissue and studied her reflection quite analytically. Again, Meg worried she was pushing too hard.

"Oh, managing, as you put it, isn't all that difficult, really," Heather said. "My grandmother on my mother's side left me a small annuity and I've made some solid investments with it." She applied a bit more blush to her cheeks. "Then I pick up the odd job here and there."

"The odd job?"

Heather smiled mysteriously. "Well, they're not really jobs. I don't punch a time clock or anything."

Meg's throat went dry. "Oh? Sounds intriguing."

Heather shrugged. "Sometimes it is. Other times it's rather routine."

"Now you've really got me curious," Meg said lightly. Curious was the ultimate understatement.

Heather rummaged through her purse again. "You don't have any sunscreen on you by any chance. I must have left mine on board."

"What? Oh, yes. I think so," Meg said, digging into her tote. "Here." She handed Heather a tube. "Anyway, you were saying?" she prodded.

Heather squeezed a small dollop of the white cream onto her fingertips and began spreading it over her face. "Saying? Oh, about how I pick up a buck or two here and there. Well, let's see. I've done a bit of modeling for a friend of mine who's a clothing designer. I was a courier for an international banker my mother dated for a while. I helped my college roommate get her Soho restaurant off the ground. And then there was Guy."

"Guy?"

"The fellow I made an ass of myself over. I worked for him for a while."

"What did he do?" Meg asked.

Heather's brow furrowed. "To be perfectly honest, I'm not quite sure. He's the one I was thinking of when I said some of the work was intriguing."

"What work exactly did you do?"

"Well, I—" Heather stopped abruptly. "You know we've been in here a positive age. I bet our fellahs are going to start worrying that we've flown the coop. We better go join them, don't you think?"

Before Meg had a chance to respond, Heather was already making her way toward the door. As she started to pull open the door, Heather glanced back at Meg. A shadow of sadness had swept over her features.

"Sometimes we do things we later wish we hadn't," Heather said in a whisper. "But there's never any going back, is there? Once a deed's done it's done."

With that, Heather spun back around and headed out the door. Meg felt rooted to the spot as she stared after her.

WHILE HEATHER AND MEG were deep in conversation in the powder room, Lars and Noah were making small talk on the terrace.

"So tell me, Lars, what brings you on this cruise?" Noah asked as they sipped their piña coladas under a brightly striped red-and-yellow umbrella at a rattan table set for four.

"A gift, you might say," Lars replied. "A friend took sick after planning the trip and suggested I go in her place. I love the sea and am fond of traveling. Then, too, as it turned out I had to be in New York on business shortly before the departure date of the cruise, so it was quite convenient."

Noah smoothed back a strand of hair the breeze had blown onto his face. "What sort of business are you in?" he asked casually.

"I started a small export business a few years ago, and it has developed into a thriving enterprise, I'm happy to say."

"Hmm. What do you export?"

Lars took the wedge of pineapple he'd removed from the rim of his piña colada and bit into it. "Mmm. Marvelously sweet."

Noah smiled. "Right."

Lars took another sip of his drink. "You were asking me about what I export."

Noah shrugged. "Just making conversation."

"Well, it's nothing very exciting. Craft items. I travel a good deal, interesting various companies around the world in Scandinavian crafts. I'm pleased there's been growing interest."

"I guess you fly mostly, so taking a cruise like this must be a nice break."

"Oh, sometimes I travel by ship. I'm not a man who likes to feel rushed. Life is too short, don't you think?"

Noah gave a thoughtful nod.

Lars stretched his arms over his head. "Ah, this is a perfect day. Glorious landscape, an excellent drink— and such pleasant companions." He smiled slyly at Noah. "You must admit we've snatched the two most beautiful women on board."

"I won't argue with you there," Noah said.

"Very different, though."

Noah gave him a questioning look.

"Heather and Meg. Both very striking in their own ways and—" Lars paused, an enigmatic smile curving his lips "—both trouble in their own ways, I suspect."

"Trouble?" Noah quizzed.

"Ah, here they are now," Lars said brightly, rising as the two women approached the table. And leaving Noah's question to hang in the air unanswered.

THERE WERE NO RENTAL CARS left in Marigot, either.

"It's silly, anyway," Heather said amicably. "No reason we can't ride back together." She paused for a moment, slipping an arm through Noah's. "Naturally we don't all have to stay glued to each other for the whole afternoon."

Lars slipped an arm around Meg's waist. "There's a dinner-dance on the ship tonight. If we meet here at the car at five, we can get back to the ship in time to change for the evening."

Meg and Noah shared a quick look.

"Fine," Meg muttered.

"Yes, fine," Noah echoed.

"Let's go up to the old fort," Heather said to Noah. "I hear there's a spectacular view of the port from there."

"And what would you like to do, Meg?" Lars asked in courtly tones.

Give you the third degree, she thought. Aloud she said, "Let's browse through the shops, shall we?"

"A fine idea," Lars said.

The two couples parted, Noah and Heather heading for the fort on top of the hill, Meg and Lars strolling down the Boulevard de France along the Baie de Marigot. The ambience along the bustling boutique- and café-lined thoroughfare was a colorful mix of West Indian and French. After looking around a few shops, they came to a jewelry store.

Meg paused at the window, pointing to a diamond-studded platinum necklace. "Pretty, isn't it? What do you suppose it costs?"

Lars shrugged. "I am not a good one to ask. I have no idea what such things are worth."

Is that so, Meg thought.

"Let's go in and find out," she said brightly.

Lars smiled broadly. "You are clearly a woman who can't resist baubles."

She grinned. "I do love jewelry. Don't you?"

"Love it? I don't think for men it's the same thing, yes?"

"Maybe I should have said appreciate," Meg amended.

"Yes. Appreciate," he agreed, taking hold of her hand and pressing the back of her palm lightly to his lips. "But may I be so bold as to say that I find your beauty outshines even your finest jewels."

Meg groaned inwardly. *Oh, give me a break.* Olson was so corny and obvious that, once again, she questioned whether she was on the right track. Could this guy really be a clever jewel thief? Then again, maybe he was clever enough to use this ploy in an effort to throw her off his trail.

"Do you want to talk about her?" Heather asked Noah as they stared out at the port from the old abandoned hillside fort.

Noah glanced at her. "Talk about whom?"

Heather smiled. "Meg Newell."

"What makes you think I want to talk about her?"

"Weren't you thinking about her?"

"No, actually," he lied, "I was thinking about you."

"Were you?"

"Don't you believe me?"

"I'm not sure. You and Meg seemed to have hit it off rather well."

"Things aren't always what they seem, Heather," Noah said.

"No, I suppose that's true," she said quietly, then took hold of his hand. "Come on. The view is lovely, but I've seen enough. Let's go do a bit of shopping."

They were just starting down the Boulevard de France when they ran into Paul. He did not look very happy to see the two of them arm in arm.

Heather smiled uneasily. "Hi."

Paul glanced at Noah. "Mind if I borrow Heather for a few minutes? There's something I want to talk to her about."

Heather started to protest, but Noah smiled amiably. "No problem. I've got a few gift items I need to pick up. Why don't I do a bit of shopping and we can meet back here in, say, an hour?"

Heather's eyes kept drifting back to Paul. "Well, I—"

Paul flashed Noah an appreciative smile. "We'll be at that café across the street."

NOAH STEPPED into a shop a short distance from where he'd left Heather. He walked to the window and looked out. Heather and Paul had already crossed the street and were heading for one of the outdoor tables. He found himself hoping that, for Paul's sake, he was wrong about Heather.

"Looking for anything in particular?"

Noah spun around at the sound of Meg's voice. He glanced at her, then scanned the shop. "Where's your boyfriend?"

"Lars got waylaid by Barbara Friers. She insisted on dragging him off to a bookstore to show him her latest novel, which was on display."

"How did you escape?"

"She didn't even notice me. I think she's got a crush on the Swedish hunk." Meg's smiled wryly. "Unless, of course, they're in cahoots."

"Does this mean Heather's now off the hook?"

"Of course not," Meg said emphatically. "She's very much on the hook. I've never met anyone harder to pin down." She smiled faintly. "Well, maybe there've been one or two others. Speaking of Heather, where is she?"

"Look for yourself," Noah said, pointing out the window to the café across the road.

"Damn," Meg muttered as she saw Paul and Heather sitting together. She shot Noah a look. "Was that your doing?"

"It's out of my hands and yours, Meg," Noah said quietly.

"I don't want to see him getting hurt."

He put a hand on her shoulder. She compressed her lips.

"Come on. Let's go someplace where we can talk for a few minutes."

They strolled side by side along a stretch of deserted beach, not speaking for a while, breathing in the moist freshness of the sea air. Meg stared down at the sand, watching their feet stepping in rhythm.

"So what's your take on Lars?" Noah asked finally. "You think he's your jewel thief?"

"I keep vacillating. He doesn't fit my expectations. He doesn't seem smart enough or suave enough."

Noah grinned. "Considering you thought I was your villain, I'm flattered."

Meg smiled. "Then again, his smartest move may be to play dumb." She glanced at Noah. "What about Heather? You think she's your blackmailer?"

Noah considered her question for a few moments. "I'm not sure. I can't get a good handle on her."

"We had an interesting little chat in the powder room," Meg said. "She's definitely been involved in something she's not too happy about. And there was this fellow, Guy something, who she was wild about. He may have been the one to indoctrinate her into the world of crime. Lars could have stepped in to pick up the slack after her boyfriend dumped her."

"She just doesn't strike me as the criminal type," Noah persisted.

Meg gave him a rueful look. "But I did?"

He grinned. "You have an air of danger and mystery about you. I knew the moment I set eyes on you that you were the sort of woman who took risks. I was right about that."

Meg felt her cheeks heat up.

Noah drew her to a halt. "Are we simply going to ignore what happened between us?"

"No, I suppose we can't," Meg admitted, then looked at him with more resolve than she felt. "So we might as well talk about it and...and get it over with."

"You make it sound very easy," Noah murmured.

"I'm trying to be sensible." She started to walk again.

He grabbed her arm and brought her to a stop again. "Passion isn't sensible, Meg. Or easy. Or something we can talk ourselves out of, if that's what you hope to do."

Meg opened her mouth to speak, but she didn't know what to say. All she finally managed was "Damn," before his mouth reached hers.

The instant his soft lips touched hers, her resolve crumbled. All she could think about was the desire for him that simply would not stay put. He pulled her close. Her arms slipped around his neck, then down his back, then up under his shirt. The fragrance of the salt air, the feel of the tropical breeze, the sight of the aquamarine water lapping the shore all felt heightened to Meg, as if her physical contact with Noah had the power to intensify the elements.

When they separated, she felt his absence sharply.

"This isn't helping matters," she mumbled.

"One matter has nothing to do with other matters," he said huskily.

She gave him a quick look, then focused her gaze on the bay. "I don't compartmentalize very well. And besides . . ."

"Yes?"

Her gaze returned to his face, her expression a mix of vulnerability, fear and defiance. "Oh, Noah, what's the point?"

"The point? The point is that we're wildly attracted to each other," he murmured, trying to draw her back into his arms.

Meg impeded his efforts. "An attraction neither of us can afford. An attraction that could interfere with what we're doing here in the first place."

"We don't have to let it interfere, Meg," Noah persisted.

"And when the ship docks?"

A pall fell over them both.

"Look Meg, if what you're asking—"

"No, you don't get it, Noah. I'm not asking for anything. I value my freedom and independence as much as I'm sure you value yours. All I'm saying is that when we do dock I'll be off on my next assignment heaven knows where and you'll have another job waiting for you back in London. And that will be that.''

"That's more than a week away," Noah said with a sense of urgency in his voice. "Are we supposed to spend the time we have together pretending we don't feel what we do feel for each other?"

Meg tried desperately to ignore the rapid beat of her heart. She tried to ignore what Noah was saying, how good he looked, how wonderfully he smelled, how incredible he'd made her feel last night.

Somehow, she managed to get control of herself and gave him a sober look. "Yes, that's precisely what we should do. Neither of us can spare time out for a . . . brief romantic interlude.''

Noah's gaze skidded away from Meg's face and he stared off at the horizon. Meg was right and he knew it. So why couldn't he get a grip on himself? He'd never before let a woman interfere with an assignment. And this assignment was vital. One of the most crucial of his entire career.

So why in blazes couldn't he get her out of his mind? Or worse, out of his heart? Was that the real issue here? Was this more than mere attraction? Was it possible that when they did dock he wouldn't want it to end? Was he beginning to fall in love with this woman?

Love. The very thought filled him with trepidation. Love meant commitment, responsibility, obligation. Love meant his whole life being turned upside down and inside out.

Meg was caught up in the same panic. She, too, sensed there was more here than physical attraction. If she let herself she could fall in love with Noah Webb. She could feel it already beginning to happen.

Love. The very thought tied her stomach in knots. Love was nothing but disappointment, heartbreak. Love took you to the highest peaks, then pushed you over the edge without a parachute. A great ride while it lasted, but she was definitely not up for the crash landing. "We better go," she said finally. "Lars will be looking for me. And I think the less time Paul spends with Heather the better."

"Right," Noah said flatly.

For a moment they dared a last look at each other, the tropical sun beating down on their faces, the water lapping at their feet, the breeze blowing their hair about. A sea gull flew overhead. They both looked up, watching it fly off toward the horizon. Then resolutely they turned away from the bay and headed back.

MEG FOUND LARS sipping a drink at one of the outdoor cafés on the boulevard. With him was Louanne Percy. Lars rose as Meg joined them at the table.

Louanne smiled at her. "Lars and I were just playing detective," she said in her sexy Southern drawl.

"What do you mean?" Meg asked cautiously.

"Louanne is thinking who is the jewel thief aboard the ship," Lars explained.

Meg eyed Louanne. "And have you come up with a suspect?"

Louanne's gray eyes sparkled. "Well Lars and I were debating whether it's a passenger or an employee. Naturally, I imagine the employees must have a thorough screening, so my bet is on one of the passengers. Lars disagrees."

Yes, he would, Meg thought, turning to Lars. "You think it's an employee then?"

Lars shrugged. "I have my suspicions."

"Suspicions?" Louanne exclaimed. "Don't be modest, Lars. You do have one particular suspect in mind. Why keep it a secret from Mrs. Newell?"

"Well, I do not like to spread rumors. I have no proof," Lars demurred.

Louanne had no such compunctions. "He thinks it's that sexy athletic director," she said. "And even though he doesn't have proof positive, he has seen the fellow skulking around."

Meg was all ears. "Really?"

"Well, not me personally. But I did hear—"

"Clara Schmidt told Lars she saw what's his name—Alex, that's it—coming out of Noah Danforth's suite the other day," Louanne said conspiratorially.

Meg made a mental note to warn her brother to cover his tracks better. "Well, we should let Captain Simon know so he can question Alex," she said.

"If you want my theory, I think Clara Schmidt lied to Lars. I think she wanted to throw suspicion off the real thief," Louanne said.

"And who might that be, gumdrop?" Alan Delacore asked as he came up behind his fiancée.

Louanne looked up at the new arrival on the scene, having to squint because of the sun. "Where have you been all this time, sugar?" she pouted.

Meg was curious to know the answer to that question herself. Although Lars still topped her suspect list, Delacore wasn't far behind. If he'd been off somewhere for any length of time and there was another robbery aboard the ship today, she'd have to think seriously about moving Delacore to the head of her list.

Delacore sat down between Louanne and Meg, but his attention was focused fully on his fiancée. "You want to know where I've been, do you?" He reached his hand into the pocket of his white linen jacket and pulled out a thin rectangularly shaped box wrapped in silver paper.

Louanne's eyes widened as he set the box in front of her. "Oh, sugar, you shouldn't have."

Delacore chuckled. "Go on and open it. Then say that."

Louanne excitedly tore at the paper, revealing a teal blue velvet box. "Oh, I just love presents."

Delacore winked at Lars. "The way to a man's heart may be through his stomach, Olson, but the way to a woman's heart is—"

Louanne's exclamation of delight cut Delacore off. She pulled out an exquisite gold-and-ruby bracelet. "Isn't it just the most beautiful thing you ever saw?"

Delacore leaned over and planted a kiss on Louanne's lips. "No, gumdrop. You're the most beautiful thing I ever saw. The bracelet's a mere runner-up."

Louanne threw her arms around her fiancé. "Oh, sugar, if you spent all this money it must mean you aren't worried about your silly investments anymore."

Meg's eyes shot to Delacore. She saw his expression turn grim as he drew away from Louanne. He was clearly not pleased by Louanne's comment about his financial state.

The waitress approached and Delacore ordered a whiskey and water. Meanwhile Louanne slipped on the bracelet and held her hand out to admire it.

"Isn't he just the sweetest man in the whole wide world?" she purred.

"He's very generous," Meg said.

"Yes, you are a lucky woman," Lars added.

Meg gave her date a sideways glance. Was that a glint in the Swede's eye? Was he thinking Louanne's new trinket might make him a lucky man soon enough?

Delacore slung an arm over the back of Louanne's chair. "So, what's this you were saying about Clara Schmidt covering up for the real jewel thief?" he asked her.

"Well," Louanne said in a hushed drawl, "I personally think it's that husband of hers."

Delacore laughed. "Dr. Schmidt? Come now, gumdrop, the man's a world-renowned scientist. He won the Nobel prize."

"Go on and laugh if you want to. Barbara Friers happens to agree with me. She says it's always the quiet ones you have to watch out for. And she should know. She writes all those books about criminals, doesn't she?"

"If you ask me," Delacore said, "she's the one I'd be suspicious of."

Lars gave the former ambassador a puzzled look. "Mrs. Friers? But she was the one who was robbed."

"Right," Delacore said. "And she's the one who's going to collect the insurance money. I'm certainly not one to spread rumors myself, but I say there's a strong possibility we've got a neat little scam operating here. And you can bet the husband's in on it, too."

"Why would they bother?" Meg inquired. "They certainly seem to have tons of money."

"Oh, she makes plenty on her books," Delacore granted. "But I happen to own stock in some Hollywood studios and one of them is—or I should say, was—CineCom, Horace Friers's company. Let's just say it was a smart move on my part to cut my losses when I did. Friers puts on a good front, but he's hurting. And I'd lay odds he's poured his wife's earnings into the company to try to keep it afloat. Only there are too many holes to be plugged up and the banks are looking the other way. It's amazing," he mused, "what people will resort to when their careers are on the line."

"Interesting," Lars said. "And what do you think, Meg?"

"About Horace Friers?"

"About who you think is the culprit," Lars said.

"Well, I...don't know. I suppose it could be desperation driving the thief. Then again..." She paused deliberately.

"Yes?" Lars was the first to press for the rest of the sentence.

"Oh, I'm sure whoever it is, is enjoying the fruits of his labors," she said dryly, "but I think there's also the element of excitement and daring. I think the jewel thief may be someone who loves a good challenge." She smiled with feigned innocence. "Maybe I've watched too many movies."

"Or read too many of Barbara Friers's books," Alan Delacore suggested.

Louanne pursed her lips. "I don't know. It sounds like a good theory to me. And so romantic."

"I guess that's the problem," Meg said. "There's no shortage of good theories. It seems like almost anyone could be the thief."

"Even your barrister?" Lars prodded.

"Oh, he'd be perfect!" Louanne exclaimed. "I mean if I were going to cast someone as a suave debonair jewel thief in a movie, I'd choose him."

"I agree," Lars said with a faint smile.

He would, Meg thought.

CHAPTER ELEVEN

MEG AND EVERYONE ELSE along her corridor was awakened at around eight the next morning by Louanne Percy's shrill shrieks. Meg bounded out of bed, snatched up her robe and, barefoot, made a beeline for the hall. Louanne, her hair in huge pink rollers, clad in nothing but an almost sheer mint green nightie, was out there in the corridor, yelling at the top of her lungs, "I've been robbed! I've been robbed!"

"This is an abomination," Barbara Friers sputtered, wrapping her robe around her ample figure. Her husband, Horace, already dressed in a running suit, stood just behind her. He looked extremely agitated.

Meg saw Heather, dressed in a bright red tunic and short black running shorts, pop out of her door, which was diagonally across the hall from Louanne Percy's suite. She didn't pop out alone. Meg felt her heart sink right to her stomach when she saw Noah, in T-shirt and running shorts, step out of the room after Heather.

Anger, jealousy and hurt swept over Meg. She caught Noah's eye for an instant, then deliberately looked away.

Meanwhile an out-of-breath Alan Delacore came racing down the corridor toward Louanne.

"Now, now, gumdrop," he soothed as soon as he got to her.

Louanne collapsed against him.

"My beautiful new bracelet," she sobbed. "And my engagement ring. The awful beast."

"He broke into *your* safe, too?" Barbara Friers asked. "Don't tell me this character has ESP or something. How did he figure out your code?"

Louanne bit her bottom lip. "He didn't. I...didn't. I mean I didn't have them in the safe. I was so tired when we got back from sight-seeing and I had this terrible sunburn..."

Much of which, Meg noted, was quite visible. So did Delacore, who took off his light tan jacket and wrapped it around his fiancée's shoulders.

"And I had this awful headache. I took some aspirin and I was just going to lie down for a few minutes. I meant to—"

"You didn't, Louanne," Alan Delacore scolded sharply. "Even after I warned you not to leave your jewels just lying about? After the woman right next door to you gets robbed?"

"Don't scold me, sugar," Louanne pleaded before breaking into another fit of sobs.

Captain Simon, crisp in his navy-and-brass uniform but looking harried, came rushing up. Barbara Friers wagged a finger at him. "What kind of a ship are you running, Captain? I demand that something be done about this."

Simon caught Meg's eye for a moment before turning to the agitated novelist. "I assure you we're doing everything in our power—"

"We?" Barbara Friers countered. "Who exactly is *we?*"

"Myself and my security staff," he said calmly.

"Well, it's my opinion, Captain, that your security staff could do with some beefing up," she said archly.

Meg swallowed hard. She was sure Captain Simon had to be thinking much the same thing.

"BUCK UP, LOVE," Noah said softly as he came up behind Meg. She was standing at the railing at the far end of the deserted Promenade Deck. It was lunchtime and most of the passengers had retired to the dining room for the luncheon buffet.

She stiffened as she felt his hand on her shoulder.

"It isn't what you think, Meg. About me and Heather. I didn't miss that look in your eye when you saw us coming out of her room together this morning."

Meg put on her sunglasses, hopefully preventing him from seeing anything else in her eyes. "I'm only thinking about one thing," she said flatly. "Nabbing a jewel thief. Everything else is...extraneous."

"I didn't spend the night with her, Meg."

"I didn't ask."

"No, you wouldn't. Any more than I would ask if you and Lars spent the night together. Even though Chet did see you arm in arm with the Swede entering his suite about one in the morning."

"I left at two," she said tightly.

"I didn't ask."

"No, you didn't."

"As for Heather..."

She opened her mouth to protest, but he cut her off.

"I happened to have come to call on her about five minutes before Louanne came bursting out into the corridor announcing she'd been robbed. When I saw Heather to her door last night, she suggested we go jogging this morning. And she said there were some things she wanted to talk to me about. I was hoping she'd decided to come clean. Unfortunately we never did get to take that jog or have that talk."

He paused for a moment, then smiled roguishly. "Not that you asked."

Meg shot him a hard look. "I'm glad you can take this all so lightly. Captain Simon informed me a few minutes ago that if I don't crack this case before we hit St. Kitts tomorrow, he's going to request that the company fly in a new team."

Noah sighed. "My people aren't exactly happy with my progress, either."

"Do you really think Heather was about to confess?" Meg asked him.

"I think she's got something on her mind, but I'm not sure what it is."

Meg hesitated. "Tony had a look around her suite while we were all on Saint Martin. He didn't find anything suspicious. Of course, she most likely would have everything stuck away in her safe. He wasn't able to crack the code, but..."

"Yes?"

Meg hesitated, debating how much she should reveal to Noah. Somewhere along the way she had gotten into her head that she had to prove to him she was as good—no, better—at this game than he was. He'd been the one to lay down the gauntlet, but she'd been only too eager to pick it up. Now she felt a bit childish about the whole thing. Even if they were both too independent and opinionated to work together, it was to neither of their advantage to work against the other.

"Tony's quite talented with electronics and that sort of thing," she finally said. "Yesterday when we were all on Saint Martin, he planted miniaturized surveillance cameras in several suites. Heather's, Lars Olson's, Alan Delacore's. If any of them open their safes we should be able to pick up the codes and have a look-see when they're out of their rooms."

Noah smiled broadly.

"What's so amusing?" Meg demanded.

"Chet Carson's done much the same thing," he said. So now there are two cameras in each of those suites."

Meg's eyes narrowed, suddenly remembering Noah's break-in of her suite, finding him at her open safe. What was it he'd said when she'd asked him how he'd managed it? *I have my ways.*

"You had one of those cameras in my suite right from the start. That's how you knew the combination to my safe. You were...watching me."

"I assure you I was most respectful," Noah murmured with a boyish shamefaced grin. "I always closed my eyes when you were, shall we say, sans apparel. Well, almost always."

Meg glared at him. "You really love your work, don't you?"

"Don't you love yours?" he countered. "Am I to assume you didn't have brother Tony place one of those cameras in my suite?"

"No, I didn't," she said, but then found she couldn't lie to him. "We'd planned to, but you made your move on my suite before we had the chance. Afterward, well, there was no need," she admitted.

Noah smiled at her. It was incredible how much alike they were. "Now see—" he leaned a bit closer "—if we'd joined forces as I'd suggested we wouldn't be duplicating operations."

Meg could feel herself starting to lose ground. Yet if they did join forces she was still convinced he'd insist on running the show. "I'm quite satisfied working with my own team," Meg declared stoically.

Noah grinned. "You mean you're quite satisfied being the boss."

Meg compressed her lips. "Let's not start that again. I suppose only time will tell whose expertise will win out."

Noah's eyes danced. "So, it's a contest, is it?"

"You're the one who thinks your experience and training are superior to mine," Meg challenged.

"So I do," Noah said glibly. "Not that I don't wish you well, love."

Meg's mouth twitched. "Are all British agents so smug, Mr. Danforth II? Or are you unique?"

"I'd very much like to think I'm unique. I'd very much like to think you think so, as well," he added with a disarming smile.

Meg found herself responding to that smile despite herself. "Unique and impossible."

He surveyed her in much the way he might a fine painting. She was looking especially enchanting today in her sunflower yellow sundress that highlighted her amber eyes. Once again she was wearing the pearl necklace and matching earrings, the huge diamond ring. But the jewels in no way outshone her loveliness.

"Did you really think I would spend the night with Heather?" he asked in a low voice.

Meg stared intently at him. "In the line of duty...maybe. That was why you seduced me—at first, anyway, wasn't it?"

"Ah, Meg, it wasn't that simple even from the first." His smile held a hint of melancholy. "I'll tell you something. I've always prided myself on having a bloody good instinct for emotional survival. Granted, I haven't always kept my libido in check, but I've never let my feelings—my emotions—get me in too deep." He hesitated. "Until now."

Meg looked away. "Don't say any more. This is crazy. Neither of us wants to get . . . entangled. Not to mention that my whole career is on the line. And so is yours. We simply can't let this happen."

"No, you're right," he echoed. "We can't."

Meg gave Noah a closer inspection to see if he was being facetious, but he seemed quite earnest.

She sighed. "Then it's settled. We'll end it here and now. You'll go your way . . ."

"And you'll go yours."

"Yes," she said in a whisper.

"Naturally if I get a lead that might help you . . ."

"Or if I should get one that might help you . . ."

"Yes."

They both smiled, but neither of them looked the least bit happy.

SEAN WAS OFF between lunch and dinner and hurried back to his cabin to keep watch on the monitors connected to the miniature surveillance cameras his brother had placed in the suites of Heather St. John, Alan Delacore and Lars Olson. He hadn't been watching for more than twenty minutes when Heather St. John entered her suite.

Sean became instantly alert. Heather was alone and she looked on edge. He observed her pacing her sitting room for several minutes, then coming to an abrupt halt, turning and sitting down on one of the armchairs, picking up a magazine from the coffee table. After thumbing through it for a minute or two she tossed it down on the floor, threw her head against the back of her chair and closed her eyes.

Sean sighed, thinking she was drifting off. Then suddenly her eyes sprang open and she rose from her seat.

"Yes, yes," Sean muttered. "That's it," he encouraged as she started across the sitting room in the direction of her safe. He drew a little closer to the monitor, snatched up a magnifying lens with one hand, a pen with the other.

She seemed to be debating as she stood right in front of the painting concealing the safe. Sean could feel his impatience start to mount. "Come on, Heather. You know you want to get a little look at your cache."

Sean held his breath, waiting. Just when he thought he was about to strike gold, Heather turned away from the safe, went over to the bar and poured herself a drink. He watched with mounting frustration as she finished it off quickly and left the suite.

"Damn," Sean muttered.

ALEX SAUNTERED over to the StairMaster where Louanne Percy was working up quite a sweat. It was midafternoon and the health club was empty but for the two of them.

"I was sorry to hear about your being robbed," he said.

Louanne pursed her lips, not altering her vigorous stepping. "You'd think...it was all...my fault...the way Alan's been...going on," she said between spurts of catching her breath.

"Your fiancé?"

Louanne came to a stop and let out a great weary sigh. Alex handed her a fresh towel. She dabbed at her damp face.

"You'd think he'd be more worried about me than a few pieces of jewelry," she said irritably. "What if I'd woken up while the thief was in my room? Why, he might have... Heaven only knows what he might have done."

"You never heard a thing?" Alex asked, keeping in mind that he had to be careful not to appear to be pumping her for information. Louanne, however, seemed perfectly happy to have found a sympathetic ear.

"No. I'm a very sound sleeper. And to be honest, I did have a teeny-weeny bit too much to drink last night. Which I blame entirely on Alan."

"Why is that?" Alex asked as he watched Louanne check her readout on the machine.

She gave him a distracted glance, then tossed the towel around her neck and stepped off the machine. "He knows I have a low tolerance for alcohol. But for some reason he kept refilling my glass all through dinner, then insisted we have a nightcap in the lounge before we turned in. I ask you, is it any wonder I practically passed out when I got back to my suite? If you think about it, it's amazing I even had the energy to take my ring and bracelet off."

She gasped and put her hand to her heart.

"What's wrong?" Alex asked.

"I just had the most dreadful thought," Louanne drawled. "What if I had been wearing those jewels? Why the thief might have... Oh, it's too awful to imagine."

"I see what you mean," Alex said sympathetically.

"Then again . . ." Louanne's voice trailed off, but Alex observed the cunning glint in her eye.

He waited expectantly. Louanne impressed him as the type of woman who, once she got talking, wasn't likely to stop. His impression proved accurate. He had only to wait a few moments before she tilted her head and smiled coyly. "I suppose this is a terrible thing to say, but do you know what I thought when I first woke up and saw that stuff missing?"

"No," Alex answered because Louanne also impressed him as a woman who rarely asked rhetorical questions. "What did you think?"

"I thought it was Alan," she whispered conspiratorially even though there was no one in the health club to overhear.

Alex feigned a puzzled expression. "You thought your fiancé stole the jewels? Why in heaven's name would he do such a thing?" He and the rest of the Delgado brood could have supplied an answer to that one, but Alex was definitely curious to find out what Louanne Percy thought Alan Delacore's motive might be.

"You know," she said as if Alex was a little slow. "To teach me a lesson."

"To teach you a lesson?" Alex echoed.

She tsked. "He'd given me this big lecture just the other night about being sure to lock up my jewels in my safe before going to bed. And then after that impossible woman next door to me was robbed, I'm sure he thought I'd be extra careful. Well, I started thinking after I woke up and found the jewels missing that Alan might have come back into my suite in the middle of the night—oh, not to rob me, of course. To, well, you know." She smiled and blushed at the same time.

Alex pretended to be a bit embarrassed. "I think I can guess."

She giggled, but then sobered quickly. "Anyway, I thought that maybe when he came in and saw I'd been real careless again and left the ring and bracelet out, he snatched them so I'd realize just how big a risk I was taking by not locking my valuables in the safe."

"Well, I suppose that would have been one way to teach you a lesson," Alex mused.

Louanne frowned. "When I told Alan I suspected he'd done it and why, he was positively livid I would even think such a thing. He said in that deep baritone voice of his, 'I hope you haven't gone around blabbing that ridiculous theory all over the ship.' As if I would," she said airily.

Alex had to fight back a smile. "No, of course you wouldn't."

"I'm parched," she said, heading over to the juice bar.

Alex followed her, stepped behind the bar and poured them both tall glasses of fresh-squeezed orange juice. On Louanne's invitation he joined her at one of the marble-topped tables in the corner of the club.

She sipped her juice slowly, then set her glass down. "This cruise wasn't my idea, you know. Alan was the one who talked me into it. He loves cruises."

"Really?" Alex murmured. "Takes them a lot, does he?"

"I guess. I've really only known Alan a couple of months." She smiled prettily, displaying toothpaste-commercial white teeth. "I guess you'd describe what we had as a whirlwind courtship. I was completely flabbergasted when he proposed less than two weeks after we met. Not that I wasn't thrilled. I was completely enthralled by Alan. He's such a dynamic forceful man. Always knows exactly what he wants and goes after it until he gets it. Not that he had to work very hard to get me. I said yes without even a moment's hesitation."

She did hesitate now. "He didn't tell me that his divorce wasn't final until after I said yes. And he didn't tell me we'd have to wait ages to get married because of some messy custody business with his ex."

She sighed. "I don't get it. He was the one that went on and on about how a cruise would help relax him, but honestly, he's been so uptight ever since we left New York. I probably shouldn't be telling you this," she said with a shrug indicating she actually had few qualms about it. Probably, Alex thought, because he was merely the *help*. "But I think some of Alan's investments have gone sour and he's worried about them. Then there's his greedy ex who's simply trying to take the poor man for all he's worth..."

"'...TAKE THE POOR MAN for all he's worth,'" Alex repeated late that night in the sitting room of Meg's suite where he and his siblings had gathered for a briefing. He'd already filled the team in on everything else Louanne had said, including the Southern belle's theory that her fiancé had ripped her off to teach her a lesson.

"He may have ripped her off, but I bet that wasn't his reason," Paul said.

Tony rubbed his beard. "I'm sure Delacore's got a key to Percy's suite, so it would have been a piece of cake for him to enter in the dead of night. And know she wouldn't wake up since, as she told you, Alex, he'd made sure to get her good and soused. It would be nice if we could narrow down the time of the break-in. Delacore was in the casino until after 3 a.m."

"Winning or losing?" Meg asked.

"It was up and down," Tony said. "He had luck at roulette but started losing at the craps table. Looked to me like he broke even by the time he left."

"What about Olson?" Alex asked Meg with a teasing smile. "How late were you two...together?"

Meg rolled her eyes. "We *talked* in his suite until a little after two."

"That puts Olson off the hook, then," Tony said.

"What do you mean?" Meg asked, taken aback. Even though the circumstantial evidence was piling up against Delacore, the more time she spent with the Swedish hunk the more she got the feeling he had this ability to let her see only what he wanted her to see— and that what she was seeing wasn't him at all.

"Your Swede showed up at the casino a little after two and he hung around there all night," Tony informed her. "He finally shuffled out of the place at eight-thirty this morning, a good twenty minutes after Percy discovered she'd been robbed."

Meg scowled. "Damn. I was so sure it was him."

"Hey, you can't be right every time," Paul said pointedly.

Meg knew he wasn't only talking about Olson but Heather St. John.

She focused back on Tony. "Wait a sec. You weren't on duty at the casino till eight, were you? How do you know Lars was there the whole time?"

"I got off at six and I checked with Liza, one of the croupiers who was on till nine this morning. She says Olson stayed put till eight." Tony's expression hardened. "The bastard even had the nerve to proposition her."

"Curious," Meg mused.

Tony gave his sister a sharp look. "What's that supposed to mean?"

"Just that I've never observed Lars giving the eye to any of the female staff before," Meg said. "He's always gone where the money is."

"Okay," Paul said, "so we can tag the Swede as a possible fortune hunter, but with his airtight alibi we can't tag him as our jewel thief. So we've got Delacore to consider, for one."

"And what about Horace Friers?" Sean asked. "If what Delacore told you about Friers's studio about to go under is true..."

"It isn't," Meg said. "I sent out a couple of faxes and got the latest scoop back a few hours ago. Delacore was either wrong about Friers's studio folding or he didn't have the latest word. According to a recent article in one of the film trades, Friers's studio just got an infusion of a large amount of capital from a German investment group."

"I say Delacore was deliberately trying to muddy the waters," Alex declared.

"You think he's our man?" Paul asked him.

"I think he's our best bet," Alex said.

Sean seconded that opinion. So did Tony.

All four of them eyed Meg.

"I don't know," she said. "What if Olson was getting edgy and decided to set up an ironclad alibi for himself?"

"You mean his supposed accomplice might have pulled the latest heist?" Alex asked her.

"She means Heather," Paul said harshly.

"I mean someone other than Lars," Meg said evenly. "And that someone could be Heather." She'd already shared the unsettling conversation she and Heather had had in the powder room of the restaurant on Saint Martin the previous day. None of her brothers, not even Paul, could deny there was something bothering Heather St. John. But Paul strongly disagreed as to what it might be.

"Look," Paul said, "I know she's got some stuff on her mind, but I tell you she isn't in cahoots with Olson. Or Delacore. Or whoever the damn jewel thief is."

"Okay," Meg granted. "Maybe Heather isn't in cahoots with the jewel thief, but there's still the matter of Noah's blackmailer," Meg reminded him gently. "She did spend time in London recently. She was involved with a man there. It could have been the finance minister. Maybe she didn't even start out to set him up. Maybe...things got out of hand. Maybe she needed money. Or maybe someone else put her up to it. For all I know—"

Paul's mouth twitched. "You don't know anything about her," he said sharply. "You certainly don't know her like I do," he added in an impassioned voice.

"Come on, Paulie," Alex soothed. "How well could you know her? It's been less than a week. Maybe you've spent a few hours with her here and there, but—"

"I happen to be in love with Heather," Paul said fervently. "And I happen to think she just might be in love with me.'' He rose to his feet and strode across to the door leading out of Meg's suite. He gave them all one last glance as if daring any of them to say another word.

No one did. What could any of them say?

CHAPTER TWELVE

ELIOT HARPER woke up in a cold sweat in the middle
of the night. He was having a terrible dream that a
hurricane had struck and the ship was under siege.

Only it wasn't a dream. The ship was rocking and
swaying mightily, the wind was howling fiercely, and
water was actually slapping against their porthole.

Panicked, Eliot shook his wife awake. "Elaine, get
up. Get up. Quick. Get ready."

"Ready for what?" she answered groggily after
several shakes.

Eliot was already out of bed. Or at least he attempted to get out of bed, but the ship listed sharply
to the right and he fell back onto the mattress. "We
may have to abandon ship. I've got to check the
emergency instructions posted on the door and make
sure I know where our lifeboat station is."

"You already know where it is," Elaine muttered,
still half-asleep. "We had a drill our second day out."

"Elaine, don't you understand? This has nothing to
do with drills. We're in the middle of a torrential hurricane. Oh, didn't I tell you this would happen?" he
moaned. "Didn't I say, not once but dozens of times,
'Elaine, this is not a good season to take a cruise to the
Caribbean.' This was when there were all those hurri-
canes—"

"This is not the hurricane season," Elaine grumbled, trying to pull the covers back up over her shoulders.

"Elaine, you must get up," Eliot insisted, his voice quivering with anxiety even as he tried mightily to stay as calm as possible under the circumstances. "We must get our valuables out of the safe. I know the captain said that in an emergency we must leave everything behind, but..."

Elaine rolled over to face her husband. She did feel the boat listing, but she assumed there was nothing very serious to worry about. "Will you please be calm, Eliot. It's just a little storm. Why, they haven't even sounded the alarm. I'm sure if there was even the slightest bit of danger—"

The rest of her sentence was drowned out by seven short blasts followed by one long blast of the ship's whistle.

Eliot Harper shouted, "Aha!"

Elaine Harper promptly fainted.

"WHY DO CATASTROPHES always happen in the middle of the night?" Horace Friers groused as he hunted in the dark for his slippers. The power was out.

"Well, at least you managed to wake up this time," Barbara said, slipping on her robe. "Remember that time in Japan—"

"Please, Barb. Not that again."

"Okay, okay."

"Let's just stay calm."

"You don't think we'll actually have to abandon ship, do you?" she asked anxiously.

"I certainly hope not," Horace said, an edge of panic in his voice. "And to think I was actually considering doing a remake of *Titanic.*"

"Oh, Horace, I keep thinking about the new book I'm working on now. *Dangerous Curves.* There's this scene in it where Sam Dunne and Rita Arnot are on a tramp steamer chasing a nefarious arms dealer and they're forced to abandon ship because they hit this iceberg and they're in these icy waters and Sam's arm gets gnawed off by a shark—"

Horace grabbed his wife's hand and squeezed it. "Calm down, Barb. We're in the tropics, for heaven's sake. Our ship isn't going to hit an iceberg. There are no icebergs in the Caribbean." As for sharks, that was another matter altogether. Horace did not want to think about sharks.

"That's cold comfort, Horace," Barbara muttered as the pair made their way across the suite holding on to the walls so they wouldn't lose their balance.

By the time they made it to the door, Barbara was crying softly.

"It's going to be all right," Horace said. "Think about your new book coming out and all the hoopla..."

"Especially if it's published posthumously," she wailed.

LOUANNE PERCY met up with the Frierses out in the corridor, which was now dimly lit by the emergency generator. Louanne was shaking badly and clearly terrified.

"We're going to die," she sobbed. "We're all going to die!"

Oddly enough Louanne's hysteria had a calming effect on Barbara Friers. The novelist immediately pulled herself together and grabbed hold of Louanne's arm.

"Nobody's going to die. It's just a little storm. We'll all be fine. Just fine."

Alan Delacore made his way down the corridor by gripping the railing. As soon as he got to Louanne, he put his arms around her and strongly seconded Barbara Friers's pronouncement that there was nothing to worry about.

"I've been on ships a dozen or more times when we've had squalls a lot worse than this," Delacore assured them all. "We're going to stay calm and get to our lifeboat stations now," he added in a take-charge manner. "I'm sure we'll ride this little storm out and be back in our beds within a couple of hours at the most."

PAUL WAS ALREADY on his way to Heather's suite before the whistle blasts went off. He'd been caught in enough storms aboard ships to know it was only a matter of time before the alarm was sounded. The storm really wasn't all that bad as storms at sea went, but he knew that as a safety measure everyone would be required to meet at the lifeboat stations, don their life jackets and prepare for the possibility of having to abandon ship.

His knock on Heather's door coincided with the first blast. He knocked again before the second one went off so that she'd hear it. Her door opened on the fifth whistle blast. She was standing there in a white cotton nightie, a robe clutched against her chest, her tousled red hair cascading around her shoulders.

Paul was swept up in a current of longing, even though he knew these were not the feelings he should be having at a time like this. But then he saw Heather's soft unguarded expression and knew she was caught up in the same whirlpool of desire.

Wordlessly they fell into each other's arms, clinging to each other. Tears streamed down Heather's face and Paul kissed them away. Then his lips found hers and nothing else mattered; nothing else existed. They basked in their deep fiery kiss, swayed with it, drank it in and wanted it to go on forever.

"Oh Paul, Paul," she cried when they finally broke away.

"It's okay, baby. It's okay. Everything's going to be okay," he murmured. "I'm never going to let anything bad happen to you."

"Paul, I've got to tell you—"

"Not now, baby. We've got to get to our lifeboat stations—"

But she was pulling him back into her suite. "No. If anything bad does happen . . ."

"It won't. I promise."

"Please, Paul. Please let me tell you. I've got to do it now before it's too late."

His heart heavy, his emotions twisting his gut, he nodded, letting her lead him into her suite even though he desperately didn't want to hear her confession.

He reached for her as they stepped inside, but she held him off. The tears had dried and she was calmer now. "Paul, I've done some things I'm terribly ashamed of. Once you know, you probably won't want anything to do with me ever again."

"Heather, that won't happen. I love—"

"No, don't. Please, Paul. Don't say it."

"Okay, Heather," he said softly and calmly. "Tell me. Just tell me straight out."

"First, I want you to know that I vowed never to fall in love again after . . . after Guy."

"Because you loved him so much?"

She fought for composure. "It wasn't love. It was . . . obsession. And that obsession nearly destroyed me. In the end I hated him. But not nearly as much as I hated myself. I don't deserve love. I don't deserve a man like you, Paul. You're decent and kind and everything a woman would want in a man."

"Hey," he teased softly, "you're going to give me a swelled head."

"No, don't joke, Paul. I mean it. I felt something for you almost from the start. That's why I tried to avoid you. I . . . I don't deserve you."

"Heather, you're breaking my heart," he said, his voice etched in pain.

"I've done so much lying, Paul. I don't want to lie anymore."

Paul smiled wistfully. "Maybe it's time for us both to do away with the lies."

She gave him a curious look, but then steeled herself to tell him the truth she'd been running from for months. "When I first met Guy I was dazzled by him. But after we'd been seeing each other for a short while he told me he was involved in a business venture that required his getting his hands on a great deal of money. He knew that I had no money of my own since I'd told him that my father had cut me off, but he . . . he knew this venture capitalist who he thought would—under the right circumstances—invest the needed funds."

Fearing the worst, Paul tried to stop her from going on, but she was adamant about getting it out.

She shut her eyes even though the room was so dark Paul was a mere shadow. "Guy told me that this man had taken a fancy to me. I didn't know until after, I swear, that they'd actually... struck a bargain. Guy and I went out to this... man's country estate for a weekend and... and when I woke up the next morning Guy was gone."

She swayed, only partly due to the constant side-to-side motion of the ship.

Paul went to grab hold of her, but she stepped out of his reach and huddled against the wall, her arms wrapped around herself. "He came into my bedroom—"

"Heather, you don't have to tell me this. Whatever happened, it doesn't matter."

"He asked me how much I loved Guy. I told him I didn't think I could live without him. I... I did feel that way back then. And he told me that this was my chance to prove just how deeply I cared for Guy."

She clutched her stomach. "God help me, I was so crazed at the time I actually believed him. I actually let him..."

She couldn't go on. Racking sobs broke from her and this time Paul overtook her and pulled her against him.

"Is that it, then?" he asked. "Is that all it is?"

"All? Isn't it enough? I'm so ashamed. I'm so horribly ashamed," she sobbed.

"Oh, Heather, I love you. And if you love me, then what we have is new and clean and fresh. And forever. Only first..."

She looked up anxiously. "What is it?"

Paul hesitated. He knew this was a serious breach. He also knew he believed Heather. And more important, he knew he loved her. "I have some secrets that need telling, too...."

A GOOD FIFTEEN MINUTES after all the passengers had scurried to their lifeboat stations to don their life jackets and prepare for the possibility of having to abandon ship, Noah and Meg practically collided in one of the deserted corridors.

He gave her a sharp look. "What the hell are you doing here? You should be at your station."

"You should be at yours," she countered.

"You are the most stubborn woman—"

"Oh, stuff it," Meg muttered, trying to get by him. He latched on to her arm. "Where are you going?"

"Where are *you* going?"

"I asked first."

"How childish," she said, snickering.

"This is ridiculous."

"You're telling me."

"You're going to Olson's suite."

She gave her head a defiant shake. "If you already knew, why'd you ask? And I suppose you're off to shake Heather's suite down."

"How very clever we both are."

The boat listed sharply to the right and before Meg could grab the railing she fell against Noah, who fell against the wall. Immediately his arms went around her waist.

She tried to pry herself free. "Really, Noah, this isn't the time—"

"Have you considered," he murmured, "that there might never be another time?"

"Oh, please, it's just a little storm," she muttered.

He tilted up her chin, forcing her to look at him. "What if it isn't? What if these are our last moments on earth?"

He buried his lips in her hair and her heart hammered against her chest. "Noah, this isn't fair. You can't do this to me."

"One never knows, love," he whispered by her ear. "If this was it, I'd tell you, Meg. I'd tell you you've turned my world upside down. I'd tell you you were the most desirable, the most bewitching, the most alluring woman I've ever had the misfortune to run up against."

"A misfortune? Well, that makes me feel just grand," she said.

Noah exhaled a ragged breath. "I'd tell you I love you, Meg."

Her breath jammed in her throat. "What?" she gasped shakily.

"I'd tell you I love you," he repeated, saying each word slowly so that there could be no question of her hearing correctly.

Tears threatened to spill from her eyes. She felt a crazy twist of emotions—joy, frustration, anger.

She shoved her hands against his chest and tried to push away from him. "Oh, sure. Sure, that's what you'd tell me if these were our last moments on earth. But what if they aren't? What then?" she charged. "Oh, you're a piece of work, Noah Webb."

Noah released her and threw up his hands. "I give up. I bare my bloody soul to you and all you can say in return is I'm a piece of work?"

"What do you want me to say? That as long as this ship goes down and we go down with it, I'll admit I love you, too? Well, I won't," she said, her chin jutting defiantly.

He smiled disarmingly. "You won't say it or you won't admit it?"

Meg felt cornered. She pressed her lips together. Saying anything would only make this whole affair more complicated. And it was far too complicated as it was.

Noah, however, was like a man possessed. He wouldn't let it go. "You do love me, Meg. So get it off your chest, why don't you?"

"I am not going to have this discussion with you now," she said archly. "This ship is not going down, these aren't our last moments on earth, and we both have more important matters to attend to."

"Oh, Meggie, Meggie. You are tough. I admire that in a woman."

Before she could stop him, his lips captured hers, his kiss hungry, passionate. And Meg, suffering from the same hunger, couldn't keep herself from responding in kind.

Finally she pulled back from him, her breath shallow, her forehead damp. "I think we better get back to work."

He nodded, but his hand moved to her throat for just a moment to savor the quickened beat of her pulse and the soft satin of her skin.

TONY HURRIED DOWN the corridor to Liza's cabin. When he knocked on her door there was no response. He tried the knob and to his surprise the door gave way. He figured Liza had probably left in such a panic that she hadn't closed the door fully. He was about to turn away and head for his lifeboat station when he heard a noise inside the cabin.

He was instantly concerned. Liza could have tripped and fallen in the darkness trying to get out of her cabin. He flung the door open. A large shadowy figure standing by the small wall safe spun around as Tony entered.

"What the hell?" said a masculine voice as Tony's flashlight temporarily blinded him.

"So, it's you," Tony said dryly. "Looks like the jig's up, buddy."

"It is for one of us, but that one isn't me," the intruder said with a confident chuckle.

That's when Tony saw the gun in the guy's hand.

And that was just the beginning of his problems. A sound behind him made him turn his head. Before he got to see who the new arrival was, however, something hard came crashing down on the side of his head and everything went black. He hit the floor and was out cold.

The pair stared down at the body slumped on the floor, the man cursing under his breath.

"Damn it. Didn't you see I had everything under control?"

"No, I didn't see you at all!" Liza Hamilton snapped. "Why do you think I came back? I got worried."

"Since when have I ever given you reason to worry?"

"All right, all right," she said as she watched him kneel down to check the damage she'd wrought. "It's just that when I saw Tony here, I thought he must have discovered the truth and . . . and that the jig was up."

She swallowed hard, clutching the metal flashlight that had served as a weapon. "Is he...dead?"

"No. You merely knocked him out."

She exhaled a sigh of relief.

He looked up at her with a sardonic smile. "Don't tell me you actually fell for this jerk?"

"No, of course not. I just never...knocked anyone out before."

"And was I right to suspect him?" he pressed.

"Yes, you were right," she answered flatly.

"I'm always right, darling. That's something you should know by now."

"Okay, okay," she said irritably, flinging back her hair. "Did you get everything? The jewels, the letters, the negatives?"

"Really, Liza, your sudden lack of confidence in me is most disconcerting."

"What do we do about Tony?"

"What we do is get rid of him."

Liza blanched. "Oh, no. Hold on. Blackmail and robbery's one thing. I mean, let's face it. We never hit on anyone who couldn't afford to pay."

"You're a regular Robin Hood, darling. Steal from the rich and give to the... Well, steal from the rich, anyway."

"What I'm saying here is that murder is another thing altogether. I'm not having any part in it."

"Did I say murder?"

"You said we'll get rid of him." Liza said.

"Temporarily, darling. Just until we land in St. Kitts where we shall quietly disembark and fail to return to the ship when it sets off again."

"You sound awfully confident that we're going to ride out this storm."

"Trust me, darling. It's a mere squall. We're already riding it out. Can't you feel that the ship is listing less and less?"

Now that he mentioned it, Liza did realize they weren't swaying as much. Nor was the wind howling with the same ferocity.

"Which means," he added gruffly, "we've got to hurry before everyone gets back from their lifeboat stations."

"Just what do you have in mind?" Liza asked.

"We'll tie your boyfriend up, gag him and stow him away in some quiet out-of-the-way place where it'll take a while for him to be found."

"But what if he's found too soon?"

"You worry too much, darling."

Liza couldn't argue with him there. After a year of working together this was the first time there'd been even the slightest slipup. And she had more worries.

"Even if he isn't found until after we've gotten away, he can identify you," she said anxiously. "And even if he didn't actually see me, I'm sure he can put two and two together. After all, this is my cabin."

"Once we're happily settled in Brazil where there are no extradition agreements with other countries, it won't matter in the least," he assured her as he pulled a sheet off her bed and began tearing it into strips with which to tie Tony up.

Liza knelt down and put her hand on his arm. "You mean it? We'll settle down? This is the end of it?"

He smiled and paused for just a moment to plant a kiss on her lips. "We've got more than enough to live quite comfortably, wouldn't you say?"

"Yes. Oh, yes," Liza agreed emphatically. "But I thought..."

"You thought I was greedy. You thought I'd never want to stop."

"Yes," she admitted sheepishly.

He stuffed a wad of the torn sheet into Tony's mouth, then winked at her. "I might even make an honest woman out of you."

Liza smiled tremulously. "Do you really mean that? You want to marry me?"

"Of course I mean it. Now help me settle our stowaway in a nice quiet little spot and then scurry on back to our game plan."

IT WAS CLOSE to five in the morning and dawn was just breaking over the horizon when the all-clear whistle blast sounded. The crew returned to their respective stations and most of the greatly relieved passengers shuffled back to their rooms. A few, however, still shaken by the experience, stopped at the Renaissance Room for a drink. Or two.

Alan Delacore, one of the first to arrive, ordered two whiskeys right off the bat. And a brandy for Louanne.

"You're not still upset with me, sugar," he coaxed as he took hold of her hand.

"You abandoned me," she drawled in a little-girl voice.

"I didn't abandon you, darling. Why, you were so much on my mind I dashed out of my suite empty-handed so I could get straight to you and make sure you were safe. I didn't leave your side for an instant until I got you to our lifeboat station and helped you on with your life jacket, now did I?"

"No, but—"

"Gumdrop, be reasonable. I just got a bit nervous because I'd left some papers in my suite I felt better having on me, so I dashed back there for a minute to—"

"You were gone for more than a minute," she said, pouting. "It felt like a lifetime."

"That's just because you were scared."

The waitress arrived with their drinks. Delacore swigged down one whiskey and then lifted the brandy snifter to Louanne's lips. "Here, take a sip. You'll feel better."

"I don't like brandy and you know it, Alan."

"Think of it as medicine. You need something to help settle your nerves."

Louanne couldn't argue with him there.

ELAINE HARPER regarded her husband with amazement as they reentered their cabin.

"Eliot Harper, you are remarkable," she proclaimed.

Eliot smiled sheepishly. "Now really, dear—"

"The way you took charge like that. You were so incredibly brave. I always thought I'd be the calm one in a crisis and, instead, there you were, like a knight in shining armor, stilling my fears, comforting me..."

Eliot glowed with pleasure. In truth, he really didn't know what had come over him. For the first time in his life, instead of his usual panic in the face of calamity—or near calamity in this case, thank goodness—he'd suddenly felt capable of taking charge. Perhaps it was because Elaine had passed out and he'd had to set aside his fears and concentrate on reviving her. But even after she'd come to, she'd been so frightened he'd had all he could do to get the two of them to their lifeboat stations. Elaine's hands were trembling so badly he'd had to help her on with her life jacket. And even though the safety chart, which he had, naturally, committed to memory, indicated that each person should first put on his or her own life jacket before coming to another passenger's assistance, he'd rather gallantly, if he had to say so himself, helped his wife with hers before donning his own.

Elaine smiled at him in a way she hadn't smiled at him in years. More years than he could remember. And he thought, *Why, she's still quite pretty.*

She patted the side of the bed. "Come here, Eliot."

Eliot beamed. Maybe a cruise was just the thing, after all.

HORACE AND BARBARA FRIERS had returned briefly to their suite to dress, then headed over to the lounge where they joined up with Lars Olson, who was nursing a Scotch at a corner table.

"Well, that was a scare," Barbara said as, uninvited, she took a seat opposite him.

"I got a little worried about you, Lars," Horace said. "Didn't see you at our lifeboat station."

Lars scowled. "I didn't go to the station. I spent my time trying to hunt down Meg."

"Did you find her?" Barbara asked.

"No, as a matter of fact I didn't."

Horace frowned. "Maybe something happened to her. Don't you think we ought to report this to the captain?"

Barbara nudged him. "No need."

Horace gave his wife a puzzled look. "What?"

"Over there."

Both men turned to the lounge entrance where Barbara was discreetly pointing.

Walking in together were Meg and Noah.

Horace reached over and gave Lars a sympathetic pat on the back.

"Look's like the Brit beat you out, fellah."

"Yes," Lars said with a melancholy sigh, "it does look that way."

MEG SPOTTED LARS as soon as she and Noah entered the bar. Noah steered her to a secluded table way across the room. He motioned for the waitress and ordered himself a martini. Meg ordered a glass of milk. Warm.

"Stomach in a bit of a snarl, love?" Noah asked sympathetically.

Meg frowned. "I don't get it. I didn't find a thing in Olson's safe." Nor had she had time to make it to Delacore's suite before the all clear had sounded.

"I came up empty-handed, as well," Noah said, not mentioning that he'd had to hide out in a recess in the corridor until Heather and Meg's brother, Paul, made their exit from Heather's suite. The pair came out arm in arm, looking for all the world as if they were floating on cloud nine. Not an easy feat, considering the way the ship was swaying.

"They could have hidden it all somewhere else on board," Meg said gloomily. "It could be like trying to find a needle in a haystack."

"Well, they'll have to collect the goods before they leave the ship."

"Something tells me they may make a run for it when we hit St. Kitts later this morning," Meg said. "I saw a manifest showing there's a cargo ship that's docked in St. Kitts right now and heading for Rio this morning at eleven. We dock in St. Kitts at 10:45 a.m.''

Noah nodded solemnly. "It does sound like a tidy plan.''

It wasn't the waitress who brought over their drinks, but Meg's brother Sean, who was dressed in waiter's attire and made extreme effort to avoid having anyone else see his face and question why the dining room maître d' was waiting tables in the lounge.

The instant Sean approached Meg knew something was wrong. She was right.

Sean leaned toward her as he placed the glass of steaming milk in front of her. "Drink up fast, Meggie. We're gathering at the captain's quarters on the double.''

"What is it?'' Meg asked anxiously.

He hesitated for a moment, his gaze taking in Noah and then returning to Meg. "Tony's missing.''

CHAPTER THIRTEEN

"ARE YOU SURE Tony's missing?" Meg demanded.

They were gathered in the captain's sitting room— Meg, Captain Simon, Sean, Alex and Noah, who'd insisted on tagging along. Meg hadn't argued. Everyone but Meg was seated. She was too upset to sit still and was pacing the room.

"I've covered the whole damn ship," Sean said. "He was supposed to be at my lifeboat station and didn't show up. I went down to his room and he wasn't there."

"I checked the casino and all the other public rooms," Alex said.

"What about that croupier?" Meg asked, trying to remember her name. "The one Tony . . . got friendly with."

"You mean Liza Hamilton," Sean said. "No luck. I spoke to her first thing. She says the last time she saw him was around midnight in the casino. She got real upset when I told her I couldn't find him."

"Maybe you shouldn't have told her," Noah said.

"Why not?" Alex charged. He wasn't all that thrilled to have Noah there in the first place. As far as he and his brothers were concerned, the British secret agent had two strikes against him. One, he was butting in on their territory. Two, he was likely to break their sister's heart. However much Meg denied it, her brothers all knew she'd fallen for Noah hook, line and *stinker*.

"It's just that we don't want to create a general panic," Noah said evenly.

"He has a point," Meg said gently, putting a hand on Alex's forearm. "But what's done is done, so let's all just think about what to do next. We're all on edge."

She paused and scanned the group. "Where's Paul, by the way?" One missing brother was more than enough to be worrying about.

"He said he'd meet us here," Sean said.

As if on cue, there was a knock on the captain's door. It was Paul. He wasn't alone.

Paul held up his hand to ward off any arguments as he ushered Heather into the room. "It's okay. She knows everything."

"Paulie, are you nuts?" Alex said in disbelief.

"I don't believe this," Sean said in much the same tone as his brother.

Captain Simon looked disconcerted, but said nothing. Neither did Meg or Noah. The silent threesome, however, looked no more pleased than Meg's two vocal brothers.

Paul put a protective arm around Heather's shoulders.

Heather managed a tremulous smile. She was clearly nervous.

"I'm not your jewel thief," she said quietly to Meg. Then she looked at Noah. "Or your blackmailer."

Her eyes skidded back and forth between them. "I swear to you both I'm innocent. You can go through my things, whatever . . ."

Meg gave Noah a sideways glance.

He cleared his throat. "I've already done that."

Paul's eyes narrowed. "And found nothing, right?"

Noah shrugged. "That doesn't mean—"

"Because there was nothing to find," Paul cut him off.

Meg sighed. "Try to look at it from our perspective, Paulie," she said softly.

"How about you trying to look at it from ours?" he countered.

Heather leaned closer to Paul. "Please, just hear me out. I've done some things in the past I'm ashamed of, but they weren't criminal."

"And they're also nobody's business," Paul said emphatically.

Sean threw up his hands. "This is nuts."

Alex scowled and cracked his knuckles.

"Paul told me that Tony's missing," Heather said. "I'd like to help."

Meg shot Heather a look. "You have any idea where he might be?"

Heather sighed. "No. But I'll help you look."

"Great," Alex muttered.

There was another knock on the door. The captain opened it. Chet Carson, still in his steward's uniform, gave the group a grim look.

Meg's breath held. Had Tony been found? Was he . . . ?

Noah saw Meg go white and knew immediately what she was thinking. "Is it Tony?" he asked Chet quickly.

"No. No, still no sign of him."

Meg let out her breath. Her brothers let out theirs.

"Then what is it?" Noah asked sharply.

"We've got a general panic brewing among the passengers," Chet informed them.

"I don't understand," Captain Simon said.

"I do," Meg said. "Word's out about Tony."

Sean looked down at the floor. He knew he was probably responsible for the buzz having started, thanks to his questioning Liza Hamilton.

The captain, who looked as if he'd aged a good five years since they'd left New York, gave the group a haggard look. "Well, I'd better see what I can do to calm everyone down."

The others in the room all knew the captain didn't stand much of a chance of doing that until they found Tony. Not to mention the jewel thief.

As Simon headed for the door, Meg called out to him. "There's one other thing. It's not going to make the passengers any happier, I'm afraid."

Captain Simon turned slowly back to her, knowing it wasn't going to make him any happier, either. "What?" he asked.

"We can't dock in St. Kitts," she said. "Not unless we find Tony and apprehend the jewel thief within the next four hours."

"But that's impossible," the captain argued.

"Meg's right," Noah said. "If we dock, there's every chance our thief will make a run for it."

The captain aged another year right before their eyes. "This is awful. Simply awful. Four hours, you say? Well, then, what are you all doing sitting here?"

It was a damn good question.

WHEN TONY CAME TO, he found himself on a hard floor in a dark narrow storage room. Thanks to the thin crack at the bottom of the door that let in a little

air and even less light, he was able to make out stacks
of cartons piled against one wall. And as his head
started to clear a little he could hear a kind of contin-
ual chugging sound.

Was it coming from the engine room? No, he decided. What he was hearing wasn't a ship's engine. He
tried to think, believing that if he could place the
sound, it would help. Not that he was sure exactly how
it *would* help since he was bound and gagged, making
it more than a little difficult to get anyone's attention.

He winced in pain. The right side of his head was
throbbing. What had hit him? And who? Not that he
didn't have a pretty good guess....

"A PERSON DOESN'T get himself temporarily misplaced," Barbara Friers said with a mix of righteous
indignation and fear. Robberies, storms at sea and
missing persons were all well and good in a novel—
especially in one of her novels—but having them happen to her in real life was another story altogether.

Captain Simon pressed his palms together as he
stood in the center of a group of about thirty anxious
passengers who'd gathered in the ship's breakfast
room. While they were all seated at tables, their
breakfasts in front of them, hardly anyone was eating.

On the surface the captain was the picture of calm,
but behind that facade he was as unnerved as the lot
of them. Maybe more so. Until now, his record as a
ship's captain had been exemplary. Not one black
mark.

"The captain didn't say the man was temporarily
misplaced," Alan Delacore said in his statesman's

voice. "He simply said he hasn't been accounted for as yet."

Louanne clutched her fiancé's hand. "He could have had an accident. It could just be an accident, couldn't it? I mean, just because he's missing doesn't mean—"

"That a foul deed's been committed?" a reed-thin middle-aged woman who was traveling with her bridge group piped in apprehensively from one of the tables.

Clara Schmidt's eyes widened. "Are you saying the casino manager has been murdered?"

"I bet this Tony fellow caught the jewel thief in the act," Horace Friers declared, "and the thief had to do him in to protect himself."

There was a chorus of gasps from the passengers.

Dr. Schmidt frowned darkly. "How could something like this happen?" he demanded of the captain.

"Please, everyone," the captain entreated. "Nobody's said anything about murder. If everyone would just stay calm..."

"I agree with the captain," Lars Olson said firmly. "For all we know this man may have had a bit too much to drink and passed out in some quiet corner. No doubt he will come to by the time we reach St. Kitts, and all this panic will have been for nothing. Am I not right, Captain?"

The captain sighed. *Not right* said it. "About St. Kitts..."

"NOW WHAT?" Liza demanded. "If they don't find Tony they're not even going to dock in St. Kitts?"

"Will you take it easy and keep your voice down?"

"Oh, who's going to hear us over here?" They were standing in the shadows behind a rarely used stairwell on the lower deck.

"You're the one who knocked him out in the first place," he reminded her.

"I didn't have much of a choice, did I?"

"True. We couldn't very well have left him to go merrily off and report us."

"Maybe I could have convinced him not to say anything," Liza said. "I just wish I knew what we're supposed to do now."

He drew her into his arms. "Will you leave everything to me?"

She wrapped her arms around his neck, clinging to him out of fear, not passion. "I'm scared. If they do find Tony before we're supposed to dock in St. Kitts our goose is cooked, because he can finger us. And if they don't find him we'll never get to St. Kitts. And that means we won't be able to get on that cargo ship for Brazil, and that means—"

"There are other alternatives."

She looked anxiously up at him. "What do you mean, other alternatives?"

"Leave that to me."

Liza shivered. There was something about the way he said that . . .

"ANYTHING?" MEG ASKED anxiously, looking from her brothers to Noah and Chet. They'd all broken up after leaving the captain's quarters to scour the ship and had met back in Meg's suite to report their findings. Only there were no findings to report.

Meg was greatly disheartened to see glum looks all around.

"I say we do it again, but we work in pairs this time around," Noah suggested. "Sometimes two heads can prove better than one."

Alex and Sean teamed up, and Chet suggested he and Paul join forces. Paul nodded but insisted that Heather join them, as well. Chet was agreeable. What better way to keep on eye on a woman who was still, in his mind anyway, a possible suspect?

"That leaves you and me," Noah said to Meg after the others took off.

She gave him a distracted look. "If anything's happened to Tony, I'll never forgive myself," she muttered darkly.

Noah took her hand. Despite the tropical heat, it was like ice. "This isn't your fault, Meg."

"Yes, it is. Tony wasn't even going to join us for this assignment. He'd gotten this job offer in Las Vegas at one of the big casinos to head up a security team there."

"And you talked him out of it?"

"No. No, I told him to take the job," Meg said quietly.

"So how is any of this your fault?" Noah said, confused.

"Well, he knew how important this assignment was to me. I didn't have to say a word for him to know I could use all the help I could get."

Noah lifted her chin so that their eyes met. "Even mine?"

Meg had a hard time meeting Noah's gaze, but it proved even harder to look away. "Especially yours," she admitted in a small voice.

"Oh, Meg," he whispered as he cupped her face and kissed her. The touch was light at first, but the tenderness lasted only an instant before they were kissing in a frenzy that was part desperation, part lust and part panic.

Meg's lips trembled when she and Noah broke apart. "If these were our last moments on earth," she confessed, "then I'd tell you . . . I love you."

"My father used to say," Noah said with a disarming smile, "that you should live each moment like it's your last."

Tears spilled down Meg's cheeks. "Oh, Noah, I just don't want to think that Tony's last moments..." She couldn't finish.

Noah drew her into the comfort of his arms for long moments, just holding her, rubbing her back, smoothing her hair. Then he dropped a kiss on the top of her head. "Tony's okay. Don't ask me how I know. Call it a secret service agent's intuition. Now brighten up, love, and let's go find that errant brother of yours."

Noah's voice held such a ring of confidence it was contagious. Suddenly Meg knew that's exactly what they would do.

LIZA CLASPED HER HANDS in her lap like a schoolgirl as she sat in Tony's office. Her gaze skidded warily back and forth between Meg and Noah.

"Why are you two asking all these questions about Tony, anyway?" she demanded petulantly. "Since when are you part of this investigation?"

"We've both had some experience in finding missing persons," Meg said ambiguously, not wanting to give too much away. "So we offered our services, and you could say the captain appointed us as temporary deputies."

"You and Tony were lovers, weren't you?" Noah queried Liza, shifting the focus back on her.

"So what if we were?" Liza challenged. "That's no crime."

"No one's accusing you of a crime," Meg said. Not yet, anyway, but to say the least her suspicions about the croupier were mounting. As much of an effort as Liza was making to stay cool, Meg could feel the effort. Why would effort be required if Liza had nothing to hide?

Noah lifted his leg and rested his foot on the chair beside Liza, leaning in toward the croupier to scrutinize her more closely. "You wouldn't happen to know a woman by the name of Alison Baker by any chance?"

Liza's expression didn't change even a fraction. "No. Never heard of her."

"Spend any time in London recently?" he asked.

"No. I've never been to London," Liza said impatiently. "And I don't know what London or this Alison Baker has to do with Tony being missing." There was a distinct edge to her voice now. The effort taking its toll?

Noah and Meg exchanged glances.

Liza popped up from her seat. "Look, I'm as worried about Tony as anyone aboard this ship," she said, suddenly teary. "We had something ... special."

"Had?" Meg asked, her heart feeling as if it had just been clamped in a vise.

THE PAIN IN TONY'S HEAD was beginning to dull a little and he concentrated more on what that chugging noise might be. He even managed to get closer to the door by rolling over on the floor several times, which was no mean feat.

He placed his ear against the side of the door, ignoring the sweat pouring down his face. Unlike the rest of the ship, this room wasn't air-conditioned and it had to be well over 110 degrees. His shirt and trousers clung to his damp skin. Curiously, even hotter air seemed to be streaming into the room from the crack at the bottom of the door. And that sound—ca-chug, ca-chug, ca-chug. Steady, constant, loud.

Listening harder, he realized he was actually hearing two separate mechanical sounds. There was the ca-chug, ca-chug, but there was also a second sound, similar but lower pitched.

And then it came to him. Washers and dryers.

The laundry room was on the other side of that door. And that meant there had to be launderers in there. Now if he could only figure out some way to bang on the door to draw someone's attention. The problem was, not only was he tied hand and foot and gagged, but even if he could thump on the door, who'd hear him over the racket of all those machines?

MEG AND NOAH checked the corridor to make sure no one was in sight, then used the purser's passkey to slip inside Liza Hamilton's room. Liza was on duty at the casino, so they didn't have to worry about her interrupting them.

Because the croupier's room hadn't been monitored, access to her safe was not going to be easy, but Noah set to work on it while Meg began searching the rest of the room.

She was going through Liza's small desk when she looked over at Noah and asked, "You really think she's your blackmailer? Because my gut feeling is she's involved in those jewel thefts."

"As we've surmised all along, our gal's very likely multitalented when it comes to the criminal arts. She certainly fits the physical description the finance minister gave me. I'm not proud to admit it," Noah confessed, "but I completely overlooked her because she was on the staff. Lyons seemed so sure she'd booked passage on the *Galileo*. He must have overheard her mention the ship and just assumed, because of the amount of money he'd already coughed up, that she'd travel as a first-class passenger. I really could kick myself."

Meg smiled at him. "Don't be so hard on yourself. I didn't suspect her, either. So neither of us is perfect."

Noah's blue eyes sparkled provocatively. "No, but you, love, are more perfect than you think."

It was a corny remark, but she knew Noah meant it. And it gave her a temporary but much needed lift.

She cleared her throat, sensing him watching her as she continued rifling through Liza's desk drawers, slamming each one shut as she went along.

When she finished with the last drawer she said despondently, "Nothing here. How are you coming along?"

Noah's attention was on the safe. He'd donned a stethoscope and was listening intently as he tapped out possible code letters.

"Hold it," he murmured. "I think . . ."

He grinned broadly as the safe door swung open.

Meg hurried over. As she and Noah peered inside they shared an all-too-brief moment of expectation.

The safe was empty.

"Damn," Noah muttered.

Meg glanced over at the narrow bunk. "Help me lift the mattress."

They ended up pulling the whole bed apart. And once again came up empty-handed. Discouragement and frustration were etched on both their faces.

"Maybe she's passed the stuff to her boyfriend," Noah suggested.

"Tony was her boyfriend," Meg reminded him.

"No, I'm afraid Tony was the dupe," Noah said gently.

"Unless we're altogether wrong about her," Meg muttered as she looked down at the floor. Suddenly she dropped to her knees and gasped.

Noah thought she'd become unexpectedly ill and he kneeled down to her. "Meg. Meg, what is it? Are you all right?"

She lifted something off the floor and held it out in the palm of her hand for Noah to see. It was a small gold coin.

"It's Tony's," she said.

"Are you sure?"

Meg nodded. "Yes. See the little nick? It's his lucky piece. He always keeps it on him."

Noah didn't want to rain on her parade, but he had to point out that, since Tony and Liza were lovers, there was every reason to believe he might have dropped the coin during a tryst.

Meg began examining the floor more closely. "Look," she said in a low hoarse voice as she pointed to a tiny splattering of brown spots on the gray floor.

Noah examined the spots. He didn't have to say what he thought they were. What both he and Meg felt quite certain they were. Blood spots. Tony's blood.

Noah put his arms around Meg. She was trembling badly. He pressed his lips against her hair. "We'll make Liza talk," Noah said. "She probably just coshed him and knocked him out. We'll make her tell us where she and her boyfriend stowed him. Just hold tight."

NOAH GAVE the assistant manager of the casino a hard cold look. "What do you mean she isn't here? She's supposed to be on duty until ten this morning. And it's not even nine yet."

The dark-haired, well-tanned young male assistant shrugged. "She said she had a headache and needed to go back to her cabin to lie down. She did look kind of pale."

Noah returned to the entrance to the casino where Meg was waiting to give her the bad news about Liza. It was clear the croupier hadn't returned to her cabin or they would have run into her. So the question was, where had she gone off to? And why?

They stared at each other, neither knowing what their next move should be, when Meg felt someone tap her on the shoulder.

"Excuse me. My name's Eliot Harper. I'm one of the passengers and I . . ." He hesitated.

Elaine Harper, who was standing beside her husband, gave him a little nudge.

"Not to think we were eavesdropping, I assure you . . ." Eliot said in response to the nudge.

"Well, of course they don't think we were eaves-dropping," Elaine said. "We simply happened to overhear you mention Liza Hamilton."

"She's the pretty croupier who runs the roulette table, isn't she?" Eliot asked, feeling a need to confirm that was the woman in question.

"Well, of course it's her," Elaine said impatiently. "She was wearing her name on one of those brass pins."

Meg clutched Eliot Harper's sleeve. "You haven't seen her, have you?" Her voice was quick and urgent.

Elaine Harper was practically drooling with curiosity. "What has she done? Is she involved in the disappearance of the casino manager? In the jewel thefts?"

"Please," Meg said. "Have you seen her?"

"Time is of the essence," Noah said dramatically.

Elaine Harper's eyes widened. "I knew there was something sneaky about her. Just like I knew about the two of you. Oh, I knew you'd get together before this cruise was over." She nudged her husband again. "Didn't I tell you, Eliot? Go on. Tell them."

Eliot grabbed his wife's hand before she managed yet another poke in the ribs. Then he gave Meg and Noah a sober look. "We saw Miss Hamilton leave the casino a few minutes ago," he said.

"You didn't happen to see which way she went?" Noah asked.

"Of course we did," Elaine said eagerly.

Eliot and Elaine stepped out onto the deck with Noah and Meg on their heels. They both pointed toward the stern.

Meg eyed the short portly man with curiosity. "What made you pay such close attention to where the croupier was going?"

The professor flushed. "Well, she is . . . quite attractive."

Noah smiled. "We understand."

"That may have been your reason, Eliot, but it wasn't mine," Elaine said haughtily.

"What was your reason?" Meg asked.

Elaine Harper's brows furrowed. "She looked quite agitated. Like something might be terribly wrong."

She elbowed her husband. "Isn't that what I told you, Eliot?"

Noah and Meg didn't hear. They were already racing down the deck.

WHEN LOUANNE SWEPT into the main lounge frowning and looking all around, Chet Carson approached her.

"May I be of assistance, Miss Percy?" he asked.

Louanne gave the steward a distracted glance. "It seems that everybody gets lost on this miserable boat."

"Have you lost someone in particular?" Chet prodded.

"Of course I've lost someone in particular," she snapped. "I've lost my fiancé. He said he was going to meet me by the pool twenty minutes ago."

She stamped her foot. "He knows how I hate to be kept waiting. And what with everything that's happened you'd think he'd be a little more sensitive to my needs."

Before Chet could respond, she stormed off in search of the errant Alan Delacore.

TONY ROLLED and heaved his shoulder against the door yet again. He was sure he'd be black-and-blue for days.

That was, if he had days.

He decided to give his right shoulder a rest and with great effort shifted his position so that he could ram the door with his left shoulder.

After a few tries, he had to rest. He was practically drowning in sweat and, thanks to the gag in his mouth, his throat was raw as sandpaper and it was all he could do to fight back the nausea.

He closed his eyes. A minute later they sprang open. It took a couple of seconds for him to fully grasp what was happening.

The door was opening.

Tony couldn't believe it. One of the laundry workers had actually heard him. Or maybe they'd just run out of supplies and were coming into the storage room for more detergent.

What did it matter? The important thing was he'd been saved.

As the fluorescent light from the laundry room flooded the dark storage area, Tony had to shut his eyes against the sudden brightness. When he opened them slowly, all he saw at first was the white laundry worker's uniform. Then he saw the gun in the man's hand. And last he saw the smirking smile on his abductor's all-too-familiar face.

In the next instant, the door shut and the room was once again bathed in darkness.

"You don't look too comfortable, Tony," his abductor said with mock sympathy. "I'm happy to tell you I've come to put you out of your misery."

CHAPTER FOURTEEN

THE PIERCING SCREAM echoed throughout the main lounge. For an instant everybody froze. Then they rushed en masse onto the deck to see what had happened.

Barbara Friers was shaking like a leaf and still screaming. "He's dead. Oh, my God, he's dead." With that pronouncement, she fainted.

Meg and Noah, who were racing along the deck in search of Liza Hamilton, came to an abrupt halt when they heard the novelist's anguished cry. Meg gasped and turned white with terror.

"IT'S ALAN DELACORE," Captain Simon announced as he knelt down beside the body stretched out at the end of the first-class corridor.

Louanne screamed.

"It's all right," the captain quickly assured her. "He's not dead. He's just unconscious. Someone give me a hand and let's get him into his suite."

Chet Carson assisted the captain. As they carried him into the suite, the former ambassador's eyes fluttered open.

"Laundry," he croaked before he proceeded to black out again.

Meg and Noah, standing nearby, shared a look. Then they raced out of the suite.

"YOU WILL AGREE this is for the best." A dry chuckle. "But then whether you agree or not is beside the point," Lars Olson said with aplomb as he stood there in his borrowed laundry worker's uniform.

"You know too much," the Swede went on with a gloating smile, "and therefore you must be eliminated. I suppose if I really did mean to settle with Liza in Rio, it wouldn't matter. But I'm on a roll and have no intention of settling down. Especially not with a woman like Liza. I'm afraid she's become a liability, as well. Poor Liza."

Lars Olson pointed the gun at Tony's head. "If you're a man of faith, this is the time to say your prayers...."

The Swede's finger was just about to squeeze the trigger when the door to the storage room burst open. Noah made a leap for Lars and the gun went off, the bullet embedding itself in the far wall.

The two men struggled while Meg raced over to Tony. She quickly pulled the gag off his mouth and began untying him.

"Boy, you can't imagine...how glad I am...to see you," Tony croaked.

"About as glad as I am to see you," Meg said with unbridled relief.

Her relief was short-lived.

"Hold it right there," a throaty female voice said from behind Meg.

Meg spun around to see Liza Hamilton holding the gun that Lars Olson had lost in his struggle with Noah. The two men, in the meantime, were still going at it and Noah clearly had the upper hand.

Until Liza threw her arm around Meg's neck, dragging her to her feet, and pointed the gun at Meg's temple.

"Get away from him," Liza warned Noah. "Or your girlfriend's dead."

Noah let go of Olson.

"Okay, take it easy," Noah told Liza. "You don't want to do anything crazy."

Lars Olson chuckled. "I wouldn't bank on that, Danforth."

The Swede rose, dusted himself off and approached his girlfriend. "All right, baby. I'll take over from here."

"Liza, listen to me," Tony said in a raspy voice. "He's handed you a bill of goods. He doesn't plan to settle down in Rio with you like he told you. You've become as big a liability to him as the rest of us here. He can't afford to have you around any more than he can afford to have us around. Don't give him the gun."

"You're pathetic," Lars sneered at Tony as he stretched out his hand to Liza. "Give me the gun, baby."

"Think about what Tony's telling you, Liza," Meg said quietly. "It makes sense. Think about it."

There was a moment's hesitation on Liza's part. No one made a sound or even took a breath.

And then the croupier smiled tremulously at her lover and handed the gun to him.

"You're not going to... kill them, are you?" Liza asked Lars only after he had the gun in his hand and it was already too late.

Actually it was precisely what Lars intended to do, but his plans were interrupted by the arrival of Chet

Carson, Captain Simon and Meg's three other brothers.

Thinking fast, Lars grabbed Meg, and much like Liza had done before, held the gun to her temple.

"I'm sure none of you wants to see this lovely woman's brains splattered all over the room," Lars snarled.

"Steady there," Captain Simon entreated.

"I'm quite steady, Captain," Lars informed him.

"If you harm so much as a hair on her head..." Noah warned.

Lars laughed. "Ooh, I'm just cringing with fear." He sobered quickly. "Now everyone get over against the wall. All except you, Captain. I've got a job for you."

"What kind of job?" Simon asked icily.

"I want you to get on your radio and arrange for a helicopter to take me and my lovely hostage on a flight to Brazil."

"Aren't you forgetting one other passenger?" Liza murmured.

Lars gave her a regretful smile. "I'm afraid not, my sweet. Your boyfriend here was right. I feel we've grown apart these past few days."

"Lars, you don't mean that," Liza gasped. "You can't. You love me. You said you wanted to marry me."

"I lied," he said breezily.

"Lars," Liza pleaded now, "you can't leave me here. I'll be arrested. I'll go to jail. Just take me with you to Brazil. We don't have to get married. We can split up as soon as we touch down."

"I'm sorry, baby. But I've truly grown bored with you."

"You bastard," Liza hissed.

"Too bad it took you so long to figure out," Meg muttered only to feel the barrel of Lars's gun press into her temple.

"You wouldn't give me the time of day till now, Mrs. Newell," Lars sneered. "Now, I'm going to have your undivided attention for several hours while we're being flown courtesy of SeaQuest to the coast of Brazil."

"And then?" Noah asked grimly.

"Once the chopper's put down on Brazilian soil, I will have grown weary of the beautiful Meg and will have the pilot deliver her back to you."

"What guarantee do we have that—" Paul started to ask.

Olson cut him off. "None. But you're in no position to barter."

A sardonic smile lit his face. "Which reminds me," he added slowly, turning to Noah, "I have a little job for you, too. While the captain is arranging for our transport, you, my friend, will busy yourself gathering the valuables and ready cash from the rest of the passengers."

He glanced at his watch, which was on the wrist of the arm draped across Meg's neck. "It's now ten-fifteeen. One hour, my friends. The chopper and the valuables in one hour or Meg here won't see eleven-sixteen."

He motioned the captain and Noah to get moving.

Noah hesitated, his eyes meeting Meg's. He knew she was scared, but she didn't show it. He didn't show it, either, but he was just as scared. If anything happened to her...

No, he wouldn't allow himself even to consider that possibility. He had to do something to ensure that nothing did happen to her. Noah didn't know yet what that something was, but he'd figure it out. He had to.

Somehow, in that brief shared glance, all of what was in Noah's mind—and in his heart—got conveyed to Meg. Even though she knew her situation was dire, she felt buoyed. And whatever happened, even if these proved to be her last moments, she was glad of one thing. She was glad she'd told Noah she loved him.

"Time's ticking away, Danforth," Olson jeered.

A smile flickered on Noah's face before he turned away from Meg. An idea had come to him. An idea that just might work.

No, he thought. *Might* wasn't good enough. It *had* to work.

Barbara Friers was irate. "It isn't fair. He's already taken most of my jewels. He could at least let me keep my wedding band. It isn't worth—"

"Barb," Horace cut her off sharply, "give the ring up. It's certainly not worth someone's life."

The novelist flushed. "I'm sorry. You're right, Horace." She took off her wedding ring and dropped it into the sack Noah was being forced to pass around to the passengers, all of whom had gathered with their valuables in the main lounge on Lars Olson's orders.

Olson, with Meg in tow, stood near the entrance to the lounge in view of the landing pad on the deck. He kept glancing out to see if he could catch sight of the chopper. Twenty minutes had passed since the captain had radioed for one.

AFTER EXITING with Noah, Meg and the captain, Lars had locked Chet, Heather, Liza and the four Delgado brothers in the laundry storage room. The men worked at breaking down the door while Liza sat cross-legged on the floor, sobbing her eyes out.

Heather put a hand on the croupier's shoulder. "Look, maybe if you turn state's evidence on Lars, the court will go easier on you."

"I loved him!" Liza cried. "I truly thought he loved me."

Heather's gaze strayed to Paul and she smiled faintly. "Well, maybe you'll be luckier next time around."

"Yeah," Liza muttered glumly. "Like in ten years."

There was a cracking sound and the door gave way. Light streamed into the room.

Liza sprang to her feet and made a dash for the open door even though there wasn't very far she could go.

"Not so fast, sweetheart," Tony said bitingly as his fingers clamped around her upper arm.

"Please help me, Tony," Liza whimpered.

"Right. Like you helped me," he muttered sardonically.

ELAINE HARPER was dropping her sapphire brooch into the sack when the chopper could be heard whirring overhead. Olson leaned out to check on the landing just as Noah had counted on him doing.

Fast action was essential. Noah quickly shoved the sack into the hands of the unsuspecting Eliot Harper, who was standing beside his anxious wife. Then, he quickly ducked through the crowd and headed for the side exit. He was gone by the time Olson turned back to the gathered group and started to address him.

"Okay, Danforth…" It took a few seconds for him to realize Noah had vanished. He muttered a curse, thinking at first that Noah had run off with the valuables. Then he spotted the sack in Eliot Harper's hands.

"You," Olson shouted, pointing a finger at the portly professor.

Eliot's knees were knocking together as he clutched the sack. "Me?"

"Bring that sack over here," Olson ordered. "Make it fast."

Eliot nervously obeyed nearly tripping over his feet. Meanwhile Olson scanned the group for Noah one more time, but then gave up. It really didn't matter about him anymore. About any of them. Now that he had his hostage, a superior cache of jewels and money and a way out, he was set.

"Time to fly," he said to Meg in a buoyant voice, stepping out with her to the deck just as her brothers and Chet Carson were about to spring on him.

They were a few seconds too late. Olson grinned triumphantly as he made them step over to the railing. "Say goodbye to everyone, Meg."

Meg's eyes swept over her brothers. She tried to smile, wanting to somehow reassure them, as Noah had somehow managed a minute ago to reassure her, that she was going to make it out of this mess okay. Only she had no idea how she was going to pull it off, so her attempted expression of reassurance fell flat. She saw fear and worry reflected in the eyes of all of her brothers. Probably the same emotions they saw in hers.

"Move it, baby," Olson ordered her, shoving her in the direction of the chopper which had now landed.

As Olson had specified, the chopper had only one pilot. He was wearing dark goggles, a Red Sox baseball cap and a blue nylon flight jacket. He motioned for them to climb on.

Olson shoved Meg up into the chopper. He was so busy gloating over how well his extemporaneous plan had worked out he hardly gave the pilot a second look.

Meg, on the other hand, gave the pilot a very long look. Suddenly she felt airborne and they hadn't even lifted off.

Nor were they about to.

"Hey, Lars," Meg said, having to shout over the din of the chopper. "You forgot something."

"What's that?" he demanded.

Meg lifted up her hand, waving the ruby ring she wore in his face.

Olson's eyes lit up, a greedy smile curving his lips. "Well, now. Isn't that kind of you to remind me."

Meg pretended to have difficulty getting the ring off her finger.

Olson muttered impatiently and grabbed for her hand. In the same instant he snatched Meg's hand to pull off her ring, another hand curled into a tight fist, and landed a knockout punch to the side of the jewel thief's jaw.

Olson's eyes widened in shock for one moment before he passed out cold.

Meg sprang forward in her seat and threw her arms around Noah, who had exchanged places with the real pilot while Olson had been busy looking for him in the lounge.

A HALF HOUR LATER, the chopper, now being flown by the real pilot, took off with Olson, but without his stolen cache and without his hostage. Instead, he was wedged between two of the ship's security officers who were flying their prisoner back to Puerto Rico where authorities from the U.S. would be picking him up.

Liza Hamilton, meanwhile, was put under house arrest until the *Galileo* docked in St. Kitts; she would then be flown back to London to face charges. All of the letters, photos and negatives involving her and the British minister had been reclaimed. Noah, himself, oversaw their destruction and faxed the good news to British Intelligence.

A few minutes before the ship docked in St. Kitts, the Delgados, Heather St. John and Noah gathered once more in the captain's quarters. Chet Carson, still in his steward's uniform, entered carrying a bottle of champagne. He poured glasses for all of them.

The captain, looking remarkably youthful once again, smiled in triumph. "All's well that ends well," he toasted.

Everyone tapped glasses and drank.

Paul turned to Heather as he proposed a second toast. "How about toasting our upcoming wedding?" His expression was awash with adoration.

Heather blushed. "Just how upcoming is it?" she asked tremulously.

Paul grinned. "I take it that's a yes?"

Meg and Noah shared a glance, but the only expression they could see in each other's eyes was bittersweet. They had both confessed their love, but what they couldn't do was precisely what Paul and Heather seemed able to do with so little effort—commit.

Heather smiled. "Yes. Oh, yes, Paul. I'd marry you this very instant if it was possible."

Captain Simon cleared his throat.

All eyes turned to him.

ELAINE HARPER rummaged through her purse. "Now where are my tissues?" she muttered as she and Eliot took their seats in the main lounge.

"You aren't coming down with a cold, are you, dear?" Eliot asked with concern.

"Of course not. I feel perfectly fine," she said. "I feel absolutely wonderful. But you know I always cry at weddings."

Eliot smiled, recalling that his wife had even cried at theirs.

Elaine found a few crumpled but unused tissues and she smoothed them out on her lap. "It's lovely that Paul and Heather are tying the knot," she said, "but I must say I'd hoped it would be Meg and Noah. If ever a pair were hopelessly in love..." She sighed.

Eliot slipped his arm around his wife's shoulders.

She looked over and smiled at him, then lovingly patted his cheek.

He reached for one of her tissues. "Do you mind?"

Her smile deepened. "Not in the least."

BARBARA FRIERS had chosen a flamboyant floral print dress embellished with a long mint green scarf tossed around her neck. She also took great joy in flaunting her diamond necklace and diamond-and-ruby earrings for the occasion. Now that the jewel thief had been apprehended, she, like so many of the other passengers—all of whom were attending the wedding—no longer feared wearing the jewels they'd brought along on the cruise.

Horace Friers sat beside his wife, looking quite dashing in his blue blazer with brass buttons over a custom-tailored pale blue shirt, white linen slacks and white boat shoes, once again sporting his diamond-and-gold pinkie ring.

"I always did suspect the Swede, you know," the novelist said.

Horace merely smiled.

"I do think he'll make a wonderful villain for my next novel," she went on. "The girlfriend will need some work, though. That croupier really lacked the necessary panache. All that wailing and sobbing. No, that would never do."

"It might add a touch of realism," Horace suggested. "After all—"

"Really, Horace, some things are fine for real life, but that's the beauty of a novel, don't you see? I get to make her any way I want her. And that being the case, I'd like to see her more defiant, more cynical. I'd have her punch him right in the nose when he announces he's going to dump her. Or better still, kick him in the..." She grinned. "Well, I'm not sure my editor would keep that part in."

"We can do it in the movie," Horace assured her.

Naturally there was a movie in it.

"ARE YOU SURE you're feeling fine now, sugar?" Louanne cooed as she was led into the main lounge on the arm of her fiancé. Like the rest of the guests attending the wedding, the Southern belle and the statesman had dressed to the nines for the occasion. Louanne was entrancing in a perfectly peachy wisp of a silk chiffon dress and a dashing little black hat with a matching peach band around it. Alan Delacore wore a pale yellow shirt with a paisley ascot fitted into the open collar, a white linen jacket and gray trousers.

The former ambassador patted Louanne's hand. "I keep telling you, gumdrop, I'm feeling great."

He ushered her into one of a pair of empty seats on the aisle. She smoothed down her dress as she sat. "I still don't understand how it happened," Louanne said.

Delacore entwined her fingers in his. "I saw Olson dash out of his cabin in that laundry worker's outfit. The next thing I knew he was coming at me like a madman." He sighed. "A simple matter of being in the wrong place at the wrong time."

A hand fell on Delacore's shoulder. "Or you could say," Dr. Schmidt said in his thick Hungarian accent from the seat right behind, "that you were in the wrong place at the right time. That was how, was it not, the day was saved?"

Louanne beamed. "How well you put that, Dr. Schmidt."

"Please," the botanist said, "call me Franz."

Louanne smiled radiantly. "Don't you just love cruises, Franz?"

"RELAX, PAUL," Sean said as he watched his brother agitatedly pace the floor of the small anteroom beside the main lounge. Paul was dressed in a full tuxedo, right down to the red cummerbund and matching red bow tie.

"You're not getting cold feet, are you, Paul?" Alex asked.

Paul stopped dead in his tracks. "No, but I'm worried Heather will. What if she's changed her mind? What if she thinks this is nuts?"

"It is nuts," Tony said, but he was smiling.

Paul pressed his hand to his chest. "My heart's racing. I just hope the rest of me can keep up with it."

Alex rested a hand on his brother's shoulder. "You'll survive. Think of all the other grooms who managed to live through their weddings."

Sean grinned. "Even most of the brides somehow survived."

"Right, right," Paul muttered seriously.

"What happens after the honeymoon?" Tony asked.

Alex chuckled. "Slow down. Poor Paulie's still worried about making it through the wedding."

"No, I mean it," Tony said. "Are you coming back, Paul?"

Paul gave Tony a puzzled look. "What do you mean, am I coming back?"

Tony shrugged. "Well, I was just thinking that once you were married, you might want to settle down. Or at least Heather might want to. How's she going to feel about your being at sea for weeks at a stretch on assignments?"

Paul scowled. "I don't really know. I just assumed..." The rest of the sentence trailed off while he pondered the predicament. After a minute his face broke into a wide smile. "Why can't we just add one more investigator to the team? Heather's smart as a whip and I bet she'd be terrific."

The other brothers shared a look.

"How do you think Meg will take to it?" Alex asked.

"I don't know," Tony said, "but I don't think this is a good time to ask her. She's got enough on her mind."

"What do you mean?" Paul asked, but then answered his own question. "Oh, you mean Noah."

Tony, Sean and Alex all nodded in unison.

MEG WAS HELPING the bride get ready for her big moment. While they hadn't come up with an actual wedding gown, Heather had brought along for the cruise an exquisite watercolor-washed pastel print crepe dress with a scallop-collared matching jacket. Substituting for a veil, Meg had taken one of her own white silk scarves and artfully draped it over Heather's hair. The effect was beguiling.

"Any hard feelings?" Meg asked, glancing not at Heather but at her reflection in the mirror.

"Hard feelings about what?" Heather asked.

"I did think you were Olson's sidekick."

Heather nodded. "So you did."

"Paul, on the other hand, was convinced of your innocence right from the start," Meg felt she should add.

Heather smiled dreamily, then turned and hugged Meg. "I have no hard feelings. I think we're going to become very good friends."

Meg felt greatly relieved as she nodded agreement.

"You look beautiful," Meg said, stepping back to survey her soon-to-be sister-in-law.

Heather's smile was radiant. "Thanks. What's even more important, I feel...beautiful inside. I don't think I've ever felt this happy in my life."

Meg stared at Heather in wonder. "You seem so incredibly sure of what you're doing. Aren't you the least bit worried? I mean, you hardly know Paul. Marriage isn't something to take...cavalierly."

Heather grasped both Meg's hands. "Believe me, I'm anything but cavalier. I didn't say yes to Paul on a whim. That yes came from deep within my heart. Is it written in stone somewhere how long it's supposed to take for two people to fall in love?"

Meg shook her head. "No, but—"

Heather looked her square in the eye. "Some people can feel it the very first instant they set eyes on one another. Even if they don't want to admit it to themselves."

Meg felt her cheeks heat up. "I should go see if—"

Heather refused to let go of her hands. "You do love him, don't you, Meg?"

Meg gave a short exhalation of breath. "It isn't that simple for me."

"Love isn't simple or hard," Heather persisted. "Love just is. Do you love Noah, Meg?"

She looked down at the floor. "Yes, but I'm just not ready to settle down. And neither is Noah," she quickly added, omitting that he hadn't asked her to settle down with him in any event, so this conversation really had no point. Clearly for some people love led directly to marriage while for others it led . . . nowhere.

Meg stepped out on the deck to give Heather a few minutes to finish up her makeup and have a bit of time to herself before the big event. She crossed to the railing and cast her gaze to the lovely green isle of St. Kitts. The ship was docked, and after the wedding everyone would disembark and spend the day touring the island just as the cruise brochure had promised.

Another day in paradise. Meg tried to smile, but she couldn't quite manage it. She should be overcome with joy. High Seas Investigators had brought the jewel thief to justice. Albeit with a little help from the British secret service.

Now she did smile as she thought about Noah's masquerading as the pilot, knocking Olson out. If not for his quick-thinking action she might be in Brazil this very minute. Instead of gazing at a beautiful tropical paradise, she would have been staring down the barrel of Lars Olson's gun.

Noah had saved her life. There was no doubt about that. So maybe, she told herself, that explained her heightened emotions and the teariness that kept threatening her. The aftereffects of what might have been. Maybe what she was really feeling toward Noah now was more gratitude than love.

Fat chance.

"Pretty island, isn't it?"

At the sound of Noah's voice, Meg spun around to see him reclining on one of the slatted wooden deck chairs.

"I didn't realize you were out here," Meg said breathlessly even though there was no reason for her to have any trouble breathing. No reason other than her heart was racing as if she'd just finished a marathon run.

"How's the bride doing?" he asked nonchalantly.

"Oh, fine. She looks beautiful," Meg said, trying to respond in kind but not quite succeeding. She was feeling anything but nonchalant at the moment.

Noah's gaze slowly traveled down Meg's body, taking in the simple coral jersey dress with a floral silk sash that hugged her beautiful figure to perfection. She wore no jewels. Now that the thief had been caught, she'd returned her borrowed gems to the ship's vault for safekeeping.

"You look beautiful, too," he said, rising from the chair and starting toward her.

"Don't," Meg said, holding up her hand to halt his advance. "Let's just leave things as they are." She couldn't quite look at him.

Noah folded his arms across his chest. "Where exactly *are* things, Meg?"

"You know what I'm trying to say," she said, her voice edged with frustration. She turned her back to him, gazing once again at St. Kitts. "Will you fly back to London with Liza?"

"Yes. That's part of the job," he said, coming to stand beside her at the railing. They stood shoulder to shoulder, maybe an inch or two apart. It might as well have been a mile.

She nodded.

"What about you?" he asked.

Meg's hands rested on the railing. She could feel them trembling. "Another assignment."

"Already?"

"Captain Simon got a fax from his head office. The boys and I are sailing from Athens on the thirtieth and we dock in Istanbul on the eighth."

"Sounds delightful."

Meg smiled winsomely. "It's a living."

"One you're very fond of," Noah pressed.

Meg turned to face him.

He could see her moment of hesitation.

"Yes. Very fond," she murmured finally.

He smiled. "This has been quite a week," he reflected, his blue eyes never leaving her face.

Meg smiled. "And some."

He took hold of her arm. "Let's walk."

"We don't have much time. The wedding—"

"We have a few minutes. One turn around the deck."

They walked in silence for a minute or two, Noah continuing to hold Meg's upper arm as if he was afraid she might suddenly flee.

She glanced at him. "When's your flight back to London?"

"There's a commuter flight from St. Kitts to Puerto Rico this afternoon at four. And then we catch a six-o'clock flight back to London by way of New York."

Four that afternoon. It was almost noon now. Four hours. Four hours and he'd be gone. Her steps faltered.

Noah gripped her arm more firmly, slowing their pace.

"What will you do once you've gotten Liza to the authorities back in London?" she asked.

Noah stared straight ahead of him. Looking at Meg literally made his heart ache. All he could think was that once he flew out of St. Kitts he would be flying out of Meg Delgado's life forever.

"The chief's sending me to Tokyo on a new assignment," he said flatly.

"Tokyo," she repeated inanely. A universe away from Greece and Turkey. "I've been there a couple of times. Great city. The sushi's something else. Have you ever tried—"

He stopped abruptly and shook his head. "What are we doing, love?"

"Making small talk," she said quietly.

He turned to her then, not only looking at her, but searching her face, his eyes lingering on her mouth. "I don't want to make small talk," he whispered. "I want to make love to you."

He'd caught her completely off guard. "What? Where? When?"

She laughed nervously.

"Anywhere you say. Now," he said urgently, pulling her into his arms, his mouth coming down hard on hers. All he could think about was that she tasted so good, that he wanted her so much, that if ever there was a question of living for the moment this was the moment he lived for.

Meg felt as needy and desperate with longing as Noah did. She wrapped her arms around him, kissing him back with equal fervor. He might have carried her off right there and then to his suite but for the loud whistle blast that brought them both sharply back to reality.

Meg gasped. "Oh, God. Paul's wedding. It's about to start. And I'm the maid of honor."

CHAPTER FIFTEEN

THE PIANIST from the ship's lounge played "The Wedding March." The captain, looking extremely dapper in his shiny white uniform, stood under a canopy of flowers. To his side stood Paul, with Tony as best man next to him. Meg led the procession down the aisle. Behind her came the bride with Alex on one side of her and Sean on the other. The passengers, seated on both sides of the aisle, smiled and nodded approvingly as Heather passed by them. Whispered oohs and ahs could be heard throughout the audience. Elaine Harper was already dabbing at her eyes. Eliot had his tissue at the ready.

Meg's eyes fell on Noah for a moment as she walked past him. He was seated in the front row and his eyes met hers, a tender smile on his lips.

Meg's legs felt rubbery and she had this sudden urge to cry. What was the matter with her? Surely she didn't wish that this was *her* wedding, that Noah was standing there in front of the captain waiting to say his "I do." Marriage was as far from her plans as, well, as she knew they were from Noah's. Neither of them were the type to settle down. Both of them had avoided commitment like the plague up till now.

For some strange reason Meg found herself remembering her high-school graduation day, remembering especially the valedictorian's speech. Funny, the name of the girl had slipped her mind and yet she could recall whole flashes of the girl's speech. A few lines in particular ran like a refrain in her head:

> ... that this summer will be different from those carefree summers of the past. When this summer comes to a close we will all be going our separate ways. A time of parting. A time of fond but sad farewells ...

It wasn't summer now, but thanks to the tropical island climate it might as well have been. And for her this time aboard the *Galileo* had been as different as night from day. She'd fallen in love for the first time. Only now that she was experiencing what love was really like did she understand that what she'd felt for Jonathan or any other man in her past had been only a poor imitation of the real thing.

Heather had been right. Meg realized nothing was written in stone about how long it should take for two people to fall in love. For some it could be a lifetime; for others an instant.

Still, just as in that valedictorian's speech all those years ago, this too, was a time of parting, a time of fond but sad farewells....

Meg felt the tears begin to roll down her cheeks. She was glad she was standing off to the side of Paul and Heather with her back to Noah. Yet she could feel him staring at her, feel the power of those magnetic eyes, feel his longing and, yes, his love.

"... Paul, do you take Heather to love and to cherish..."

Meg's eyes welled with more tears. This was crazy. Pretty soon she'd be sobbing.

"I do," Paul said in a voice brimming with adoration and joy.

Meg's lips were quivering. She had to get control of herself. She couldn't spoil this special time for Paul and Heather.

"...and Heather, do you take Paul to love and to cherish..."

To love and to cherish. Suddenly those words seemed the most meaningful words Meg had ever heard. To love and to cherish. To be loved and be cherished. Was there anything more important?

Again she slid back in time to graduation day, remembering her dreams of adventure and derring-do. That was all she'd wanted—danger, excitement, risks.

What about now—now that she had all that. Was it enough? Would it continue to satisfy her as it had in the past?

"I do," Heather said with absolute confidence as she gazed lovingly at Paul.

Meg's eyes were riveted on the pair as the captain pronounced them husband and wife. She saw the tender way her brother enfolded his new wife in his arms and gently kissed her lips. However long they'd known each other prior to this moment, Meg felt certain they'd spend the rest of their days together living happily ever after.

Heather and Paul were still in their tender embrace when a cry of alarm echoed from the back of the main lounge. The pair sprang apart and everyone turned to see why the ceremony had been so rudely interrupted.

An agitated young security guard rushed down the aisle heading straight for the captain.

Meg watched intently as the guard whispered something in the captain's ear. The captain turned white.

Noah was already on his feet and hurrying over to the captain.

"What is it?" Noah demanded. "What happened?"

The captain's eyes rose to the ceiling for a moment, then his gaze dropped to the floor. "She's escaped."

"What?" Meg exclaimed.

"Liza Hamilton has escaped," the captain said with a mix of exasperation and distress.

Noah shifted his focus to the nervous guard. "When? How?"

"The young man rubbed the side of his head. "I brought her a cup of tea and a nice hot scone at nine this morning. And just as I was turning to leave, she clobbered me. I think it was a lamp. I caught sight of it out of the corner of my eye, but it happened so fast..."

"So, she jumped ship a little after nine," Noah cut in, then checked his watch. It was twelve-fifteen.

"Three and a quarter hours," Meg calculated. "She could have swum to St. Kitts, hopped a jet and be anywhere by now." She gave Noah's arm a sympathetic pat.

Noah cursed under his breath.

"If it's any comfort," the captain said to Noah, "there was one flight to Nevis at eight this morning, and there aren't any other scheduled flights out of St. Kitts until four this afternoon."

Meg looked at Noah. That was the flight he and Liza were supposed to be on.

"We can contact the local police and have them put men at the airport to keep an eye out for her," the captain finished.

"I'm afraid it's small comfort," Noah said. "She could have as easily taken a boat to one of the other islands and gotten a plane from there."

"It depends," Meg said.

Noah scowled. "Depends on what?"

"Well, on what time she actually jumped ship. And on how much cash she had on hand. My guess is not much, unless she had some well hidden in her cabin. I made her hand over her pocketbook before she was locked in there. I've got her credit cards and most of her cash. Without either, how far could she really get?"

Noah impulsively pulled Meg into his arms and kissed her square on the lips. "I adore you, love."

"Hey," Paul complained, "you guys are horning in on our wedding here, or have you forgotten?"

Meg grinned. "Quit griping. You got to tie the knot before you were so rudely interrupted." She looked from Paul to the rest of her brothers. "Time's awasting, boys."

"And gal," Heather said.

The Delgado brothers all smiled enthusiastically, but then looked at Noah. Meg followed their gaze.

She realized Liza Hamilton wasn't High Seas' assignment. The croupier-cum-blackmailer was strictly Noah's. She and her team were jumping the gun.

She smiled sheepishly at Noah. "That is, if you want our help."

Noah arched a brow. "Are you actually going to make me say it?"

"You bet I am," Meg said, her amber eyes sparkling.

Noah sighed in mock surrender. "Yes, yes. I very much want your help. All right. Are you happy now?"

Meg grinned. "Happier."

St. Kitts was all of thirty-four miles long and, at its widest point, only six and a half miles. If Liza Hamilton was still on the island, the group felt they stood at least a fair chance of finding her.

Their first order of business was to spread out along the harbor in Basseterre, the capital on the southern tip of the island, and inquire about what boats had left the dock between nine and twelve-fifteen that day, and whether anyone remembered seeing a woman who fit Liza's description departing on any of them.

After spending close to an hour asking questions down at the harbor, everyone met at the Circus, which was really the town's round square, in the center of which stood a tall green Victorian clock tower. The clock read one thirty-five. Two hours and twenty-five minutes until the only flight out of St. Kitts that day was scheduled to take off. The flight that Noah, with Liza Hamilton in custody, was supposed to be on.

The reports from all concerned were uniformly discouraging. A number of schooners and fishing trawlers had left port during the past three-plus hours, but no one down at the harbor recalled seeing a woman fitting Liza's description.

"She could have stowed away," Chet Carson suggested glumly.

"Or seduced some sucker into giving her a free ride," Tony muttered.

Alex gave his brother a sympathetic pat on the back. "Don't forget that if you were a sucker at least you were in good company. Liza managed to reduce a government minister to mush, as well."

Noah winced. Wait until his chief heard the bloody bad news. Okay, so at least he'd seen to it that all the evidence was destroyed, but returning to London without the culprit of the crime was not going to win him any favor, that was for sure.

"If only we knew what she was wearing," Heather said.

Meg snapped her fingers and then gave her new sister-in-law a hug. "That's it!"

"That's what?" Heather said, saying aloud the question on all their minds.

"Don't you see?" Meg said excitedly. "If she jumped ship—meaning she had to swim to shore—she must have been wearing a bathing suit."

Everyone nodded.

"Well," Meg went on, "she wasn't likely to wander around the island in a bathing suit."

"Are you saying she must have gone into one of the shops to buy something to wear?" Heather asked.

"Hey, brilliant thinking, Meggie." Alex beamed and ruffled her hair.

"Yeah!" Sean said excitedly. "So the next move is to check out the boutiques. Surely a saleswoman will remember a gal wearing nothing but a bathing suit coming in to buy a dress."

Noah shook his head. "But she didn't have any credit cards or any money, you told us," he reminded Meg.

"I didn't say she went into a shop to buy a dress," Meg said with an enigmatic smile. "I said all she had on was a bathing suit."

Chet scowled. "So?"

"So," Meg said brightly, "where would a woman wearing nothing but a bathing suit and having no money be likely to go?"

There was silence for a few moments. Then Noah's face broke out in a big grin. "The beach. She'd be hanging out at a beach. Very likely giving some rich tourist a sob story in order to milk the poor bloke out of enough dough to make her getaway."

"So what are we waiting for?" Meg said.

They raced to a moped shop near the harbor. Since there were only a few mopeds left for rent, they doubled up. Heather and Paul headed for the beach at Frigate Bay, while Alex and Chet zipped off to Friars Bay. Sean and Tony drove to Conaree Beach, two miles from Basseterre. That covered the main nearby beaches, leaving Meg and Noah to consider other possibilities.

Meg looked up from the guidebook she was thumbing through. "There's a classy little private resort not far from here that might be just the kind of spot Liza would choose. It's on a secluded beach and you have to take a launch to get to it. Probably easy enough for her to latch on to some guest heading out there and go aboard. If I had to choose a spot to hide out in here in St. Kitts, this one would certainly be high on my list."

Noah leaned over and dropped a kiss on top of her head.

"What was that for?" she asked.

He smiled. "For being so bloody clever."

"Coming from someone with so much experience and training in the field, I take that as quite a compliment," she replied with a teasing note.

"You're never going to let me forget that, are you?"

"No. Never."

Their eyes met and held, each thinking the same thing but neither daring to say it aloud. If they parted, she wouldn't be around to never let him forget it. Funny how they could take so many risks when it came to their professions, but were so fiercely protective when it came to their hearts.

Meg checked her watch. "There's a launch leaving for the resort in ten minutes. If we hurry we can catch it." Even as she said the words, a part of her didn't want to hurry. If they did, and if they found Liza quickly enough, Noah would still have time to make it to the airport by four and fly off. Fly out of her life forever. Okay, so their parting was inevitable, but did it have to be so rushed? There wouldn't even be time for a proper goodbye.

Noah hesitated, the same thought running through his mind. Even now, however, he couldn't dismiss his professional duty.

"Right," he said quietly but firmly.

THE LAUNCH, carrying twenty passengers including Meg and Noah, arrived at the dock of the exclusive Sugarcane Cove resort at just past two o'clock. The resort, which consisted of a main lodge and about two dozen bungalows, sprawled along the beachfront and was backed by a small mountain. While the place had an informal air, the tanned and sleek-looking guests bespoke money. They were clearly part of the fashionable set.

"Let's go right down to the beach and have a look around," Noah said as they stepped off the launch.

"It would be nice if we spotted her lying right out there in the open catching some rays," Meg said, but her voice lacked enthusiasm.

The cove-front beach was a ten-minute walk from where the launch docked. They probably could have made it in five if they'd jogged. They didn't.

In the center of the secluded white-sand beach was a bamboo bar encircled with a dozen stools. Half the stools were occupied. None by Liza Hamilton.

"Shall we split up?" Meg asked as she slipped on a pair of sunglasses and scanned the beach. No sign of Liza.

Noah, who was also wearing sunglasses, shook his head. "No, I think it would be better if we stick together. It may take two of us to nab her."

Meg nodded. "If she spots us before we spot her she might try to make a run for it."

"Not many places to run," Noah said.

Meg looked back at the low-slung lodge and the bungalows, then beyond that to the small mountain with sugarcane climbing the slope. "I wonder how good she is at rock climbing."

"How good at it are you?" Noah asked.

"Excellent," Meg said flippantly.

He grinned. "I thought so."

Meg smiled back, but then her expression turned serious as she gave his torso a close scrutiny.

"Are you questioning my athletic prowess?" he asked.

"No, your attire," Meg said, then glanced down at herself. "And mine." They were both still dressed in their wedding clothes. "We stand out like sore thumbs. Liza will spot us in a flash if she's here."

Noah glanced back at the main lodge. "Maybe they've got a clothing boutique."

Fifteen minutes later, Noah and Meg exited the lodge and headed back down to the palm-lined beach. Noah was wearing a pair of black bathing trunks and Meg was wearing a rather skimpy hot pink bikini. Not her first choice; not really a choice at all. The selection was very limited and that was the only suit available in her size. Despite her personal objections, Noah seemed delighted by it.

"If only we weren't here on business," he murmured, putting on a black cap with a visor, which he'd purchased along with the trunks to further disguise his appearance.

Meg donned a wide-brimmed straw hat, which she pulled low over her face. What with the sunglasses both she and Noah wore, it was unlikely Liza would spot them quickly.

If indeed Liza was there. Or anywhere on St. Kitts. At three-thirty, the group was scheduled to meet back at the clock tower in Basseterre, someone hopefully having their escapee in tow. It was now nearly two-thirty.

Meg estimated they had twenty-five minutes to search for Liza, get to the launch and make it back to Basseterre on schedule.

They spent ten minutes covering the beach. At one point, Meg nudged Noah and pointed to a woman stretched out on her stomach. She had the same color and style of hair as Liza, as well as the same shape.

"You circle round to her right and I'll come up on her from the left," Noah said.

Meg nodded and they separated.

A minute later a very irate woman who was most definitely not Liza cursed them for waking her from her snooze.

Noah and Meg apologized profusely and backed away. They continued their search for another few minutes, but came up empty-handed. After a brief stop at the bar for a couple of glasses of papaya juice, they decided to head back to the lodge and check the lobby, perhaps ask some of the staff if they'd noticed anyone fitting Liza's description hanging about.

Ten minutes later, they were dressed once again in their wedding finery and were chatting with one of the bellhops, a handsome blond-haired expatriate from New Jersey. The young man was observing Meg thoughtfully. She was glad she was no longer wearing the skimpy bikini.

"Looks a bit like you, you say?" he asked.

"Yes," Meg said. "We're about the same height, similar hair, but hers is a bit darker and maybe a trifle shorter."

The bellhop tapped his lips with his index finger. "Probably a dozen or more female guests here at the resort would fit your general description."

"She'd have arrived some time this morning," Noah offered. "That would eliminate some guests, surely."

The bellhop nodded slowly. "Yeah, I guess that's right."

Meg glanced at her watch. It was now almost two forty-five. If they didn't catch the three-ten launch back to Basseterre, they'd be late for their scheduled rendezvous at the clock tower.

"Wait a minute."

Meg and Noah looked expectantly at the bellhop.

"There was this beautiful broad..." The young man gave Meg a sheepish smile. "Sorry."

Noah grinned. "No apologies necessary."

Meg elbowed him.

"Anyway, like I was saying, there was this very attractive tall young woman who I noticed down at the beach at around eleven this morning. I don't recall seeing her before, so chances are she did arrive some time today."

The bellhop paused.

"What is it?" Meg pressed.

"The thing is, she wasn't alone," the bellhop said. "She was with this guy. Actually the reason she's standing out in my mind isn't only that she was a real looker, but because she was way taller than her boyfriend. And maybe twenty years younger. I saw them walking hand in hand down to the bar on the beach. Like a couple of lovebirds."

The bellhop glanced over at the desk. "Well, I gotta go. Hope I was some help to you."

"Just a sec," Meg said. "You don't know the man's name, by any chance, do you?"

The bellhop thought for a moment. "No. I wasn't the one who took his bags so..." He shrugged.

"Could you describe this fellow in a bit more detail?" Noah asked.

The bellhop tipped his cap back a little. "Like I said, kinda short and old. A paunch. Oh, and he's kinda bald—tries to hide it by combing hair over the spot. You know what I mean."

Meg and Noah nodded.

The desk clerk was decidedly reluctant at first to give out any information about a registered guest, but then Noah showed him his secret-service ID. While not still under British rule, St. Kitts was affiliated with Britain.

The dapper middle-aged clerk's demeanor instantly changed. He was suddenly intent on helping. "Short, you say? Likely in his forties? Balding? That might be Jason Barnes in bungalow seven. Yes, now that I think about it, I do recall seeing him with an attractive brunette earlier today."

"Bungalow seven?" Noah confirmed.

"Yes. Would you like me to ring him?"

"No, that won't be necessary," Noah said firmly. "We'll just trot over there and surprise him."

The clerk's thick eyebrows knitted together. "Oh, dear, I hope there won't be any trouble."

Noah assured him there wouldn't be. He had his fingers crossed behind his back. So did Meg.

CHAPTER SIXTEEN

BUNGALOW SEVEN sat on a grassy knoll near the far end of the beach. Like all the bungalows, number seven had a fair degree of privacy and was embraced by fragrant frangipani, bougainvillea and hibiscus. Hummingbirds flitted from flower to flower.

Meg and Noah conferred behind a huge poinciana tree that hid them from view of the bungalow.

"We could be way off base," Meg said.

"There's only one way to find out," Noah replied.

"Why don't I skirt around the back of the bungalow?" Meg suggested. "If she is inside she might try to make a run for it from one of the back sliding doors when she realizes we've tracked her down."

Noah slipped his hand in his pocket. "Maybe you should take my gun."

Meg compressed her lips. She knew how to use a gun, but her work rarely called for one, which suited her just fine. "No. Don't worry. If Liza makes a break for it, I'll be able to stop her. I'm a brown belt in karate."

Noah smiled. "A woman of many talents."

Meg's heart lurched a little as she thought how he hadn't seen even half of her talents. And likely never would.

"Are you ready?"

Meg's head jerked up. "Definitely."

He cupped her chin and kissed her firmly on the lips. "For luck."

Meg had a feeling they were going to need it.

JASON BARNES gave Noah an indignant look as he stood at the door to his bungalow, refusing to allow Noah admittance. "I don't see that it's any business of yours whether I'm entertaining a woman," he said sharply.

"If the woman inside your bungalow is Liza Hamilton, then it's very much my business," Noah said in a low voice, flipping open his billfold to show the man his ID.

Unlike the desk clerk, Jason Barnes, a wealthy American businessman, was not impressed by Noah's credentials.

"I am not entertaining a woman by the name of Liza Hamilton," he said archly, and started to close the door in Noah's face.

Noah stuck his foot in the jamb.

"Look, you don't have a warrant—" Barnes started to say as Noah, running out of time and patience, barreled his way into the foyer of the bungalow. No sooner had he entered than he saw a woman dash for the sliding door in the living room that led out to the patio.

Meg saw Liza Hamilton burst onto the patio and started for her. She stopped short when she saw the kitchen knife Liza brandished.

"Stay away," Liza warned. She was wearing a man's belted raincoat, no doubt swiped from Jason Barnes's closet.

Noah, with Jason Barnes at his heels, came running out onto the patio moments after Liza raced out.

Liza was now dashing across the grassy lawn beyond the patio and heading straight for the mountain.

"Watch out," Meg warned Noah. "She's got a knife."

"I don't understand," Jason Barnes muttered as he watched Meg and Noah set off in hot pursuit of the woman who'd introduced herself to him as Alison. "What's this all about? What did she do?"

Liza began scrambling up an overgrown mountain path with Meg and Noah only a few yards back. At one point Liza slipped and Noah managed to get close enough to snatch hold of her ankle, but she spun around and cut his arm with her knife. Instinctively he let go of her.

"Are you okay?" Meg asked worriedly as she saw the blood oozing from the wound.

"It's nothing," Noah told her, keeping her behind him on the narrow path to prevent her from getting cut by Liza's knife.

"Watch out," Meg shouted as she saw a large rock rolling at them.

To dodge it, they were both forced to take a flying leap into the brambles.

"Damn," Meg muttered as she started to her feet. Then she looked at Noah and saw his blood-soaked sleeve.

"Nothing?" she said angrily, grabbing hold of his arm.

"Not now, Meg," he said, shaking off her grip.

"I've got to stop the bleeding," she said adamantly, quickly and efficiently using the sash she'd been wearing around her waist to fashion a tourniquet.

"She's getting away," Noah said impatiently.

"This'll only take a second."

In reality it took closer to twenty seconds, and by then Liza was no longer in sight. They continued up the mountain path for several minutes hoping to spot her again, but they didn't.

"She must have cut a detour somewhere," Noah muttered.

"Look, I'm sorry, but I couldn't very well let you bleed to death," Meg said.

"I'm not blaming you. It's my bloody fault. I shouldn't have stood there arguing with Barnes for so long. I should have burst right into the place and surprised her."

"Look," Meg said excitedly. She pointed to a figure way below them. Liza had managed to find a route that led her back down the mountain toward the resort.

Noah and Meg charged down after her, slipping and sliding as they went. During one slip, Meg heard the seam of her dress give way practically to the waist. Well, at least she had the bikini on under it.

Liza was doing plenty of slipping and sliding herself, enabling them to gain on her. Noah warned Meg to watch out for the knife Liza still brandished. Noah himself needed no such reminder.

In the end, they both made a leap for Liza just as she reached the foot of the mountain. The brunette tumbled face forward, her weapon flying from her hand. It was Jason Barnes who came scurrying over to retrieve the knife.

"This woman stole five hundred dollars from my wallet!" he declared with outright indignation.

Noah, who was putting a pair of handcuffs around Liza's wrists, looked up at the businessman and smiled wryly. "Consider yourself lucky."

Meg grinned. She couldn't have put it better herself.

IT WAS THREE FORTY-FIVE by the time Meg and Noah, with Heather in tow, made it to the clock tower in Basseterre. Meg's brothers and Heather were greatly relieved to see them, but alarmed at their ragged and bloodied appearance.

"We're all right," Noah assured them.

"I'm all right," Meg corrected. "But Noah's going to need stitches for that gash."

"There isn't much time," Alex said, pointing to the clock. "The airport's only five minutes away and Noah can still make that plane if he hurries."

Meg felt her throat go dry. It was all happening too fast. He couldn't race out of her life like this. Without even a few minutes to say a private farewell. But how could she buy more time?

As it turned out she didn't have to. While she was struggling to figure out a way, Noah suddenly swayed against Alex and came precariously close to passing out. Meg gasped in alarm.

"Forget the airport," Alex said firmly. "We better take him to the hospital. They'll have to catch the morning flight out."

Tony, Sean and Chet took charge of Liza Hamilton. They'd have to place her under house arrest on the ship again until the next morning, but this time they'd add a second guard and warn both of them never to turn their backs on their prisoner.

Meg and Alex hailed a cab to take Noah to the hospital. Paul and Heather offered to go along, but Meg told them they'd postponed their honeymoon long enough. Noah, grumbling that all this fuss over a little cut was "bloody ridiculous," added that going to the hospital was bad enough; he didn't want to arrive with "a whole bloody entourage."

"All right," Paul said, putting an arm around his new bride. "You win."

Noah gave him a crooked smile. "No. You're the one who won."

Noah's gash required sixteen stitches. The doctor in the small emergency room suggested that his patient might want to spend the night in what he referred to as the infirmary, but Noah insisted he felt well enough to return to the ship and spend the night in his own suite.

When the threesome stepped outside into the hot sunshine, Alex suggested getting something to eat, since it was nearly six o'clock. Then he saw the flicker of a frown on his sister's face. He didn't need a brick to fall on his head.

"Damn. I forgot," Alex said. "I already made plans with . . . some guys from the ship to meet them for dinner. Gee, I'm sorry about that, but I really don't think you'd want to join a mess of rowdy characters. . . ."

"We wouldn't dream of mucking up your plans," Noah said, smiling gratefully at Meg's brother.

Alex winked and took off on the double.

"Well," Meg said.

"Well," Noah echoed.

She spotted a little café across the street. It seemed pretty casual and, since they still looked grubby, she thought it a safe bet.

While at the hospital she and Noah had cleaned up a bit, and one of the nurses had even given Meg a needle and thread to sew the ripped seam in her dress. And she'd run across the street to a small souvenir shop to get Noah a clean shirt. All she could come up with was a black T-shirt with a poinciana tree on it and Welcome to Paradise emblazoned in red across the chest.

Meg pointed to the café. "What do you say?" she asked Noah.

"Fine," he said, both his voice and his manner subdued.

"Unless you're in too much pain?"

Oh, he was in pain all right, but it had nothing to do with his stitched-up arm. "No. I'm so hungry I could eat a horse," he lied.

"I don't think there'll be any horse meat on the menu. At least I hope not." Meg's attempt at flippancy fell flat.

They sat at a small table on the patio overlooking the harbor. They could see the *Galileo* docked a short distance away. When the waitress came over, Noah ordered a traditional West Indian chicken-and-rice dish, along with a beer.

"Same for me," Meg said just because she couldn't focus on the menu. Or on anything really, except that even though she'd gotten a twelve-hour reprieve, her joy at having this extra time with Noah felt, at best, bittersweet. Maybe it would have been easier if he *had* caught that plane and dashed like a whirlwind out of her life.

After the waitress left to put in their orders and get their drinks, Meg found herself at a loss for words. She couldn't make small talk now. Any more than Noah could. So what was there to talk about? Well, a lot really, considering they hardly knew anything about each other. They'd shared passion and tenderness, but neither of them knew anything about the other's past.

There were many things she found herself wanting to know about Noah—what he'd been like as a child, what his first schoolboy crush had been like, what his family was like, how he'd decided to become a British secret agent. Endless questions spun in her mind, yet she couldn't bring herself to ask a single one of them. She was afraid knowing him better would only make the pain of losing him worse.

She gave a little start as she felt his hand move over hers as it rested on the table. She looked at him, letting her eyes linger on his face as his blue eyes stared unwaveringly into hers.

Even scruffy and bedraggled, wearing that ridiculous T-shirt, Noah was the most handsome man she'd ever seen.

The waitress brought their beers. Reluctantly his hand left hers, but he kept his gaze fixed on her as if afraid she might vanish if he looked away for even an instant. But then he was the one who would vanish in another twelve hours. Unless—

"Meg."

Her glass of beer was cupped between her hands, but she hadn't yet taken a taste of it. She set the glass back down on the table, but didn't let go of it.

"Yes?" Try as she might, she couldn't conceal the hint of expectancy in her voice.

Damn it, Noah chided himself. *Have a little bloody courage.*

His lips parted, but somehow the words wouldn't come. He couldn't count the times he'd risked his life in the line of duty. Yet now he felt like a complete coward.

He lifted his glass and took a large swallow of beer. Beads of sweat had broken out across his brow despite the cooling breeze.

"Are you feeling light-headed?" Meg asked with concern.

Noah blinked several times. "A little."

"You need to get some food into you and then you'll feel better."

He shook his head.

Meg was puzzled. "You don't want to eat?"

He gave her a pained look. "I won't feel better."

Meg felt her eyes mist over. "Neither will I," she whispered.

When their dinners arrived a few minutes later, they both ate what they could. Not that the dish wasn't excellent or even that they weren't hungry; neither of them had eaten since breakfast. They simply didn't have the heart for it.

As they left the café, the sun was setting and the wide palm-lined streets, bordered by rows of white colonial houses and shops, were bustling with tourists. While St. Kitts wasn't at all a nightlife mecca, there were a couple of small casinos and a disco at one of the hotels. Mostly people just strolled along the streets and harbor, browsing in the shops, chatting with newfound friends.

The ambience was warm and cheerful, but Meg and Noah felt alienated from the general mood.

"Let's go back to the ship," Noah suggested.

"Yes," Meg said quietly.

Few of the passengers had yet returned to the *Galileo* when Noah and Meg boarded. They passed the piano lounge. He glanced at her.

"Do you want a nightcap?" he asked.

"No."

He walked her silently to her suite. They stood there at her door. She felt awkward and uncertain. Not to mention miserable.

"You should get some sleep," she said without inflection. And without meeting his eyes. "You've lost a lot of blood."

When he didn't respond she put her hand on the doorknob. Before she could open the door, his hand was over hers. "Who are we fooling here, love?"

A heartfelt smile curved her lips. "No one."

And then she was in his arms and he was opening her door. Clutching each other in an embrace that was filled with longing and need, they practically fell into the suite. Eager and hungry, they tore at each other's clothes, tossing them helter-skelter, moaning and gasping, kissing greedily, roughly. Living for the moment. And loving every moment of it. Loving the taste, the touch, the feel of each other.

"Your arm," Meg whispered with alarm as they toppled naked and entwined in each other's arms onto her big bed. "I don't want to hurt your arm."

"It isn't possible," he whispered back before his lips found hers again and a wild crazy sweetness shot through them both.

When his mouth left hers it traveled to her breasts. The feel and taste of her warm erect nipples was like nothing on earth. Nectar of the gods. He shivered with delight as her silky legs encircled his thighs, her hands skimmed down over his body and she whispered his name in his ear over and over in a soft loving refrain.

He was shaking and he couldn't control it. He had never felt this good and this bad at the same time. He wanted to give her everything he had to give, but he was afraid he could never give her enough.

Tears spiked his eyes as he entered her and she cried his name. He could feel her closing around him; feel himself getting lost within her until he was part of her very being. He buried himself in her, wanting to stay connected to her always and yet feeling the pain of the inevitable separation even as he experienced a bliss beyond compare.

THE WEST INDIAN SUN was streaming through the picture window of Meg's suite the next morning. Even before she opened her eyes, her arm instinctively reached out to the other side of the bed for Noah.

Only he wasn't there.

Her eyes flew open to confirm what she already knew.

He was gone.

She looked at the clock on her bedside table. Seven-fifteen. He was already airborne. And he hadn't even said goodbye.

She began to cry softly, realizing that their entire brief time together had all been about saying good-bye.

CHAPTER SEVENTEEN

ONE OF THE NINETY-TWO passengers or crew aboard the sleek luxurious S.S. *Northstar* was believed to be involved in a ring smuggling ancient Greek icons, a number of which had surfaced in various Turkish ports of call, including Bodrum, Kusadasi and Canakkale. Not coincidentally, each of these ports were stopping points on the Windstar cruise from Athens to Istanbul. High Seas Investigators, minus Paul who was still honeymooning with Heather in the Caribbean, had been hired to smoke the smuggler out if he was on board as suspected.

For this assignment, Meg was again masquerading as one of the A-list passengers—Miss Maria Laurenzi. Her plan was to let word out that her father was a very wealthy and very discreet underworld figure with a yen for fine antiquities. Especially Greek and Roman antiquities. Alex, who was acting as Maria Laurenzi's bodyguard, pretended to have a bit of a drinking problem. This allowed him to run off at the mouth a lot down at the ship's bar. To keep Alex from really getting plastered as a result of his nightly round of whiskeys, Sean was playing steward, filling and refilling his brother's glass with iced tea. Tony, doing steward duty this time round, had access to the crew's quarters, as well as the passengers' suites, so that he could do some nosing around.

The *Northstar* pulled out of the Athens dock at four-fifteen on the afternoon of March thirtieth. Meg went directly to her suite, which was a bit more compact but almost as elegant as her quarters on the *Galileo*. Once again she had a comfortable sitting room and adjoining bedroom and bath. There were no picture windows, but the portholes of her cabin were quite large allowing in the bright late-afternoon Mediterranean sunshine. A large teak console in the pastel-hued sitting area housed the VCR, CD player and color television. A shelf right below the TV slid out to form a small dining table. Beside it was a minibar stocked with sparkling water, chilled wine, cognac and an assortment of liquors.

Sean, looking very dashing in a trim white jacket with gold epaulets and black tuxedo trousers, appeared at her door a few minutes after she'd finished unpacking. He came bearing fruits—literally.

"Who are those from?" Meg asked.

Sean shrugged. "A secret admirer."

As soon as Meg took the basket of tropical fruits from his hand he ducked back into the corridor and reappeared at the door with a huge bouquet of yellow roses.

Meg looked askance at her brother. "The secret admirer?"

Sean grinned, but then a passenger stepped out into the corridor and he quickly got back into character. "Shall I set these in a vase for you, Miss Laurenzi?"

"Yes," Meg said formally. "If you wouldn't mind."

As soon as Sean stepped in and closed the door behind him, he handed her the flowers. "Maybe our smuggler's already making his move," he suggested optimistically.

Meg was dubious. "Alex couldn't have had much opportunity to spread the word yet."

"Well, then maybe it's just some rich playboy whose fancy you've struck," Sean said breezily.

Meg stared glumly at the beautiful and fragrant yellow roses.

Sean stroked his sister's cheek. "Still feeling low?" he asked softly.

She shot him a defiant look. "Who said anything about feeling low?"

"Meg," Sean coaxed.

Her defiance melted away. "He could have at least dropped me a damn postcard."

Sean put his arm around her. "Maybe he did. You did say he was heading to Tokyo. It could take several weeks..."

Meg shrugged off her brother's arm. "He didn't. It's over. I know it's over. I'm just not going to think about him anymore. We've got more than enough on our plates right now. I don't want to hear his name mentioned again. Is that understood?"

Sean thought it best not to inform his sister that neither one of them had actually mentioned Noah Webb's name. Nor did he tell her that he didn't think it was going to matter whether they did or not. Noah was going to be on Meg's mind whether or not his name was actually spoken.

All he said was, "Sure, Meg. Anything you say."

Meg sighed. "Okay, then. That's it. Onward and upward."

"Onward and upward," he echoed with a smile. It was the motto of High Seas Investigators.

After Sean left, Meg put the flowers in a vase of water and set them on the coffee table. She studied them thoughtfully. Who had sent them? A slow smile curved her lips. Probably her brothers. Even though she'd done her best to hide her misery, she knew that Sean, Alex and Tony could see through her like a plate of glass. She'd never admitted to any of them that she'd fallen in love with Noah, but the admission wasn't necessary. It was written all over her face.

She crossed to the porthole and stared out at the calm blue Mediterranean water. Usually when she started a new assignment she felt a rush of excitement, anticipation. This time she felt nothing but an awful void.

"This, too, shall pass," she muttered, turning from the porthole.

She decided to send for her dinner and eat alone in her suite. She didn't feel up to carrying out her charade that evening. She felt too drained, too down in the dumps. She promised herself she would get her act together by tomorrow. One last day to sulk and be forlorn and then she would pull herself up by the bootstraps...

She stared down at her feet. *Need a pair of boots.*

At seven-fifteen that evening Alex knocked on her door. He looked like a handsome hulk of a hood, dressed in a white dinner jacket, black silk shirt and black gabardine trousers.

He regarded his sister with bemusement as she greeted him in her pale blue silk lounging pajamas. "You can't go to dinner in that getup."

"I'm not going to dinner."

"You have to go to dinner."

"I'm eating in tonight. I've got a... a headache."

Alex smiled wryly. "Aren't you mixing up the parts of the body?"

"What's that supposed to mean?"

"It's not your head that's aching, Meggie. It's your heart."

She rolled her eyes. "Not you, too. What is this? A conspiracy?"

"Get dressed, Meg."

"Give me a break, Alex."

"Wear that hot, red backless number. You know the one I mean."

Meg gave him a wary look. "What is this? Since when do you take such interest in what I wear?"

"Hey," he said, leaning over and placing his big hands on her shoulders. "We've got a smuggler to catch, remember? And you're the bait. You want him to bite, don't you?"

Meg sighed. "What's one more bite out of my hide?" she mused sardonically.

All through dinner Meg chided herself for being so subdued. She hardly said a word to any of her dinner companions, oddly enough finding herself missing the zany bunch of characters from the *Galileo*. A week ago she'd received an invitation to the wedding of Louanne Percy and Alan Delacore. Despite his earlier insistence that they wait six months to tie the knot, they were now planning the ceremony for the following month. Meg also received an autographed copy of Barbara Friers's novel *Beyond Hope,* along with a short note promising that her next thriller, which would take place aboard a Caribbean-bound cruise ship, would be dedicated to her and Noah. The note had reduced Meg to tears.

There was dancing after dinner and Meg found herself propelled back in time to that first dance she'd had with Noah aboard the *Galileo*. That had been the start of it, she realized now. That very first time he'd held her in his arms, dancing her out onto the deck under the stars, dipping her low. That light-headed feeling she'd experienced had had more to do with her dance partner than with his dance move, she knew now.

She rose abruptly from the table and excused herself. She needed to get out of there. She needed air. As she hurriedly made her way across the dining room to the glass doors leading out to the deck, she found herself wishing she hadn't taken this assignment. She wasn't ready. She didn't know if she could handle it. She even contemplated wiring Heather and Paul to see if they'd cut their honeymoon short and join the cruise. They could fly to Rhodes...

She stepped out onto the deck, her head really throbbing now. She moved to the railing. There was almost a full moon and the sky was awash with twinkling stars.

Like that first night with Noah...

A chill ran down Meg's spine as she listened to the tune that had just started up. It was the same one she and Noah had danced to. The bloody irony of it, she thought.

"I believe this is our song," a familiar voice murmured behind her.

Meg spun around, staring at the man before her as if he was a figment of her imagination. He had to be. He couldn't be real. He was in Tokyo.

"You aren't going to faint on me, are you, love?"

"What are you...doing here?" she stammered, her heart pounding with such ferocity she was afraid it would pop right out of her chest.

"Asking you for this dance," he said, pulling her into his arms.

Meg couldn't hold back the tears as he pressed her against him. She clung to him tightly. They swayed to the music, but their feet didn't move.

"Why aren't you in Tokyo?" she whispered, still holding him tightly.

"You mean this ship isn't going to Tokyo?"

She drew back her head to look into his face. "Seriously."

He smiled. "Seriously?"

They stopped swaying to the music, but remained entwined in each other's arms. Noah heaved a sigh. "I tried, Meg. I tried to go back to the way things were before you cruised into my life. Only... I couldn't. I couldn't stop thinking about you. I couldn't stop missing you. You were the last thing on my mind when I went to bed each night and the first thing on my mind when I woke up each morning. And you were in my dreams, as well."

"Oh, Noah," she confessed. "It was the same for me."

He smoothed back her windswept hair, then tenderly cupped her face. "So I started thinking. If you were going to be on my mind twenty-four hours a day, what the bloody hell was the point of your not being with me in the flesh?"

"And was there... a point?" she asked tremulously.

He lightly kissed her lips. "No. No point at all. We belong together, Meg."

"Exactly what does that mean, Noah?" she coaxed, her pulse racing.

"You're going to make me spell it out, are you?" He was blushing. He never blushed.

"No. Just say it."

He pressed his forehead lightly against hers and exhaled slowly. "I love you, Meg Delgado. I'm going to love you for all time. And since you feel the same—and don't argue because I know you do—"

"I wasn't going to argue, Noah."

"—then we might as well—get married."

When she didn't answer, he drew away slightly and gave her a nervous look. "I didn't do that very well, did I? I've never proposed marriage before. Let me try again." He took hold of her hands and brought them up to his heart, which Meg could feel pounding heavily.

"Meg," he murmured softly, his blue eyes drinking her in as if they were in the midst of a desert, instead of a sea. "Will you marry me, Meg? If you say yes—"

"Yes," she said simply and without hesitation.

Noah couldn't quite believe he wasn't going to have to talk her into it. "Yes?"

"Yes."

"When?"

Meg's eyes sparkled. "When we wrap up this case."

Noah kissed her full on the lips, but it was quick. After all, they had a whole lifetime of kisses ahead of them. "Okay," he said. "Fill me in."

Which was precisely what she did.

EPILOGUE

PLAINCLOTHES OFFICERS from Interpol boarded the
S.S. *Northstar* at its last port of call in Istanbul and
arrested William Morgan, a key figure in an international smuggling ring. Thanks to High Seas Investigators and their special assistant, Noah Webb, the case
was cracked in record time.

Even as Morgan was being escorted off the ship,
echoes of "The Wedding March" could be heard in
the main lounge.

It was a gala affair. Meg's folks had flown in from
the United States so her dad could give her away. Her
mom had brought along her own satin-and-lace wedding gown and, thanks to the handiwork of one of the
passengers who turned out to be a fashion designer,
alterations were done and the gown—a simple prin-
cess design with a beaded trim at the bodice that gave
a jacket effect—fit Meg like a dream.

Heather and Paul had also come, flying in from St.
Kitts. Meg had asked her new sister-in-law to be her
matron of honor. Heather was thrilled.

A few other old faces were in attendance, as well.
Barbara and Horace Friers had come to witness Noah
and Meg tie the knot. A combination pleasure/busi-
ness trip. Barbara thought Istanbul would be a great
setting for a future book, which Horace's studio,
CineCom, would eventually make into a movie.

When Meg heard the strains of "The Wedding March" she felt a flash of panic. She was in a small anteroom with her mother and Heather.

"Are you sure about this, Meggie?" her mother asked.

Meg clutched her stomach. "I've got butterflies."

Heather smiled. "So did I."

"Me, too," her mom said.

Meg looked from one to the other. "Really?"

Her mom took hold of her hands and squeezed them. "Do you love him, Meg?"

Meg's bottom lip quivered. "I do."

"...DO YOU, MEGAN DELGADO, take this man, Noah Webb, to be your lawful wedded husband to love and to cherish in sickness and in health from this day forward?"

Meg looked at Noah and smiled, all the panic gone. "I do."

"I now pronounce you husband and wife. You may kiss the bride."

Noah already was doing just that.